# PAWS & PORTALS

## ELLIE WARREN

ISBN: 978-1-0686216-0-4

Cover design by Ellie Warren

First published by Curiosity Killed the Bookworm

www.curiositykilledthebookworm.net

For the Tree Keepers...

# Daisy

"Daisy! Can you get down to Ruhann? The portal squirrels are all in a flap about their trees."

"Don't call them that." Daisy Miller looked up from her desk to see her boss striding towards her. He rolled his eyes.

"It's no different than calling us monkeys. I wouldn't be offended."

"Really?" Daisy just thought it was polite not to call people squirrels.

Not that there was anything wrong with squirrels; they were cute, even if some people considered them vermin. Squirrels didn't have a whole lot of prowess beyond their vast nut storage and location expertise. The Ratatoskr had portals.

The forest-dwelling people of Ruhann kept themselves to themselves, preferring to live at one with nature over joining the modern-day rat race, no pun intended. No one had ever worked out how they controlled portal travel, and Daisy suspected the Ratatoskr didn't know either; they weren't the kind of people who needed to dissect everything. Portals just worked, and that was a blessing from the natural world. As sentient beings, you couldn't cut them up to find out how they functioned, although no doubt some had tried over the centuries.

She supposed it was hard to describe a Ratatoskr to someone without mentioning squirrels though. They did look uncannily like human-sized Sciuridae.

"Anyway, can you? They probably just got their lunars mixed up, but we can't risk the anaesthetic crop if something is actually wrong." Hari prodded her. Oh yes, her blithely ignorant boss. She suspected he had financial interest in the crop, if he was this bothered. It's not like the Ratatoskr were their customers, and Daisy had a backlog of hundreds of cases of malfunctioning magic to work through. She did not know what was going on lately, but she didn't like it. She just wanted a quiet life, getting home at a sane time, and eating cereal in front of the television.

She sighed.

"Sure. But someone needs to go check out…" She looked down at her screen. "Ah yes, Celia Blackthorn's penthouse. She says the lights keep going out at inopportune times. There's no reason a modern building like that would have dodgy wiring."

Hari's face brightened at the mention of a Blackthorn, one of the richest families in the city. He would love an in with them. Daisy was just happy not to have to deal with the fallout of whatever fault Celia could find with their service. A trip to the countryside was starting to sound a much more appealing idea already.

She hadn't had many dealings with the Ratatoskr, not many city people had even met one, but she understood they were friendly and kind. Humans were part of the ecosystem too and deserved just as much respect as a tree. While Hari might think the Blackthorns should be respected more than a tree, Daisy knew her place, and that trees were more important than money at the end of the day.

She was probably being sent to Ruhann because she was one of the few people at the Grid who'd bothered to study biology. Her colleagues mostly came from engineering backgrounds, with a smattering of physicists. They loved coming up with up with theories on magic creation, yet always failed to prove anything of any real value. What Daisy knew was trees produced oxygen, and without oxygen they would all be dead.

The trees of the Great Forest also produced a substance in their sap that numbed pain. It was crucial for healthcare, from the mildest painkiller to putting people under for major operations, and the trees couldn't be successfully farmed. It was a miracle that corporations hadn't wrestled control of it off the Ratatoskr, but they hadn't.

Daisy pulled up details of the support ticket on her console. There wasn't much to go on, just an urgent request for assistance from one of the Ratatoskr assigned to interact with human society. It implied the Grid's magic had leaked into the Great Forest somehow. The Grid's network didn't extend as far as Ruhann, so the request was puzzling. She was often supplied with the barest of information on cases, the only difference being she could usually rely on gridmail or phone calls to find out more. This time, her only option was to go in person.

"Since this is urgent, can I get a private charter?" Daisy asked.

"Not that urgent. Besides, there's that regatta on in Samaz. Good luck finding a boat on short notice."

She resisted the urge to sigh again. The quickest way out to Ruhann was by river boat, even if she was limited to the steamers. The roads were slow and indirect, without any places to charge cars. The range of newer models was ever-increasing, but she doubted she could get all the way to the forests of Ruhann on one charge, let alone return.

Even though she benefitted from reduced magic bills, she had never felt the need for a car of her own. Kirkhyrst had reliable trams and was easy enough to walk around, plus the old town wasn't designed with cars in mind. She could drive, just about, but there was very little reason to leave the city limits, not unless work sent her, and something about carrying around all that condensed magic in a small vehicle unnerved her.

So, the waterways it was. She checked the timetable, and there was a steamer leaving in just under an hour. She did the maths; if she could wrap up her visit in a couple of hours, she could get the last steamer back and be home in time to go straight to bed. What she really needed, was portal magic of her own.

Alas, humans were destined to rely on the Grid for magic. It powered their homes and transport and allowed industry to flourish. It was a marvel, really, but it did need a whole lot of equipment to function. Imagine having magic at your fingertips...

Just as Daisy was gathering up her belongings, a young, pale-faced woman walked in looking a bit lost.

"Take the intern, won't you?" Hari called over as he strode out the room.

"Hi," the intern mumbled. She looked terrified. Daisy liked to think she was a good person, deep down, yet however much she liked people in theory, she just preferred working on her own. She braced herself for a tiring day, but it's not like she'd be stuck with the intern forever; placements were only ever for a few months, and the powers-that-be tended to rotate them around departments. Whoever needed grunt work the most.

"Hey, I'm Daisy, good to meet you." She held out an elbow, and the woman gently bumped hers in greeting.

"Lima Samson. I, um... my dad said I should learn how the power works, so, um... here I am?" Lima laughed nervously.

Daisy smiled back at her—she could do this. She had been Lima once upon a time, when meeting new people was hard. Some days it still was. That's why she worked in the bowels of the Grid. Well, most of the time. Lately she'd had a lot more call-outs than usual and she was missing out on all the ongrid gossip. Idle browsing was one of the few perks of a desk job.

"I don't know how much you'll learn about power management today, since we're heading out to the countryside. There are natural pools of magic, and of course they use it in small quantities, but it's nothing like what you'd be dealing with here. On the bright side, you get to meet the Ratatoskr."

"Oh, wow," Lima's face lit up. "I would have loved to have studied ecological management, but Dad says there's no money in it, they sell the sap for peanuts—Oh no, not peanuts, that's what my dad says, I would never..." Lima flushed bright red.

"That's OK, I hear they do actually like peanuts, just like the rest of us. Just no squirrel jokes, OK?"

Lima nodded furiously, her dark hair falling in her eyes. She wouldn't have looked too out of place in the vamp bar Daisy lived above. No judgement, they were pretty chilled out neighbours. Who was she to judge those who needed a bit of O positive to stay healthy? The patrons chose to give up their blood willingly anyway. Other people's judgement kept the rent down.

She was more concerned that Lima might fry in the open sun—she didn't look like she spent much time outside, her skin was almost luminous against Daisy's bronze tone. Autumn was late coming this year, and the sun had been unrelenting.

"Maybe take a hat? This heat doesn't seem to be going anywhere, and there won't be so many places to take cover." Was that diplomatic enough?

"Oh sure, I have, er... an emergency kit in my bag. I worry a lot, so I'm, um... prepared?"

"Me too," Daisy smiled at Lima. She thought they might just get along fine.

They walked down the corridor past Hari's office where he gave them two thumbs up. He was alright most of the time, lacked a bit of tact and didn't get out from his own bubble too often, but he could have been worse. He trusted Daisy to get on with her work without breathing down her neck. She was good at teasing out the root cause of magic failures, and she couldn't think of many other places where she could put her skills to use.

Her mum loved to tell her stories of how she took appliances apart when she was little, much to her embarrassment. She wasn't sure she ever put them back together again, but her parents never got angry at her. They valued her inquisitive nature above the cost of repair. They probably kept the repair man on their street fed with their trade alone.

Turns out magic is hard to understand. It's a natural resource that ebbs and flows, and it was astonishing that humans had harnessed it at all. The reason she had a job was because it could be unpredictable at times. After more than a century of trial and error, it had become stable enough that everyone had it in their homes. In fact, most city dwellers couldn't live without it.

Combine that prevalence with an inability to fix even minor issues and you get a busy support department at the Grid. They had a whole floor dedicated to taking calls and answering gridmail, and any that weren't a simple case of user error came down to Daisy's team in the basement. She made sure her engineers had more to go on than "doohickie doesn't work" and tried to analyse patterns in the faults, hoping to further refine how they used magic.

On a good day it was fascinating work. On a bad day, it was endless data entry and arguments over who was taking ownership of tickets, passing them back and forth, or more accurately, up and down stairs.

The Grid's offices were located in an area nicknamed the Gridiron, a former warehouse district that had become the city's centre. Hundreds of small businesses touting innovative uses of magic had popped up in the shadow of the Grid, eager for their slice of the pie. Being close by gave them an air of legitimacy; some were genuinely useful, but Daisy suspected many were selling the modern equivalent of snake oil.

It was convenient for the river at least, and Daisy and Lima made their way down to the docks where the upstream steamers would depart. It wasn't quite as grand as the cruise ship port, although care was taken to make it a warm welcome to *Kirkhyrst, City of Magic*. The illuminated sign gave the impression magic came from here rather than just channelled into the Grid by people like Daisy.

The Tarac River was a hive of activity in the warmer months. Daisy enjoyed people watching, making up stories for those who passed by. Gleeful expressions signalled tourists taking in the waterside sights. Others queued for downstream steamers, the promise of sandy beaches luring tired Kirkhyrstites out to the coast and the islands beyond. It was a little late in the morning for the glum faces to be commuters, but they muttered at those blocking the pavement all the same.

A gaggle of lab-coated students dipped sample containers into the water. Daisy imagined they were hoping to discover the next big thing in aquamagic... Or just hoping not to fail a class they didn't quite understand. Maybe they were the few studying biology like she did.

She surreptitiously glanced at her young companion, who was taking in the hustle and bustle wide-eyed, as if she was fresh off a boat herself.

"So how long have you been in Kirkhyrst?" Daisy prompted, wondering if she had come in from an ambitious farming community keen to harness magic to increase crop yields.

"Oh," Lima frowned. "I've lived here all my life. I guess, I um... I never came down here. My... um... my dad... he wouldn't like it."

Daisy blinked. She barely knew anything about Lima, but she was already starting to dislike this man, who had impressed his will onto his nervous daughter. From a professional stand-point she knew she shouldn't pry, so she mentally zipped her mouth and looked back out at the river.

In a quiet spot away from the boats, a group of white robed humans bobbed around in the still water. The power of water to revive and refresh was trending ongrid among influencers, but Daisy thought there were better places to take your daily waters if you were into that kind of thing. A nice tranquil spa in the mountains or the azure waters of Samaz. The Tarac did flow through a vast city after all, and even with the best intentions in the world, unmentionables escaped into its waters now and then.

Along the riverbank, a hodgepodge of architectural styles clamoured for space and attention, from functional brick warehouses positioned for convenience, to the sleek and somewhat sterile high rises favoured by those with the money to spend on a view. Smaller houses with their own jetties were dotted here and there, leftovers from a time when space was not at a premium. The last holdouts to property developers who would just love to get their hands on prime real estate.

Those who didn't know what they were looking at might miss the ancient stone temples, blanketed green with moss, worshippers long forgotten. No one wanted to risk the wrath of a god, so they were left standing, just in case the gods actually existed. They weren't completely unloved; urban wildlife had made the vine-twined temples their home. Rats, foxes, pigeons, and an occasional bird of prey with an appreciation for on-site dinner options.

Daisy checked the time as Lima rummaged around in her oversized canvas bag. The steamer should be due any minute now; punctuality wasn't always their strong point, but no one who used them was really in a rush. Since she couldn't make her journey any faster, Daisy was determined to make the most of the day. The weather was fine, sunny but not too hot, with a fresh breeze coming off the river, and the silence between her and Lima was companionable, like they were longstanding colleagues, not acquaintances of mere minutes.

Lima withdrew a big floppy sun hat from the depths of her bag and fixed it firmly to her head. It didn't quite fit with her vamp girl aesthetic but not everyone was trying to fit in a pre-defined identity. Daisy wore faded, cut-off jeans and a scruffy t-shirt she'd picked up at a work conference, the cheesy slogan in cursive font reading *Make Every Day Magic!* Hardly dressing to impress, but she felt like those things wouldn't matter to the Ratatoskr. Hari hadn't really given her enough notice to go home and change, not if she wanted to be in Ruhann before tiffin.

The queue for the steamer was short, one family obviously setting out on holiday with their overstuffed bags and excited children, and a few solo travellers. Mostly human, but at the back was a large male shapeshifter, a wolf by the looks of his pack tattoos. Lima was trying very hard to look everywhere but at him.

"He won't bite," Daisy whispered. "Not unless you ask him to."

Lima flushed and pointedly stared in the opposite direction. Daisy had no such qualms.

The shifter's hair was dark with silver streaking through it, curling around his ears and neck. His human muscles were well defined, suggesting he didn't spend most of his time in lupine form, and his eyes were eerily golden. The expression on his face was one of mild boredom, that he had to do something so un-wolflike as queuing for a boat. He caught Daisy checking him out, and Lima not-checking him out, and smiled warmly. He was kind of cute, for a wolf.

"I have a question." Lima turned to Daisy, who made what she hoped was an encouraging face. "Why don't the Ratatoskr use their portals to come here? Wouldn't it be easier than sending a message and then waiting for us to get our arses up to Ruhann?"

"I don't think they like the city all that much. It's not exactly... natural."

"Hmm." Lima went quiet again, staring out at the water. Her posture had relaxed, just a smidgen, since leaving the office.

"You're here to learn, right?" Daisy asked.

Lima nodded.

"OK then. I want you to remember there's no such thing as a stupid question. Not knowing something is not stupid, and it's far better to ask if a wire is safe to touch than to touch it and get zapped by magic. I would know."

"Does it hurt?"

"Yes, in a weird way. It's hard to explain, but I wouldn't recommend trying it."

A few minutes later, the gentle chug of the steamer engines signalled its arrival, followed by a high whistle as it let off steam. They were one of the earliest mainstream uses of harnessed magic, replacing coal furnaces with clean energy, though essentially, they still ran off boiling water. This one, named *Selene*, was painted a cheery yellow with red waves along its hull. It was basic, but welcoming.

Selene's crew consisted of a captain and two attendants, who slid out the gangplank and tied it in place before ushering the waiting passengers on board. Daisy showed them her grid ID, granting her passage on any state run transport.

"She's with me." Daisy gestured to Lima, who was fumbling around her bag for small change. She wasn't sure if interns benefitted from the usual perks but very few people were willing to cross a Grid employee. You never knew when you might need their help. The attendant waved them both through, and they found seats on the upper deck where they could watch the world go by.

"All aboard!" the captain yelled, and they set off on their three hour journey to Ruhann.

# Lailu

THE TREES WERE SCREAMING. A cry of pain that echoed down the valley.

Traces of blue flickered up their towering trunks, bark alight with flame. Not the flame of a comforting hearth, nor the promise of a campfire to provide nourishment. No, something harder that reeked of magic. Puffs of breeze sent embers floating to another target, setting off a whimper as the next tree prepared for their fate.

A lone figure stood before the blaze, red fur illuminated by firelight, tail tip pressed to her lips. This was too soon; Tapping Day was two lunars away, and preparations for the festivities had not even begun. Seasons could be fickle, but a regenerative burn so early was unheard of.

Lailu had been sitting down to her breakfast when the news reached her. A group of Ratatoskr had gone for an early morning stroll in the Great Forest and caught the whiff of smoke. Since they couldn't find the sector's Tree Keeper—Lailu was fast asleep in her nest at the time—they'd reported it to the wardens who went to investigate without her.

She'd been honoured with the task of Tree Keeper only six lunars ago; she sincerely hoped she hadn't done anything wrong. No one had warned her of anything like this. Just the usual pests and moulds to keep an eye on. How to determine sap levels. When to give the warning that the burn was imminent. Well, she'd failed on that front.

When Lailu had finally caught on that something was wrong with the trees in her sector, she'd cornered Sylvain for more information. If she was being honest, she was hurt that the wardens hadn't woken her. She was new to the job, but how was she supposed to learn from her mistakes if she was left out of the loop? Sylvain had only muttered something about incompetent humans and rushed off to send a message to Kirkhyrst. Something about a magic leak? Lailu didn't realise magic *could* leak, it just existed. However, she barely knew anything about humans and what they did in their artificial city. A home without an abundance of nature was a terrible nightmare not worth dwelling on.

So, she did the only thing she could; she opened a portal to the Great Forest and went to look for herself. She was due to do a weekly check-up anyway. She was responsible for reporting on the forest's welfare and conditions that may affect the harvest. Her recommendations were supposed to be small things like moving Tapping Day or arranging extra nutrients to be delivered to the forest floor. She had not been expecting to see the forest ablaze when she woke up that morning.

The Great Eldur Pine Forest stretched out for miles and miles, and for as far as she could see, the trunks shimmered with blue fire, the blaze consuming fine needles as it passed by. It reminded her of the air around portals when they opened, reality breaking apart, just for a moment. The air, thick and heavy with smoke, caught in her throat. And the noise. It set her fur on edge, each hair vibrating with the frequency of anguish.

It wasn't just the desperate plea of the trees; beneath was a crackling static and an almost unheard sound of claws scraped across slate. Images of Ratatoskr kits being dragged from their nests lanced through her mind and she shook them free. She didn't need the visual message. She knew the trees were desperate, saw her as someone who could help. They were just trying to reach out to her in the only way they knew.

Lailu stepped through the pines' lifecycle in her head, trying to work out what stage they were at. A sapling would grow from the ashes of the winter before last, spend twelve lunars regrowing to their full height, an impressive achievement. The most patient of Tree Keepers could see the growth happening before their very eyes. Then came reproduction. Pine cones would form, pollen released, the moment of fertilisation wholly dependent on the luck of the wind. Tiny particles of potential drifting in the air. And sometimes up an unsuspecting nostril.

Once their offspring were released to the whims of nature, they would prepare for the burn. The cycle of life, death, and regrowth. Fire was no stranger to the Eldur Pine, but they came prepared. For six lunars they would use all the resources available to them to generate a soothing sap, pulling from the earth below and air above. For of course these majestic, living beings could feel hurt if they did not protect themselves.

The awful keening of the pines told her head what her heart already knew. There was little chance that their sap had built up enough to soften the pain of the inferno before her. Something was seriously wrong.

The least she could do was try to take back a sample for further investigation. She wasn't completely useless at her job. Lailu quickly scanned her immediate surroundings and gathered up some wide, waxy leaves from the forest floor, folding them carefully into a make-shift pouch. Countless hours spent exploring the forest meant at least her bushcraft skills were honed to perfection well before she knew what she wanted to do with her life.

"Please forgive me for any discomfort I may cause," she apologised to the nearest afflicted tree, though she doubted her presence could be felt over the flames. The scream was unbearable close-up. She attempted to muffle it, clamping her tail over her tufted ears. Using her slender, sharp claws, she scraped a small section of bark and wood into the pouch and sealed it closed with the tiniest dab of sap. It was important to be prudent with resources, especially so if the trees were dying.

No, she shouldn't get ahead of herself. She pushed the negative thought from her mind.

There wasn't anything she could do right now, certainly not by herself. She had to get back to the scurry, find out if other sectors were affected. Maybe there was something that could be done. The natural world was always able to surprise her and maybe it knew what it was doing.

The portal snapped open behind her, and with one last distraught look at the forest, Lailu stepped back into it.

* * *

"It's not the burn," Otso said, surveying the scene before them. He was a great bear of a Ratatoskr, taller in stature than Lailu, who had to crane her neck to meet his gaze. To prove his point, he threw a bucket of water at one of the burning pines. It fizzed and crackled, but the blue flame didn't waver. If anything, it burned brighter.

"I told you," Sylvain said. "There's something uncanny to it."

"I looked at that sample you took," Otso said to her. "The sap levels are low, as you suspected."

Lailu took the compliment with a small smile. Otso had been a Tree Keeper for as many cycles as Lailu had lived. He could have been a warden if he'd wanted to, but he was too fond of his role to give it up. Trees talked back less than Ratatoskr, after all.

"There's another thing," he continued. "There were strange patterns in the bark. A sort of scarring."

"Did the flames leave it behind? Like charcoal?" Lailu suggested.

"No, it was too regular for that. More like those printed fabrics we sometimes get from the humans."

"See," Sylvain said.

"Not really," Lailu said, confused about where this conversation was going. She wasn't ready to get involved with human dealings, perhaps she never would be, but the trees... The trees were her life, her calling. If she had to talk to humans to sort this out, then she would accept that burden.

"Did you send word to Kirkhyrst?" Otso asked.

"I sent a magpie first thing, requesting an investigation post haste. This whole thing stinks of human interference," Sylvain said.

Lailu thought it smelled of magic, but she let him continue.

"Should the Grid acknowledge the magpie, I'd expect someone today. It doesn't take them that long to get here with all their technological advancements," he sneered.

"Sylvain! We should accept our differences with grace," she admonished him.

"Sweet child, you are better than this old Ratatoskr. I have seen humans do too many things that defy nature to trust they mean well with it. But perhaps I am mistaken. If it is their doing, they will fix it promptly. Leaks are not friends to profits."

Lailu frowned over the strange word. She would look it up later rather than seem even more naïve in front of the warden. The scurry had an excellent library, and despite Sylvain's prejudice, the collection held many human works.

"I'm a Tree Keeper, should I not be aware of the potential for leaks, as you call them?"

"We didn't know there *was* potential. Wait and see, dear. We will have answers soon enough."

"If it was the burn, too many trees have caught to stop it now," Otso said, ignoring Sylvain. "You have to let nature take its course."

"If it's the humans, they can stop doing whatever it is," Sylvain said.

"You think?" Otso chuckled. "If they've lost control of magic, we're doomed."

It didn't bear thinking about, the idea that magic could burn out of control. Water would douse fire, but what would douse magic? A portal blazed only as long as a Ratatoskr held it open, but the magic humans traded in was untethered. A human couldn't shut it off any more than she could stop the rain from falling.

"Will the trees survive this?" Lailu asked in a quiet voice.

"Only time will tell," Otso said, patting her on the shoulder. "It's hurting them for sure, but there's no reason their cycle won't start afresh next year. They're used to this."

Lailu wasn't so sure, but she yielded to Otso's experience. She hadn't seen a regenerative burn up close before, the Great Forest being off-limits to most Ratatoskr during burn season, and she'd always assumed it was just like a normal fire. The trees before her burned cooler than any fire she'd ever felt.

"I've gotta get going. We're attempting to set up exclusion zones around the other sectors. Just in case." Otso waved and disappeared through his portal. Sylvain nodded his goodbye and followed suit, leaving Lailu alone with the whimpering trees.

They had quieted somewhat, resigned to their fate. Perhaps they'd understood their conversation, that there was nothing the Ratatoskr could do for them. She was grateful they'd stopped invading her thoughts, but their discomfort was still making her head ache.

As she turned away from the disaster, a smouldering twig snapped under her feet, disturbing something in the undergrowth. A blueish grey blur streaked out of the smoking scrub and clawed its way up Lailu's leg. It was a young male balurat, an adorable sight with its big golden eyes and soft, downy fur.

While the forest was farmed for resources, it was still a rich ecosystem providing food and shelter for thousands of creatures, from the tiniest ant to the colossal, brown bears. The first time she'd seen a bear, Lailu had been terrified, its paws the size of her head. Yet the bear had been busy picking the same berries that she and her mother had ventured deep into the forest for. They weren't that dissimilar, although Lailu was glad bears couldn't portal into her nest on a whim.

Not that Lailu ever used her magic for such things. Maybe she cheated at hide and seek every now and then, but didn't every young kit test the boundaries of their power? She sighed—those days were in the past now. She had responsibilities, an important job, one she was determined not to fail at. She very much hoped she wasn't failing.

"Hey, little cutie, you're safe," she cooed at the bundle of fur who had clambered up onto her shoulder, claws digging in a tad further than she would have liked. She knew his home was anything but safe—little white lies were a comfort when scared. It wasn't just the trees that looked to her for help; if she stayed much longer, she would have a whole menagerie of creatures to care for. "You can come home with me."

She settled the balurat into a pocket in her harness, giving him a reassuring tickle under the chin. He trembled against her chest, poor little thing. Staying there wasn't doing either of them any good. Instead, she'd go to the library and prepare herself for the arrival of the humans.

# Daisy

THE FIRST HOUR OF the journey was peaceful. As the city faded into the distance, the buildings they passed shrank in stature. On the outskirts of Kirkhyrst several towns crowded the banks of the Tarac, where the commute was still feasible and worth the compromise for the open space on offer. Beyond the towns, acres upon acres of farmland provided food for the millions of mouths downstream.

They had spent much of the journey in silence, with Daisy intermittently remembering to be a fully functioning adult and making conversation, mostly pointing out things on the riverbank as Lima drank it all in. Daisy did her best to appear relaxed, but still worried her face was doing weird things. That was the problem with always trying to outwardly portray herself as an extrovert—sometimes the façade slipped.

"You mentioned you wanted to study ecological management. Are you going to university?" Daisy inquired. The light in Lima's eyes dimmed.

"My dad says it's a waste of time. Better off getting out there, making money, making connections."

"Oh." Daisy had some choice opinions on parents limiting their child's dreams. "Well, now you've met me, that's connection number one."

"Dad will be pleased," Lima mumbled, but a trace of a smile returned to her face.

Daisy was getting up to stretch her legs when she noticed a strange gleam in the water ahead of the steamer. Perhaps it was a mirage from the unseasonal heat, but it reminded her a bit of the Grid. Not the wires and boxes that most people saw, but the inner workings where the magic was processed into a tamer form. It was slightly blue, hovering on the edge of purple, and crackled like the wrappers of those posh chocolates Hari brought into the office for midwinter. She was wondering if she should alert the captain when a scream sounded from below, followed by a loud crash.

They turned towards the sound, Lima clutching her bag as if she had anywhere to run to. Under the shouting and banging, there was a distinct sound of claws scrabbling for purchase. Before Daisy could put two and two together, a large blur of dark grey fur barrelled past them and dived under a table. Two golden eyes peered out as the wolf tried to make himself fit into the cramped space.

"Um, the boat's stopped moving," Lima pointed out. Now that the lower deck had quietened down, Daisy could tell the engines had stopped. Unusual but not unheard of if the captain thought there was an emergency. Spontaneous shifting was more upsetting for the shifter than dangerous, providing they weren't too hungry. She wondered if Lima had any food offerings in that bag of hers.

"I'm sure it's just protocol. Check no one's gone overboard, etcetera," Daisy said.

The wolf's eyebrows cycled through various expressions, settling on something close to bemused. Certainly not the look of a rabid creature. He was kind of floofy, with one ear a little crooked, giving him the impression of a large, but gentle family dog, the kind you might play rough and tumble with. His eyes were the only reminder of what he really was and as their gazes locked, Daisy blushed and looked away, remembering the shifter inside.

"Excuse me." One of the attendants, the one who'd checked her ID, stuck their head round the stairwell, getting Daisy's attention. "You wouldn't happen to mind taking a look at the engines, please?"

"What me?"

"You're from the Grid, aren't you?"

"Yes, but we're on a river... not connected to the Grid?"

"It's magic though, ain't it?"

Daisy sighed. There was no harm in looking, but she didn't hold up much hope of being able to do anything if the magic storage was breached. That might have explained the weird shimmer she saw a moment ago, but she wasn't an engineer. She mostly told the engineers what she thought was wrong, and they went and fixed it. At least it could be a learning experience for Lima.

"Come on, then." She heard a soft huffing from the wolf's direction that almost sounded like laughter.

The passage to the steamer's bridge was low and cramped, the walls lined with various pipes, valves and safety posters. In case of emergency, they did not advise asking passengers to fix the problem. The correct response was to don life jackets and get ready to bob around in the

Tarac, rather than risk getting caught up in a magic explosion. Daisy had sat through many a public safety video on the horrors of messing with magic yourself. She wasn't sure if any of the scenarios were true. Would your hands really turn to pink goo, or horns sprout from your backside? She didn't know, but it was best not to try and find out. The videos certainly did their job and the vast majority of Kirkhyrstites would contact the Grid for even the slightest fault.

At the end of the passage was a small door, plastered with several Do Not Enter and Danger of Death signs. Daisy and Lima followed the attendant through into another cramped space. The steamer's captain wasn't afforded the luxury of a spacious working environment, unlike the bridges of the cruise ships Daisy had attended to on occasion. There were personal touches dotted about, photos of a smiling woman with two children and a few crayon drawings that she assumed were meant to be of the steamer, but could have been a shoe, or cake.

The captain stood in one corner holding the operating manual, a thick tome full of diagrams and checklists, and a lot of coffee stains. Well-travelled then.

"Thank yah so much for offering to help, I'm Adam," he said, holding out an elbow. There wasn't much room for such niceties, but Daisy managed an awkward bump.

"I usually deal with tech attached to the Grid, so don't hold out too much hope," Daisy responded. "This is Lima, my assistant—you don't mind if she watches?"

"No, no, go ahead. And I understand. Anything yah can do would be amazing. I tried turning it all off and on again, but nada."

"Do you have a back-up power source?" Daisy asked. Swapping boxes over was at least within her skillset.

"Nah, sorry. Not afforded such luxuries these days. Cost-cutting, yah know?" Adam rolled his eyes.

The dashboard in front of her was quiet and dark. Steamers were relatively simple but as time went on, more and more people had ideas regarding what sort of features would make things safer and more efficient. This one was neither too old nor too new, so wasn't overwhelming to look and didn't pose a risk of imploding if she poked the wrong thing. She opened a small hatch and beckoned Lima closer.

"This is where the power source is located, see that box there?" Daisy pointed out.

"That doesn't look like it'd hold much magic," Lima said.

"No, it doesn't, but it's compressed and much more concentrated than what you'd find in the wires in your home. Makes it more dangerous if something happens to it."

"And has something? Happened to it?"

"No, not that I can tell. It looks intact and in good condition. All the wires are securely attached, no signs of corrosion."

"I take good care of my girl," Adam interrupted. Daisy rolled her eyes at Lima under the dashboard. Why were boats never male? She closed the hatch back up and turned her attention to the dashboard, which showed zero signs of life. Making sure the steamer's accelerator wasn't on, she took a breath.

"Well, here goes nothing," she muttered and flicked a few switches back and forth. The dash lit up like a Yule tree. "Are you sure you turned it off *and* on again?"

Adam looked genuinely surprised that this had worked, so maybe he had tried the first rule of problem solving, after all. Daisy's mind went back to the anomaly she'd seen in the water before they'd stopped... and before the wolf had shifted. It hadn't been a leak from the steamer as far as she could tell.

"Did you notice anything weird before it happened?"

"You mean like screaming and a wolf running loose?" the attendant interjected.

Adam looked thoughtful. "Now yah mention it, the engines stopped right when that commotion started out there."

"Interesting," Daisy and Lima said in unison.

The captain started working through one of his checklists and pulled out an incident report sheet. He wasn't too pleased to be doing paperwork, but it was important for everyone's safety to monitor incidents and look for patterns. Daisy made a note to search for similar reports when she got back to the office. She'd have to check the news and social media for spontaneous shifting events—it wasn't like shifters had a regulatory body tracking that. Or maybe they did and just didn't share it with humans. If the shifter didn't look too pissed off when he returned to human form, maybe she could ask.

# Faelan

FAELAN WAS HAVING A bit of a day. What had meant to be a quick delivery job now had him hiding under a table on a steamer heading to Ruhann, of all places.

He'd been taking a break between deliveries when Travis had slid into the chair opposite him. Travis was always very particular about packages being delivered direct into the hands of the recipient, but he paid well. The recipient in question had offices in the Gridiron, so Faelan accepted the job, knowing he'd be delivering in the area anyway. He'd drop it off, get paid a handsome fee, and be done by lunchtime. Or so he thought.

When he arrived at Anderson & Co., the titular Mr Anderson was not at his desk. His personal assistant was apologetic and offered to take the delivery, assured him she was very reliable and discrete. That wasn't the point. It wouldn't do his reputation any good if word got out that he ignored special instructions. Instructions that came with a higher price tag. He was certain Travis was exactly the kind of man to spread rumours if he was displeased.

Contracts, prototypes and samples were his usual fare. He generally turned down cargo drops, anything he couldn't easily carry by himself. He liked the feel of the streets under his feet, and the commerce of Kirkhyrst kept him busy enough. It also gave him a measure of financial independence from his pack. Thank Fenrir.

Anderson's personal assistant, Clara, was chatty, flirtatious even, and had proceeded to tell Faelan all about her boss's schedule. He had meetings out west and had left on the first steamer out of town, with an expected return in a week's time. She was quite put out that she'd had to find accommodation in Ruhann in a rush. She showed Faelan her console, the standards she'd had to lower to find the shabby boarding house, and inadvertently gave him Anderson's current location.

It was either wait it out or follow the man. He was leaning towards waiting, even though he'd have to sniff out Travis to explain the delay, which was an unappealing thought. Then he saw Astrid—with Kane—and his hackles responded. It was a stupid reaction, he knew, but he couldn't help himself. Putting distance between him and his packmates seemed the wisest choice. So here he was, sailing up the Tarac in search of a human in a business suit.

He admitted that he got a little riversick at times, but today the churning in his gut came on so suddenly and next thing he knew he was sat in a pile of his clothing while a little human boy screamed in his face. His lupine instincts kicked in and he fled, only there wasn't anywhere to run to.

The stairs seemed the best option, to put distance between him and the scared humans. The top deck was relatively quiet, just the two women from the Grid, and they of all people should be able to deal with a surprise wolf. The inner workings of the Grid were a mystery to him, but if he knew one thing, messing with magic was dangerous. And messing with magic was the Grid's whole purpose.

He'd noticed the older one checking him out while they were waiting to board. He guessed she was mid-thirties, dressed like she didn't care what anyone thought. The younger one looked a little too young to be working at the Grid already. He thought pups should take advantage of their youth and freedom as long as possible. The rest of their lives would offer more than enough opportunity for hard work.

But what did he know? Just an aging wolf about to lose his pack. Hiding from a child.

He didn't get a chance to find out any more about the women before the crew dragged them off to look at the steamer's inner workings. He'd been hoping to at least glean a little gossip, find out why the Grid was sending people out west. Most people paid no attention to shifters in their animal forms, which had proved useful on many occasion. He was too noticeable as a human, his bulk catching the attention and his eyes keeping it there.

Some, he knew, would crave that attention. He didn't. Maybe that was the reason he was where he was, not seizing the destiny laid out for him from birth. The idea of being a lone wolf hurt a little, but having the whole pack relying on him, wasn't something he needed. Her companionship, now that was something he wanted, but he had to put that behind him. For the good of the pack. For his own sanity.

Slightly hysterical laughter bubbled out of him at his predicament. The big bad wolf, hiding under a table, pining over what he couldn't have. He should probably go and retrieve his clothes since he didn't feel like he was about to shift back any time soon. His lupine form felt settled, which it hadn't done for a very long time. But if there was one thing more guaranteed to make a human child scream than a great hulking wolf, it was a great hulking naked male stranger. Fenrir help him, he didn't need a steamer ban.

Thankfully, he had thought to rig up a system to tie packages to his body, which meant they wouldn't fall off when he shifted. He usually worked in his human form, but you never knew when a wolf would be needed in a hurry. He wasn't stupid, he knew his policy of not asking too many questions could lead him into trouble one day.

He very much doubted today would be that day. Ruhann was a quiet and unspoilt land, with very few humans. Most of them just passing through.

Apparently, no one was coming to check on him. The crew must have had regular dealings with shifters, or the engine problems were a bigger concern. They weren't so far out from Kirkhyrst that a tug couldn't be sent, but they'd need to flag down a vessel travelling that way first, and it wasn't exactly the busiest time of year for river traffic. If they had to return to the city, no one would be reaching Ruhann today.

Faelan would take whatever happened as his fate. It wasn't like he had much control over the rest of his life, might as well let the whims of humans steer his path from now on.

He flared his nostrils letting the scents fill in what his eyes couldn't see. The steamer smelled of human sweat and sickly sugar drinks, mingled with traces of happiness and anticipation. A touch of faded fear. Did he cause that? They could just as easily be scared of water, or apprehensive about going to a strange land, albeit one only a few hours away from home. Minor worries and small annoyances.

It was easier to isolate the scents here than in the streets of Kirkhyrst where thousands of individual scents mingled to become one overall aroma of the city. He had grown up with it, found it almost comforting, but it was better not to parse the actual chemical make-up of it if one wanted to stay sane.

He wriggled himself free of the table, allowing himself a full body stretch while he was still alone. His ears swivelled back and forth, picking up snippets of conversation. The humans below were still talking about him, but the screaming and crying had ceased. Small blessings.

He tried to remember the last time he had shifted without meaning to. Anger or grief could trigger it, drinking too much alcohol, too. Most spontaneous shifting was among adolescent pups, their hormones running rampant. He had felt fine this morning, considering everything. Riversickness, that's all it was…

Alone with his thoughts, they kept circling around to the two people he least wanted to think about. On top of everything else, had they made him lose control of his own body too?

The wind chose that moment to blow a gust of air up off the water's surface, bringing with it odours of sediment and fish, and something sharper. A metallic tang that left Faelan's nose tingling with energy.

# Lailu

SHE HATED TO ADMIT it, but the library wasn't helping. Oh, there was plenty of information about humans, most of the books had come from them after all, but nothing told her what to do when your warden suspected humans of causing magic leaks. From the fiction she'd read, humans didn't like being accused of things; they got defensive.

She slammed shut *What Magic Gave Us: A Journey Through One Hundred Years of Innovation*. None of the books explained how humans got hold of magic, only the things it did for them. A kettle sounded quite marvellous, no more boiling water over an open fire! But those things weren't in the Great Forest, so how could they have leaked there? Sylvain must be mistaken.

Some of the more traditional Ratatoskr disapproved of the library on principle. The books were dead trees full of human lies. Lailu was more pragmatic; she could see how useful they were for sharing information, and she so loved the stories they contained. She refused to feel guilty about it, especially since the damage was already done. All their books were second-hand, cast-offs in need of a home. It was better for them to be cherished by the Ratatoskr than thrown away.

The wait was agonising. Humans travelled so slowly. She knew no one wanted to portal into the city, most believed it wasn't even possible, but could they not meet half-way? They did it with the birds, to ease their journeys when they needed to send messages.

A snore interrupted her thoughts. She'd settled the scared balurat in a nest of blankets while she scoured the library's shelves. He'd stopped shaking as soon as they'd exited her portal, the distance from the fire an instant balm. Then he'd promptly fallen asleep at her feet.

She should try and find him some food; things were always better on a full stomach. Lailu scooped him up and wandered over to the kitchens to beg a variety of scraps, hoping something would temp him to eat. She was grateful balurats were herbivores, she didn't have the faintest idea where to find meat, and she couldn't stomach killing an animal herself. She would speak with Hazel later, surely her friend would know more about the diet of the forest's residents.

She laid out her kitchen haul in front of the balurat's snout; slices of carrot, cubes of sweet rainbow beets, rings of fried halo tubers, lentils stewed in warming spices, a handful of sugared almonds, a bright green apple, and a handful of sorrel leaves picked from her own small patch of herb garden. The creature's nose twitched in curiosity.

"Go on, it's OK." Lailu nudged him closer to the feast. The balurat reached out, picked up a halo tuber and took a large bite, chewing noisily.

"Of course, the junk food," Lailu laughed. "I guess I should give you a name, if that's OK?" She didn't know if balurats had concepts of names, but a nickname to call him by would make life easier. If he was going to stay here, that was.

Visions of the strangely burning forest whirled in her mind. It wouldn't be safe for him to go back until the fire was under control. If that's what it was. She was hoping she'd unearth the details of some strange natural phenomenon in the library. Something to explain the eerie flames. Something that meant the forest was safe.

"We'll keep it simple, I shall call you Balu, since I don't know any other balurats." Balu looked up to her as he chewed on his fried ring of goodness. Lailu was quite fond of fried halo tubers too, but she couldn't live on them alone.

"Perhaps a nut, Balu?" she offered, and a small paw grasped the almond, which shimmered slightly in the sunlight. Balu nibbled on it and sighed contentedly. So, he liked sugary nuts too. He'd had a tough day, it was understandable he'd want comfort food.

Lailu yawned loudly. It had already been a long and stressful day, and it wasn't yet tiffin. Part of her wished she'd gone with Otso. She was only responsible for her sector, which he'd appeared to have written off, but if she could do anything help save the rest of the forest, she would do so gladly. Unless her responsibilities had been revoked. Scenarios ran through her head, one after another, escalating into her banishment from the scurry. She was being silly. No one got kicked out, but what if everyone blamed her? It started in her sector after all.

Balu burped and curled up among the remains of his dinner, head resting on the fast wilting sorrel. Lailu laughed. Maybe the little balurat had the right idea. It was out of his control, so why worry?

She lay back on the grass, feeling the gentle warmth of the sun against her face. Balu's rhythmic snores blended with the wind, and she felt her eyes closing.

* * *

Lailu woke with a start. She'd only meant to rest her eyes a moment, not fall asleep in the middle of the scurry. What would they think? A Tree Keeper asleep on the job while her trees burned...

She squinted at the sun, which was still high in the sky. Good, she hadn't missed lunch. All that remained of Balu's meal was a smear of stew. He'd even demolished the sorrel, all but one stray leaf now stuck to his ear. The balurat had a decidedly rounder tummy than he'd had that morning, with worryingly loud gurgles emanating from it, but she was glad he had regained his appetite.

Lailu, other the other hand, hadn't had a chance to finish her breakfast that morning, and she was famished, her stomach grumbling loudly as she brushed herself off. She was wearing a simple utility harness, the straps winding around her shoulders and legs, with loops to affix ropes to if she was doing any particularly strenuous climbing. Her thick fur meant she had little need for the kind of clothing humans wore, but pockets were an ingenious invention, so she often wore a belt around her waist with as many pockets as possible. Into one of which, she coaxed in Balu. The balurat hardly needed any more food, but Lailu didn't want to leave him unattended, and she wanted to show him to Hazel.

The scurry's dining hall was set into a hill, the walls constructed out of wood offered up by the forest. They would never fell a tree in its prime, instead waiting for boughs to break off or a fall to signal the end of its life. A diseased tree might be hurried along, but always with dignity. The resulting appearance was an organic patchwork of browns, silvers and reds, with vibrant green moss in the corners that barely saw the light of day. A hawk flying overhead might not even identify it as a building, its curves blending in with the landscape. As a communal hub, everyone was encouraged to dine together and share gossip and knowledge. It was the only enforced socialising the Ratatoskr did; if people wanted to spend the rest of their day in solitude, there was no judgement.

She looked around the hall, and her eyes found the deep chestnut fur of her best friend, currently spooning porridge into a bowl made from Ruhannian acorn husk. Lailu's stomach let out a loud gurgle.

As if the sound had summoned her, Hazel turned away from the buffet and caught Lailu's eye, gesturing over at the tables in the corner. Lailu nodded and mouthed that she'd join her, but first she needed to grab food. The porridge smelled heavenly today, laced with honey and some spice she couldn't quite place. Balu's pink-tipped nose poked out of her pocket.

"No, you don't," she hissed, pushing his head down gently. What a greedy creature he was. At least he didn't have telekinetic powers. She'd read about a species of hound from Samaz who could move their prey with their minds; no one's lunch would be safe around a telekinetic balurat!

With Balu safely stowed in her pockets, she quickly grabbed porridge and an apple before she spotted a distinctive pelt of dark fur approaching the buffet.

"Sylvain! Do you have a minute?" She rushed forward, her porridge sloshing perilously over her paws. "Ow, that's hot!"

"You must have got a fresh batch." The older Ratatoskr smiled at her. "If it's about your new found friend, it's quite alright."

"My, what? I—Oh," she spluttered before realisation dawned. "Oh, I didn't think to ask, he's a refugee after all." She patted Balu's head.

"Yes, quite so. Was there something else?"

"I—er, the humans? Have they arrived yet?"

"No. Asha is watching the dock, but she says one of the boats is late. Of all the days..."

"The fire," Lailu whispered as if saying it aloud would summon it upon the scurry. "Is it spreading?"

"Mallow saw smoke in her sector about an hour ago. Otso's trying to limit it, but... Nothing we do seems to make a difference." Sylvain shrugged, weariness showing on his face.

"It's not going to reach here, is it?" Lailu asked, wide-eyed. All the scurries were far from the Great Forest, built among non-combusting deciduous trees, but Mallow's sector bordered the beech woodland to their north.

"There's no need to be alarmist. We have a perimeter for a reason. Now, please allow me to eat, one of those chestnut buns has my name on it."

Lailu let him past, frustrated at the lack of answers. Clutching her bowl, she weaved her way over to Hazel's table.

"Good afternoon," Hazel mumbled with her mouth full.

"Not so good, but afternoon it is," Lailu sighed.

"I heard about the fire, so awful."

"Yeah, some people from Kirkhyrst are coming to investigate. Sylvain thinks it's their doing, but something just feels off. Like why would they be doing anything out here in Ruhann? We don't need their wires and gadgets."

Her friend sort of shrugged and nodded at the same time. Trees weren't her forte, but animals were.

"Hey, there's someone I'd like you to meet," Lailu said and reached into her pocket to coax out Balu, who was delighted to discover the porridge spill on her paw. Hazel squealed in delight, attracting the attention of other diners.

"Oh my, he is so cute!" Hazel tickled Balu under the chin and he squirmed in delight. "Where did you find him?"

"The Great Forest, he was running from the fire." They took a moment of silence to process this. How many others were displaced or dead because of it? In a normal cycle, those who made the forest their home would migrate to safer ground around a week before the regenerative burns started, the mycorrhizal network having sent out its alert. The presence of Balu in her lap meant they hadn't had fair warning this time.

"I was meaning to ask, what's the best diet for a balurat? He's been chomping merrily on halo rings, but I should give him something more suitable."

Hazel chuckled, "I bet he has. Who can resist the crunchy, salty goodness. They're pretty much omnivores, he would be eating berries around now in the wild, roots and leaves the rest of the year. Maybe insects, if he can catch them without putting too much effort in. He'll be OK eating our food for a while, for sure. Easy on the fried snacks, but they're good for shock."

Lailu was relieved she hadn't accidentally poisoned him with her makeshift brunch. "Could you look after him this afternoon? I need to meet with the Grid people."

"Sure. I only have garden duty. If he promises to not eat everything in sight, he can hang out with me."

"Thank you, thank you. I named him Balu, for now at least."

"Hey Balu, I hope we can be friends." Hazel scooped up Balu, turning him on his back and tickling his tummy. His paws wiggled in the air, and he chirped happily. He was in good hands.

# Daisy

DAISY AND LIMA RETURNED up deck to find the wolf sat on one of the benches, face turned to the sun, eyes closed, mouth open, tongue flapping in the wind.

"He's not what I expected a shifter to be," Lima whispered. The wolf's eyes snapped open at the sound of her voice, and Lima jumped a little. He didn't move from his spot, which gave him a good view of the passing riverbank. Lima edged back into her seat. Daisy followed, her mind still on the anomaly.

The Ratatoskr's message had said something about magic leaks. Her immediate reaction was that there was nothing Grid related out there, but the steamers travelled upstream throughout the year, passing into the borders of Ruhann, magic on board. Could the answer be that simple?

The steamers were managed by the Board of Transport, and the Grid's only involvement was supplying the power units. It wasn't her job to fix them if they were leaking all over the countryside. She peered over the edge of the boat, half expecting to see three-eyed fish swimming alongside. Still, it was in her interest to know if something funky was going on with magic at large. She took out her notebook and jotted down her thoughts.

*Anomaly in water, potential leak? Could be light artifacts caused by hot weather...*
*Steamer power failure, short term, equipment in good condition.*
*Have other steamers experienced similar issues? Run query. Would Grid even know?*
*Apparent spontaneous shifting, wolf shifter, around same time as power outage. Coincidence? Talk to shifter later.*
*Is it same issue as Ratatoskr case?*

It wasn't much, more questions than answers at this point, but it was not nothing.

"Would you like me to fetch your clothes?" Daisy turned towards the wolf. He looked at her curiously for a moment, then nodded his large head. It was a small act of kindness, but it would also give her an excuse to go and speak to the other passengers.

Downstairs the steamer was divided into indoor and outdoor seating areas, both more sheltered from the elements than the top deck. In one corner, an attendant served drinks and snacks, basic things like JojoJuice and water, but also a few regional treats like halo rings. She would have to get some on her way back; they were hard to find in the city.

The shifter's clothes were right where he'd left them, in the middle of the deck next to a family of four. They appeared a little shaken, and the youngest boy's face was tear-stained. A selection of sweet treats was laid out on their table, untouched.

"Let me just get these clothes out of your way," Daisy said as she scooped up the bundle, trying to keep the undergarments on the inside. She did not need to be touching something that had touched a stranger's nether regions. She smiled warmly at the family.

"Oh, thank you, that's so kind. We didn't think we should touch them in case..." the mother trailed off.

"It must have been such a shock."

"Oh, yes. The man—um... I guess the wolf? He looked a bit peaky and was walking past right there when—Oh it was hideous! You shouldn't say those things, I know, but it's not for little eyes to see. Why, I don't think I shall be able to sleep tonight myself..."

"Did you notice anything odd before it happened?" Daisy prodded.

"No, we were minding our own business. Why? Do you think it was provoked?"

"Oh, no reason, I just have an interest in shifters. They're so fascinating, you know." Daisy looked down at the novel the woman had put aside. "I'm writing a novel. About shifters, so I thought I could do some research... but I'm so sorry to bother you. It must be so upsetting."

"That's quite all right. I'm sure having a real life wolf on board is a real treat for your research."

Daisy was about to step away when the older boy murmured something.

"What was that dear?"

"The water went all wobbly," he said quietly.

"That's just the waves the boat creates, darling" the mother said kindly.

"It looked like lavender sweeties," he added, ignoring his mother.

"Quite the imagination these kids have. You can put that in your book too, if you like," the father chuckled.

"I'll leave you be."

"Goodbye love, thank you for..." the mother gestured at the clothes.

"No problem." Daisy turned around and headed towards the snack bar.

Lima's eyes lit up when Daisy threw a packet of halo rings in front of her. They were delicately tied with some sort of grass, hinting at their Ruhannian origin.

"I've always wanted to try these, Dad won't buy imported food." Lima took a big bite and sighed happily. "These are amazing. Did you know they tried growing them in the Sala Fields, but they just don't take? They grow all over Ruhann, like weeds. Tasty, beautiful weeds. I hope I get to see one growing."

Daisy nodded as Lima rambled on about the flora and fauna of Ruhann. Hari had thrown them together carelessly, but it was a good pairing, and Daisy couldn't think of a better partner to be taking to the Ratatoskr. Certainly better than the embarrassment Hari would have caused. She didn't know who Lima's dad was, but he sounded a bit of a nob-end; his daughter clearly had a passion for nature, and it would do her harm to stifle it in favour of a better paying job, or whatever his end game was for her.

Of course, rent in some parts of Kirkhyrst was hideous. Maybe her family needed the money. Daisy studied Lima's clothes, that they were new said little. It was the first day of her internship, and if the point was to make a good impression, they would have dressed her right, even at a cost. They were black and simple. Unidentifiable. Could be made-to-order couture or basics from the market.

Daisy wasn't great at telling the difference. Anyway, it wasn't really any of her business; it's just that Lima seemed like two different people.

"Is the steamer's power cell the smallest portable power source there is?" Lima asked.

"I've not seen many smaller ones, maybe the ones in cars, but I don't have a lot of experience with those. The Grid has some we can take out to jobs—they're a similar size. They weigh a ton." Daisy said.

"That's a shame."

"I guess."

"I was just thinking it was a shame we didn't have a way to phone ahead to tell the Ratatoskr we're running late. If we had power cells small enough, we could carry them around and make calls wherever."

"The Ratatoskr are expecting us whenever fate delivers us, and they don't use phones."

"Oh. But someone nearby might, right?"

"Hypothetically speaking, sure."

"And they could pass the message on, like we have the phone exchanges for those who aren't connected in Kirkhyrst."

"How would the call get through without wires?"

"I hadn't thought that far ahead. But it's magic, many things are possible."

"I wish I had your optimism," Daisy laughed. "There is research going into smaller power cells—my back would very much appreciate that. I'm sure some bright spark will figure out how to make voices travel through thin air if it's possible. Progress is everything to Kirkhyrst.

"Magic can't do everything though. You must remember that if you want to work at the Grid. We don't understand the innate magic inside people like shifters and Ratatoskr, but we do know it has limits when we try and tame it. A human can't just decide to be a wolf for instance." Daisy glanced over at the wolf who appeared to be listening to their conversation. She couldn't blame him; it wasn't like he could sit and read a book in his condition.

After returning his clothes, the wolf had made a kind of nest with them and settled his head on his shoes. Daisy hoped he didn't mind the smell of his own feet. She had no idea how long he'd stay in lupine form for. If it was voluntary, or if he was waiting to be off this steamer and away from scared and curious eyes.

He had some sort of package tied around his neck, indicating he was likely a courier. It was a wise idea to keep it attached to himself like that; customers would not forgive lost property just because a courier had a personal incident. The postal system promised to deliver anywhere if you had time to spare, but businesses were starting to demand more dedicated services, and couriers filled the gap. If you had the money.

She was being nosy again, trying to see where the package was going. She wasn't used to sitting around doing nothing for so long. Not that she lived an action packed life, but work took up most of her mental energy, and when she wasn't working she'd rather distract herself with a book or movie. She didn't see herself as one of those people whose work was their life, but somewhere along the way, work had taken over.

# Lima

Lima had not expected to enjoy her internship. She had agreed to it for a quiet life, one in which her dad allowed her to stay rent free in the family home. His house, his rules. Her former classmates had regaled her with tales of endless data entry and making coffee for permanent staff. Nothing of much educational value, but you could say you had "experience" once it was over, and you might just make some useful contacts along the way. The Grid was a prestigious placement that she couldn't turn down, even though she had no interest in working there.

Yet today had already been one of the most interesting days of her life. She was on a steamer to Ruhann, of all places. There was a puzzle to solve, a wolf snoozing mere feet away, and Daisy seemed open to her questions. She'd been touched by the gift of halo rings and felt like they could become friends, given half a chance. If this was what a job with the Grid was like, maybe she could stomach it.

What she'd told Daisy about her dad vetoing her education wasn't a total lie. He had put so many limits on what sort of things he was willing to pay for, Lima felt it was easier not to bother. If she was smarter, more accomplished, she could have tried for a scholarship, but without one, she was reliant on parental approval.

Contrary to popular belief, the Grid didn't require a degree to work at. They were a progressive company who offered apprenticeships to anyone with the right aptitude and attitude. Lima needed to work on the attitude part, she supposed, but it was a possibility. If rent wasn't so expensive, she'd be perfectly happy working in a cafe or bookshop, her dad be damned.

The idea that she wasn't from Kirkhyrst had tickled her. It wasn't like the whole world lived in the city, but as time went on, more and more humans ended up there. Farming, mining, even tourism, all these industries supported the burgeoning metropolis from outside. If anyone wanted more than that, all roads led to Kirkhyrst.

Lima hadn't known anything other than the city. She'd been on the usual school field trips out to the Sala Fields of course, and when she was younger, her dad had made sure she had occasional trips to the coast. She had stood on the beach and stared out at the vastness of the sea, imagining undiscovered land. She knew Samaz was out there somewhere; the archipelagic nation provided Kirkhyrst with all manner of goods that couldn't be produced closer to home and was a popular holiday destination.

The establishment of the Grid stopped humans roaming forever outwards into the world, instead they flocked together, and the Grid was their shepherd. Lima could never be the sheep that strayed; she had too much Kirkhyrst in her.

The steamer continued its journey without further mishap, the passing landscape melting from farmland into forest. Majestic Ruhannian Oaks mingled with ash and birch, painting the land greener than Lima had ever seen, not outside of documentaries. Small mammals scampered in the undergrowth, and a cacophony of birds chattered away in the canopies. There were no high rises, no glass nor concrete, just an occasional wooden house built by those who chose to live off the Grid. It seemed like bliss.

No Eldur Pines though, they didn't grow outside of the Great Forest and for good reason. Every few years they self-combusted, and a new sapling would grow from their ashes. The fire rarely spread outside the forest boundary, but a lone pine could spell disaster for a settlement.

In the distance a small dock came into view. It was a fairly rustic structure, made from rough-hewn logs with a pale canvas canopy providing a modest amount of shelter. Thick vines wound around the railings, peppered with dots of colour that gave the appearance of a string of fairy lights. On closer inspection they were bright pink flowers, their petals tilted to face the sun. It was really quite enchanting.

The steamer chugged slowly into dock and the passengers gathered belongings, shrugging on discarded clothes, ready to disembark. The wolf was standing next to his bundle of clothes with a slightly panicked expression. Did he need to shift in private? As Daisy and Lima went to leave, he let out a yip.

"What is it?" Daisy asked. The wolf stared at his clothes and back at the two women. "We're not going to watch. I'm sure the steamer doesn't go back straight away; the crew need to rest. You'll have plenty of time."

The wolf whined and nudged his shoe towards Lima.

"Do you think he can't change back yet? Is that it?" Lima suggested, and the wolf nodded and wagged his tail enthusiastically.

"We'll take your clothes ashore," Daisy offered.

Maybe they could find some sort of bag for him to carry them like his package. It must be a nightmare being a shifter away from home, away from their pack. How did they manage normally?

Lima gathered up his clothes and placed them in her miraculously spacious bag. When she was feeling fanciful, she liked to think it was magic. In reality, she'd chosen the largest bag she could find at Tor's department store. Large, and mundane.

"Just until we find something better to carry them in. I guess you're stuck with us for a while," she said to the wolf.

He opened his mouth gently, teeth hidden, in something resembling a smile. She resisted the urge to pat him on the head; he wasn't a dog. He scrambled down the gangplank with a wagging tail, and Lima followed him, stepping onto the land of Ruhann for the first time.

Awaiting them was a grey furred Ratatoskr, perched on a bench. She was a touch shorter than Lima, and her legs bent the wrong way. Lima reminded herself they were the right way for Ratatoskr; they were just different, not wrong. Tourists pointed and cooed, but the Ratatoskr was unperturbed. She did, however, raise an eyebrow at the sight of the wolf behind them.

"He with you?"

"We... er... have his clothes. Long story," Daisy said, glancing at Lima. "It's a bit mean just to abandon him here, but it's up to you..."

Lima swallowed. By taking his clothes she had inadvertently invited the shifter along, on her first day of work to boot. She hadn't thought that maybe they wouldn't be pleased to see a wolf in their midst. She hadn't really thought at all.

"I see." The Ratatoskr leaned down and stared into the wolf's eyes, long and hard. The wolf stared back, still as stone. It was not the behaviour of prey to predator. No, the Ratatoskr weren't weak or afraid in the face of their ancestor's foe. Coming to some unspoken conclusion, she straightened back up. "Let's get going then."

With nothing more than a twitch of her whiskers, the air crackled and warped, forming a bright circle behind the Ratatoskr, just large enough for them to pass through without ducking. The chirruping of the birds quietened around them, as if they knew that a wonder had occurred.

Well, it was a wonder to Lima, who held her hand up towards the portal. A slight warmth radiated from its surface, and she could feel the static brushing against her skin.

"What does it feel like?" Daisy asked. The Ratatoskr shrugged.

"To me, like stepping into a lukewarm bath, but opinions differ. Don't they always?"

"I thought you were an agreeable bunch?" Daisy mumbled.

"On the things that matter, yes, but we all experience the world as individuals. Who is to say how I experience it is the right way? Or the only way? Not me for sure."

Lima stepped tentatively towards the portal, a sensation not unlike pins and needles came over her, spreading from her outstretched hand and through her entire body. Not exactly pleasant but nothing to put her off. Not when this could be her one and only chance to experience the miracle of instantaneous teleportation. She closed her eyes, held her breath, and let the magic take hold.

# Lailu

Lailu wiped the ash from her eyes as she stood to survey her work. She couldn't bear sitting around waiting a moment longer and had gone to find Otso. He was in Mallow's sector, working at clearing the perimeter and dousing it with water. Lailu wasn't sure what good it would do. She had seen him throw the water at the flames with no success only that morning.

Still, they had dug trenches and cleared out scrub. Anything that could possibly be tinder was removed from the forest floor. A team of Ratatoskr were roped in to portal through water, just in case some of the fire decided to act like a normal burn.

The fire was spreading, without a doubt. Two other sectors had raised the alarm since lunch. While the Ratatoskr were familiar with forest fires, they weren't very practised at putting them out. Why would they be? The burn was meant to happen, so they let it. If they misjudged the timing, they would simply reap less harvest.

Lailu had turned her back on her sector with that knowledge hard in her heart. She was sorry her trees were in pain, but she had to have faith that they'd pull through.

They had no spare sap to offer them either. With the likelihood of the harvest being impossible this year, they needed to conserve their meagre stocks. She did not envy the poor warden whose job it was to break the news to the humans.

Their main concern now, was stopping the fire spreading beyond the Great Forest. They were still calling it a fire, but it was more like an inferno of magic, eating up everything it touched.

Otso had stopped digging and was staring at a nearby tree. A flicker of magic had appeared from the bark, as if out of nowhere.

"You don't think..." he said, lost in thought.

"What is it?" Lailu went to stand next to him, inspecting the tree.

"They have their own magic. If it's adding to the fire... No wonder we can't put it out."

Lailu looked more closely at the bark, being careful not to singe her fur. The first spark of magic was followed by a burst of yellow flame, which was quickly overwhelmed by the blue fire.

"Is it trying to burn itself?"

Otso shrugged. "Maybe. I forget you haven't seen a burn yet. They do spark a bit when they get going. Spark blue like the magic. But once they're started, the fire looks pretty normal. Yellow and orange, like the hearth."

"I thought we weren't supposed to come out here during the burn?"

"Ahh, that's what you tell old Sylvain. Us Tree Keepers, we like to come out here and watch. Safely, of course. You would have been invited, you know, if it was a normal year." Otso smiled sadly at her. "No one would blame you—if you decided to choose another path."

"What? No! Why would I?" Lailu spluttered.

Otso laughed. "That's the spirit. If you survive this, you'll survive anything."

"After this year, we'll need Tree Keepers more than ever; won't we?"

"True. Let's try a little experiment. See if you can find me a piece of tree that's not Eldur."

Lailu scoured the ground. They were just on the edge of the Great Forest, where other species sometimes crept in. However, they'd done such a good job of clearing the perimeter that there wasn't much left to find. She opened her portal and popped out into the nearby beech woods. They were calm and tranquil after the chaos of the fire, but she couldn't dawdle. She would help Otso with his experiment and go find out where the humans had got to. If she had to portal down to the river herself, she would.

She gathered up a few stray branches of beech and returned to Otso.

"What are you hoping to find out?" she asked.

"Just watch."

He snapped off a bough of Eldur Pine, and Lailu winced. She reminded herself that the tree would soon be consumed by fire, but she couldn't help feeling offended that a Tree Keeper would be so casual about it. Otso held out the branch to one of the burning trunks. It instantly sparked blue, followed by a yellow flame for just a moment. Then the magic took over, and Otso flung it to the ground before it could burn him.

"Now the beech."

Lailu handed him a branch. Again, he held it out towards the flame. It smoked a little as the blue flames bent around it, and eventually it caught fire. Not as quick as the Eldur, and the flame remained yellow. He dunked the branch into a bucket of water, steam hissing. When he pulled it out, the branch was charred but no longer on fire.

"That is reassuring," he said. "We should focus on protecting the deciduous trees—abandon the pines. Spread the word."

# Faelan

Faelan had been planning to peel off from his new found companions as soon as they'd deposited his clothes on dry land. Even when the younger one had vanished them into her bag, he thought could guess at where they would end up, since there weren't a lot of Ratatoskr dwellings to choose from. Worst case scenario, he could wait back at the dock to collect his belongings. It sounded like this was a day trip thing from his eavesdropping. Not that he had much choice; he could hear everyone on the steamer, the banal chitter chatter of humans with nothing to do but talk to each other.

He was starting to think Ruhann wouldn't be the worst place to get caught naked anyway. The Ratatoskr's clothing was utilitarian; something he could do with in his lupine form. They didn't tend to cover the parts humans were weird about exposing, though he certainly wouldn't want to shimmy up a tree as a naked human. He winced, thinking of the chafing.

When the portal unfurled before him, all thoughts of going his own way vanished. It was beautiful.

Anderson wasn't doing business with the technology averse Ratatoskr, that was for sure. Faelan was under no preconceptions that he might accidentally bump into him roaming around Ruhann, but he wasn't going to turn down a chance to go through a portal. Maybe's he'd find some inside info to take back to the pack. Just because he was nursing a bruised ego, didn't mean he couldn't still be useful.

That's what he told himself as he leapt into the light, a pleasant sensation vibrating through his bones. Passing through made his fur stand on end, giving him the appearance of a freshly blow-dried, pampered pooch. He shook, dislodging the static. Their guide's sleek fur didn't seem affected at all by their journey, which made sense. It was their magic after all.

On the other side of the portal was a spacious clearing, bordered by gnarled oaks and glimpses of wooden structures beneath the boughs. The Ratatoskr milling around gave them little more than a passing glance. Faelan could smell their mild curiosity, most likely aimed at the humans appearing in their midst. Regular Canis lupus were to be found anywhere there was prey, and if they recognised him as a shifter? Well, they weren't especially special, not in a place where portal magic reigned supreme.

Beyond the scents of the Ratatoskr themselves, the air felt alive in a way Kirkhyrst never did. He let his nose take it all in, the damp but not unpleasant smell of vegetation everywhere, and a wealth of life coexisting within it.

A faint odour of smoke was fleeting, there and gone again as Ratatoskr passed by. He couldn't quite parse the difference between common charred wood and Eldur Pine, and they would rely on fires for everyday life out here. They had no need to live too close to the perilous Great Forest, not with the fire risk and their ability to portal long distances. He wondered what their limits were.

A commotion rustled the bushes to their left, and five kits came barrelling out into the open. At the sight of a large wolf, they startled, but quickly regained composure. The apparent leader of the group tipped his head back, letting out an ahrooo to the sky, and his companions followed suit.

Faelan chuffed good naturedly. They were kind of adorable, with their big bushy tails too large for their bodies. Their guide shooed the kits away, and they disappeared as quickly as they had arrived. He noted that the grey Ratatoskr who had stared into his soul hadn't bothered to introduce herself to the humans. An instinct told him he was the more welcome of the three, even though he shouldn't be there.

From beneath a woven arch of hazel trees, a black-furred Ratatoskr emerged, a peppering of grey around his whiskers.

"Thank you, Asha, I'll take it from here." He dismissed their guide who scurried off in the direction of the kits. As he turned towards the newcomers, a disapproving look spread across his features. The blast of annoyance coming off him was mingled with a strong scent of anxiety, and other more complicated emotions that Faelan couldn't quite pin down.

"You at least responded to my magpie in good time. I'm Sylvain." He bowed his head slightly, not completely letting etiquette slide.

"We take magic breaches very seriously at the Grid," Daisy responded, switching into professional mode.

"That is, of course, if this is a breach. We are so far from Kirkhyrst and the reach of our network—"

"Yes, well, you humans are careless." Sylvain caught himself in his rudeness and straightened his shoulders. "Forgive me, but we are very concerned about our Eldur Pines. We are caretakers of the forest and do not wish to see it perish on our watch."

"Are you the Tree Keeper?" Daisy asked. Sylvain frowned at her, surprised she knew the term. Faelan certainly hadn't heard it before.

"No, I am one of the wardens of this scurry. The Tree Keeper responsible for the sector where the problem started is new. This is her first cycle—well, it should have been."

"What exactly is the problem? The report I was given was scant on details."

"First, I will show you the carnage," Sylvain replied, quick to get to the point of the visit.

Unlike Asha, Sylvain hadn't questioned Faelan's presence. The older Ratatoskr was impatient and brusque, and that suited him fine. He handed out pieces of cloth which the humans fastened over their noses and mouths. Faelan would presumably just have to hold his breath, as nothing was suitable for his long snout. He couldn't grumble too much; they hadn't been expecting a wolf. Did the Grid even employ shifters?

He hadn't always been such a grumpy loner. He used to have friends as well as packmates, people to go out with. Mostly shifters, many of them freeloaders, content in the knowledge their pack would have their back. Among those who did work, with real professions not just fly-by-night gigs, he couldn't recall any of them having anything to do with the Grid.

He filed the thought away as something to ask—not Astrid—he couldn't keep going to her. He'd have to ask the alphas; Luna would be happy to see him taking an interest.

A pair of earmuffs appeared in Sylvain's paws, and he slid them onto his head. Faelan blinked. Was that some sort of portal magic or a sleight of hand? A part of him wished he could ask questions right now, but then he would hardly have an excuse to stay.

"We're sensitive to the trees' suffering," Sylvain answered their unasked question. With his earmuffs firmly affixed, he opened a portal. He made it look effortless—not even a twitch of the nose or a narrowing of the eyes. Imagine having such an ability to hand. Shifting had its perks, but this? He would save so much time, visit so many places.

"Come on, no time for dawdling," Sylvain said, ushering the group through. Faelan didn't hesitate, bounding through with a happy yip. He could get used to this.

# Daisy

FOR THE SECOND TIME that day, Daisy stepped through a portal, but this time they weren't greeted by the serenity of a happy forest clearing. To borrow Sylvain's wording, it was carnage. Especially if you believed the trees were sentient beings as the Ratatoskr did. The air crackled, and the scent of smoke was thick despite nearby trees having long burned to cinder. The ground was blanketed in ash and blackened pine needles, crunching as they shuffled gingerly into place.

They had been brought to a spot with high elevation; the forest spread out before them leaving no doubt about the extent of the fire. Gnarled black shapes were silhouetted against an eerie blue light. Daisy reminded herself these trees burned naturally, and the sight wasn't too unfamiliar to the Ratatoskr, yet she could almost feel the thing that had upset them so much. The trees were in pain.

"This is not a natural fire," Sylvain shouted, overcompensating for his muffled ears.

"But—I'm right in thinking these are Eldur Pines?" Daisy asked, raising her voice.

"Yes, but the timing is all wrong. They needed another two lunars—your months, before they'd be ready. When their sap is at its strongest, they feel no pain."

"And you think the Grid is involved because...?"

"Look at the flames."

Daisy squinted at the trees in the distance. She didn't particularly want to get close to the fire, but it was hard to tell what was wrong from where she was standing. It's not like she knew what a regenerative burn looked like. Among the trees, deep channels criss-crossed the landscape.

"What are those," she asked, pointing at the lines. They looked human-made.

"Sometimes the younger trees catch before they're ready, the streams help keep them isolated. But that's not what this is. This fire resists water: it is fuelled by magic, and we can only watch them burn," Sylvain said.

Daisy took a moment to absorb that knowledge. When she looked back at the fire, she could see it. The flames had the same blue tinge as the Grid's magic. It couldn't be from the steamers, not at this scale.

"Will they grow back?" Daisy asked, her throat dry.

Sylvain adjusted his earmuffs, "Sorry, they're a bit too effective at muffling. What was that?"

Daisy repeated herself, enunciating her words carefully.

"I hope so. We'll know by Yule. If the saplings haven't sprouted by then, I don't know what we'll do. I can't get you closer to the fire; it's too dangerous. The portals can be unpredictable around so much magic."

"Is that why you never come to Kirkhyrst?" she asked.

Sylvain was caught off guard by the question and took a moment to answer.

"Perhaps the kits would be tempted, but what is there for us when we have such bounty in Ruhann?" He paused, "But yes, I imagine our portals don't open in your city due to your... interference in the natural order of things."

That shut her up.

The wolf was padding around tentatively sniffing various burnt patches. Daisy wished she could communicate with him better, find out if he scented anything odd, or useful. Eventually he would shift back to human form, and she could ask him. Lima was carting his clothes around for him, after all; it was the least he could do to say thank you.

It was a bit weird that he had followed them this far. Was it some sort of instinct to be close to people, or was that a dog thing? She supposed she would feel a bit antsy if a stranger had run off with her clothing, and she had no way of getting home. She hadn't wanted to just leave him by himself though.

A shiny black beetle scuttled out from under a half burnt log, right under the wolf's nose. He jumped in surprise. So much a for a superior snozzle. The beetle carried on as if he wasn't there, heading for greener pastures. Daisy's gaze followed the path of the insect, and as she focused, she noticed more movement, all in the same direction. The miniscule occupants of the forest were on the move.

Lima had wandered off in the direction of the fleeing insects. She was crouched down, staring intently at a line of iridescent red ants. They almost looked as if they were on fire themselves.

"Firewater ants." Sylvain came up behind her. "They are one of the few creatures that stay behind during the burn. They can withstand great temperatures, far higher than you or I. But even they flee."

"That is not good," Daisy murmured.

"Understatement of the year," Lima replied, standing up. She dusted off the ash and broken twigs from her tights. None of them had been expecting to go on a hike in a faraway forest when they'd dressed that morning, but Lima's outfit was the least suitable. Her black clothing was now dusty and smeared, a sprinkling of ash flakes coating her shoulders. If Daisy tried hard enough, she could pretend it was snow.

She busied herself showing the intern how to take magic readings with her portable meter. The levels were sky high. She didn't have a baseline for Ruhann; this could be entirely normal background magic. She surreptitiously moved the meter away from Sylvain and back again, trying to work out if he was emanating magic too. It wobbled slightly but nothing conclusive.

She had a feeling their presence alone was an annoyance and didn't want to piss him off even more. Learning more about natural magic could wait till later. If she managed to help somehow, maybe she would be welcome back to do more digging. Or maybe she was just being an arrogant, intrusive human sticking her nose into places that were none of her business. She supposed she wouldn't like to be studied either.

Standing there in the eerie remains of the forest wasn't helping her find answers. This land was untouched by human hands; she couldn't fathom a connection between the Grid and this fire. Not unless someone had come out here and literally set it ablaze with an instrument of their making.

* * *

Back at the scurry Daisy took out a map and smoothed it over the table. It showed the extent of the Grid, including its more recent additions beyond the Tarac Valley. The lines all petered out before they reached the borders of Ruhann though. The country was barely on the map, just skirting the top left corner. Any malfunction big enough to affect the Great Forest surely would have been noticed by now.

There were no roads in or out of the forest; it could be accessed by foot or by portal, and walking would take weeks from the nearest town. It wouldn't be trespassing, the Ratatoskr had no concept of such a thing, but it was a high risk area, and anyone venturing in for a hike needed to be well informed of the burn cycle. And aware of unseasonal incidents now too.

Oh gods, she hoped no one had got caught up in the fire. The skeletons of charred trees were bad enough, if it had been people... and the poor animals. Her stomach churned. Whatever the cause, it was a tragedy.

Daisy's gaze landed on a new hub around ten miles south east of the border. It was their best bet if the Grid was indeed involved. In all the history of the Grid, there were no records of mass leaks like this. Accidents happened, of course they did, but they were always localised. The magic usually dissipated into the air, only affecting anyone in the immediate vicinity.

Any leak of this magnitude wouldn't go unnoticed in Kirkhyrst. She recalled her ever-increasing workload, all the extra callouts. Were they the symptoms? Had they been losing power for months and no one, in the entirety of the Grid's workforce, had checked to see if it was leaking? She couldn't believe it.

Reams of reports passed by her desk every day, every minute fluctuation in the power scrutinised by someone. Many of the Grid's best employees were tenacious nerds who wouldn't be able to sleep until they had the answer to any puzzle. And an unaccounted loss of power would certainly be a puzzle.

Although, if everyone were honest with themselves, no one really knew what the core was doing. Yes, humans made it, maintained it, but its discovery was a bit of a fluke. The right combination of minerals attracted ambient magic; why or how was still a mystery. Perhaps the core would naturally compensate for any loss, keeping the status quo going.

Looking at Sylvain's permanent scowl, she didn't bring up the idea that the Grid could do anything naturally. Surrounded by all this wood and nature, the machinations of Kirkhyrst felt very far away.

The soft padding of unshod feet sounded out from the corridor, and a panting Ratatoskr ran through the door. Her green eyes were large and expressive, her nose wide and flat, ending in a pink snub, and her fur was a bright, glossy red, with delicately tufted ears. As she skidded to a stop, she wound her long, slender tail around her waist, and took a deep breath.

"I'm here, I'm here," she wheezed.

# Lailu

Lailu could not believe he had started without her.
Well, she could, Sylvain was generally happy to take
control of things, but she was the one meant to be caring
for the trees' wellbeing. She should get to talk to the
visitors, explain the ins and outs of tree-keeping. Sylvain
would only tell them the bare essentials. And she was
curious to meet the humans, who appeared to have
brought a wolf with them.

"Hello, I'm Lailu, the Tree Keeper," she said pointedly,
bowing briefly in the visitors' direction. "I am so sorry I'm
late, I would have shown you the site myself." She side-
eyed Sylvain but it didn't hold any venom.

"Lailu, my apologies," Sylvain offered and turned to
introduce the Grid workers. A curly haired woman, with
deep brown eyes set in a friendly, rounded face, was called
Daisy. The name suited her, daisies weren't showy flowers,
but they were pretty and well-liked. In another situation
she could imagine Daisy being a cheery person like her
namesake. Another woman, paler and younger, with hair
as dark as midnight and icy blue eyes, was called Lima. An
unusual name for a human; the goddess of doorways was

better suited to a Ratatoskr, but humans did so like to borrow things that weren't theirs.

The humans she'd caught glimpses of over the years were all sharp angles and hard edges, but these two were softer, more approachable. She guessed they came in all shapes and sizes, the same as Ratatoskr.

And then there was a big, shaggy, grey, wolf-like beast with his tongue lolling out the side of his mouth.

"And you are?" She turned to the wolf, eyes enquiring.

"Um... well... we're not sure?"

"Excuse me? You've brought an unidentified shifter into our home?" She tried not to be prejudiced, but he could be anyone. Sylvain had obviously not thought to ask his name.

"I'm sure he's fine. He just kinda got stuck with us—a friend in need and all that..." Daisy trailed off. Lailu reluctantly agreed; you couldn't just leave people flailing because you didn't know their names. She understood the trees not through common language but through something nebulous. She hadn't left Balu behind. She knew they needed her help all the same.

If they'd helped this wolf, maybe these humans weren't as bad as Sylvain made out.

Lima was rummaging around in her vast bag. "Gotcha!" she announced holding a small card. It appeared to be some sort of identification. "It was with his clothes. His name is Faelan. Faelan of the Alder pack."

Faelan barked in agreement, a soft whuffing sound.

"Good to meet you, Faelan. May I?" Lailu held her paw out, and when he nodded, she gave the scruff of his neck a thorough pat. Faelan leaned into it, and she dug her claws in enough for a satisfactory scratch. He was not unlike a much-larger Balu when he wiggled under her paws, and she was surprised he enjoyed a stranger's touch so much. Maybe he was itchy; he did have a lot of fur for such a balmy day.

The humans stood upright and stiff in their postures. A species not used to casual tactile socialising. A wolf may eat a squirrel, but a shifter and Ratatoskr could be allies, friends even. They were more than their common descendants.

With the formalities out of the way, Lailu launched into her speech about the lifecycle of the Eldur Pines. She was sure Sylvain had been curt with them, not giving them the full picture of what they did. Even with the best will in the world, you couldn't fix problems with ill-informed knowledge.

"Could the magic be coming from the trees themselves?" Lima ventured.

"What?" Sylvain furrowed his not inconsiderably bushy brow.

"Otso—he's another Tree Keeper. He had a similar idea. Not that they started it, but their own magic is adding fuel to the fire, so to speak. That's why we can't put it out." She turned to Sylvain. "You should know, we're leaving the Great Forest to it. The fire doesn't seem to affect the deciduous trees in the same way, so Otso thinks that's where we should prioritise firefighting efforts."

"Can we stay on topic? How did it start? And don't blame our trees," Sylvain said.

"Things have a been a bit off lately, our wolf friend here spontaneously shifted in front of a bunch of holidaymakers, and there's been... other stuff." Daisy tried to explain the petty grievances of Kirkhyrstites to the Ratatoskr before trailing off.

"Our steamer conked out on the way here," she added.

Lailu thought they might be onto something, but Sylvain dismissed them.

"Mechanical issues. Humans insist on overcomplicating everything. You can't compare the Eldur Pines with a boat."

"What usually triggers the burn? Light levels, temperature, chemical signals?" Daisy asked, needing to know why they were so certain it wasn't natural.

"I always thought it was sap levels, but we don't really know. It is always the same time of year, give or take a week, so it could be light related." Lailu thought for a moment. "Once one goes, the rest follow. There might be a signal. Something in their magic that sets it free. A leak might confuse them."

"Exactly!" Sylvain harrumphed.

What was Sylvain's problem? He was always a bit crotchety, especially if you caught him before he'd broken fast, but his persistence that the humans were at fault was concerning her. She wanted help from whoever was willing to give it, no matter their species.

"It is past tiffin, Sylvain. Maybe our guests would care for some refreshments?" Lailu prompted.

"Of course, of course, how rude of me. Please would you show them to the dining hall?"

Lima's stomach let out a well-timed gurgle. Yes, tiffin was a good excuse to get them away from Sylvain and talk to them properly.

The scurry was not quite a town or a single structure, but a loosely connected gathering of trees, natural tunnels, small buildings and hidden nests. Trees arched over walkways, creating shelter on a rainy day. Ratatoskr didn't force trees to their bidding, but a gentle paw may have guided one or two branches into convenient positions and let nature do the rest.

Above their heads, bridges crisscrossed the canopy, linking lookouts and resting spots. Occasionally a nest had been made high in the treetops, but most Ratatoskr preferred underground dwellings. It could get dicey up there during storm season. That didn't mean they didn't enjoy hanging out in the trees, especially at the end of a long day to watch the sun set over the forest.

Lailu was proud of the little space she'd chosen as home. It lay beneath an ancient Ruhannian Oak, which had welcomed her into its root system by enlarging the hollow only days after she'd moved in. Over time, the tree had provided cubby holes and shelves, and even a little stump she could use as a table. She thanked the oak daily for its service. Not every young Ratatoskr had such a lovely nest.

In her induction, she'd been told of a group of thrill-seeking kits who'd tried to nest in the roots of Eldur Pines between burns. She hoped none of them were out in the forest now. Every Ratatoskr had the freedom to wander the Great Forest if they wished, but technically they weren't meant to make it their home. The point of the tale was for Tree Keepers to stay vigilant and to kindly move kits on if it happened again. But Lailu's mind had dwelled on the danger of living such a life. Had the trees known to move their residents on before they regenerated? She couldn't imagine having to start over every cycle in a new nest.

They walked into the dining hall, its leafy roof arching high above. A few curious glances came their way, but most diners were too busy eating or deep in conversation to pay them much attention. Lailu must be the most curious Ratatoskr in the scurry; she was desperate to ask questions of the humans and wouldn't have quietly minded her porridge if the tables were turned.

She tried to remember what Hazel had told her about wolves. She often zoned out when her friend enthused about the minutiae of the world's fauna. She knew shifters in lupine form weren't exactly wolves, but would he be insulted at their offerings of fruits, vegetables, and nuts? A memory bubbled to the surface, several years ago half the western blueberry crop had been eaten by a pack of wolves with an exceptionally sweet tooth. She had wanted blueberry pie for her birthday, and her parents had not been able to source enough berries. The wolves had just as much right to the berries as she had, an important lesson for a young Ratatoskr to learn. She had crab apple pie instead, not as sweet but just as lovingly cooked.

"Do you need to get back to the fire?" Daisy asked.

"Honestly, there's not much I can do. My sector was the first to catch—whatever this thing is. Magic or fire. I will return once it's ran its course, but it's important we eat regularly." She patted her tummy.

"Is the scurry safe? I mean how far are we?"

"We think so." Lailu paused to do the calculations. "I'm not exactly good with your human measurements— we don't need to bother ourselves with distance quite so much. I think we're seventy miles, give or take."

"That far? Wow."

"If you don't mind me asking, what happened on your journey here?" Lailu perched on the edge of the bench next to Lima, who turned a shade of pink as fur brushed over her. What a curious adaptation, it was hardly any use as camouflage.

"First, this crumble is divine," Daisy spoke between mouthfuls and relayed the details of the anomaly and the confluence of events. "It could just be coincidence of course."

"Or not, and then it is a useful clue." Lailu sighed. "I wish I knew what to do. The trees are suffering so much."

"People keep saying that, how do you know? If that's not an intrusive thing to ask..." Daisy trailed off.

"Not at all, how do we learn if we don't ask? Passing on of knowledge is a great gift. My friend Hazel is always telling me facts about animals I have never even heard of." Lailu paused, trying to put the feeling into words.

"It's like we feel it in our bones, or a fleeting touch on our skin. The pain they're in right now, that's something else, they're screaming at us. Our ears must be more attuned to it than yours." She gestured to her elegant ear tufts, which ended in a point. "When their sap builds up, the Eldurs go quiet, like it numbs their communication, but it feels peaceful to us. That's when we know we can harvest. We never take so much as to reawaken them, that would be cruel."

"And the wood?" Daisy gestured at the structure around them.

"We wait for it to be gifted to us. They shed branches often. If we need larger pieces we wait for a death; we would never chop one down." Lailu shuddered at the thought and poked a carrot on her plate. "Can you imagine if vegetables spoke to us? We'd never eat!"

# Lima

LIMA ATE QUIETLY, ABSORBING Lailu's chatter about the natural world and the wonders of Ruhann. She thought Lailu was quite beautiful, and every time the Ratatoskr glanced her way, Lima's cheeks heated. She was hoping she could pass off her reaction as sunburn. She didn't want to waste the opportunity to get to know a Ratatoskr—if she could only get her vascular system to cooperate.

She willed the heat in her cheeks to fade and hoped Daisy would carry the conversation. Idle chit chat was not a skill Lima possessed; she hated getting her hair cut exactly for that reason. Trapped in the hairdresser's chair, she blurted out one-word answers that she worried made her seem rude. If her hair got much longer, she'd be able to sit on it.

She looked down at their plates, grateful not to have to consider the ethics of existence. She did eat meat on occasion—a greasy pizza was too hard to resist at the end of a tough day—but she did feel a bit guilty about it. This trip to Ruhann had done so much to remind her of the tasty things one could do with nuts, spices, and sugar, not an exploited animal in sight. Even the bees offered their honey to the Ratatoskr willingly, taking up residence right outside the kitchen.

"So, you said something about a new Grid site near our borders?" Lailu asked out of the blue. Lima jumped slightly. Had she been staring?

"Yes, we've been trying to expand to support some of our more remote farming communities. After we return to Kirkhyrst, we'll send a team out by car to check everything's ship-shape. It'd be an impossible journey from here," Daisy said.

"Don't be silly. I'll take you!" Lailu announced with a smile. She could prove to Sylvain that she was useful. He hadn't even thought to offer when it was obviously a thing to be concerned about. Change was important in an ecosystem, but it came with the risk of disturbances. If they could just turn something off in the Grid and stop the fire spreading, she could sleep soundly tonight.

"Do we have time before the steamer leaves?" Lima asked. Not that she was eager to return home, but she always worried about being late. Would always be the person arriving half an hour early.

Daisy checked her watch. "Adam definitely said he was running late, so we should have plenty of time."

The captain had been mumbling something about a full service check when they last saw him. Lima had no idea how long those checks took so would just have to trust Daisy on that one.

"If not, you can stay the night! My nest might be a bit cosy for all of us, but we have the treehouses if you don't want to sleep in a huddle. I don't think anyone's using them right now."

"Nest?" Lima asked, wondering if Lailu had kits of her own.

"Yes. I'm quite proud of it," she replied, her hair puffing up gently around her shoulders. "The oak has been quite kind to me, I have plenty of space... but your wolf friend is very large, and I only have one bed."

Lima's face flared with heat again. Why was it doing this to her? Any other self-respecting Kirkhyrstite would have a crush on a musician or actor. She didn't do crushes; all the conversations of who was cute and who wasn't, passed her by at school. Objectively, she could tell who was more aesthetically pleasing, but she never wanted to do anything about it. Clearly, she was just having some sort of hormonal imbalance... at age nineteen. Or she was coming down with something.

"Speaking of wolf friends, where is he?"

She looked down at the floor and saw that Faelan had vanished, leaving only a well licked plate behind. The day was getting on, and he had business to do. So did they. This wasn't a holiday, no matter how much she was enjoying it. She swallowed down the last bite of pastry and pushed her plate aside.

At least her dad would think she was taking her internship seriously if she returned late. She wasn't the type to go out drinking or dancing into the small hours. If she wasn't in her room, he'd assume she was at work. Where else would she be?

# Faelan

FAELAN SLUNK OFF WHILE the others were eating dessert. He was grateful for the plate of chestnuts they'd offered him. He rarely ate in this form, except around the pack, and he found it awkward to do in front of others, but no one watched as he chewed messily. He gazed regretfully at a plate of cakes, but he needed to be on his way and get Anderson's package delivered.

He'd forgotten he had ID on him. Some of the younger shifters wore jewellery with their names and packs on, but it felt too much like dog tags to him. He had begrudgingly agreed to carry a card with him, which now seemed a terrible idea. How was he meant to free it from his pockets without hands? Human pockets and teeth were not compatible in his experience.

But he was glad Daisy and Lima knew his name, would have something to go on if he just vanished. Or got into trouble for wandering around naked. They seemed like good people.

Before leaving the scurry, he made a last attempt at shifting. Nothing. It was almost as if he was meant to be a wolf, not a human. He imagined disappearing into the woods, never to be seen again. Would they even miss him?

When Lailu had reached out to him, it was the first contact he'd had in weeks and, starved of affection, he might have groaned a little. What could he say, he was a touchy feely being. Isolating himself from his packmates hadn't given him much opportunity for casual intimacy. He couldn't blame the humans he worked with—they didn't tend to go around petting wolves. He missed the feel of flesh on flesh.

If he shifted back to human form out in public, then so be it. He was assured that the Ratatoskr would find him something to cover the important bits if he returned to find Daisy and Lima gone. Claws crossed that he wouldn't have to make the delivery naked.

The boarding house Anderson was staying at was a good hour's trek from the dock. However, Faelan didn't know where the scurry was in relation to their starting point. He'd tried to sneak a look at Daisy's map, but the scurries weren't marked on it. Barely any of Ruhann was. He'd have to rely on old-fashioned navigation, involving the position of the sun in the sky, the lie of the land, and his nose.

The thrill of the run, through wild forests and unmapped lands, was just what he needed. It would be better than any human form of travel and far more exhilarating than a jog around the local park. He stretched out his legs and took off at a cautious lope downhill and away from the odd hybrid tree-homes that made up the scurry.

Once he'd found a steady pace, the run was effortless. The mature trees blocked out enough light that the forest floor wasn't tangled with undergrowth, and the leafy carpet cushioned the impact as he raced between the trunks. He wove between trees with a joy he hadn't felt since the whole bonding thing. He quickly dismissed the thought from his mind, he didn't want to ruin his good mood.

He leaped and yipped, scattering small rodents as he went. Deeper in the forest, the hues turned even greener, moss creeping upwards and over anything that stayed still long enough, spongy beneath his paws. A land untouched by progress.

Dust in the air tickled Faelan's nose, the scent conjuring up images of bakeries and a hearty breakfast. Ahead he could glimpse something human-made peeking between the trees.

Slowing to a trot he reached a rustic stone building with a large water wheel affixed to one side. Beyond was the mill pond, its surface as still as glass, yet when released, the water would flow through with great power, pushing on the wheel as gravity called it. This was how people lived before magic was crammed down pipes and wires.

The pond was calling to him, but this was no time to take a dip. A sodden package was not going to get him paid. He carried on, passing a few houses into an open area that might be called a village square. There was a well and a small shop, its shutters closed for the day, and the prevalence of stone and brick suggested this was no Ratatoskr settlement. He had reached his destination.

It was no wonder Kirkhyrstites came here for holidays, although really it was only within the reach of wealthier residents. The steamers were cheap enough travel, but accommodation was limited, and hosts could afford to hike prices during the peak season. Faelan was perfectly happy to sleep beneath the trees in his lupine form, but humans generally liked beds and roofs. Tents at a stretch.

He pictured human huddles littering the forest floor and chuckled.

His human form was endlessly useful in Kirkhyrst, but out here, the wolf reigned supreme.

Down a dusty track, the road widened out into what might be considered a main artery by local standards. The surface consisted of compacted stone, considerably rougher on his pads than the forest floor. A sign next to a barn-like building announced "The last stop before the wild west!"

The last stop, unimaginatively named *Frontier Lodge*, was basic but functional, playing host to traders and therefore not trying as hard as the more popular tourist destinations along the Tarac. It served as a half way point between Kirkhyrst and the sparsely populated western lands beyond Ruhann, where many an idealist set out to build their own version of Kirkhyrst. As far as Faelan had heard, they were little more than villages and ghost towns, dreams squandered and lost in the face of nature.

The land was fertile enough, and those with modest ambitions could live easily, yet without the power the Grid provided, another great city was unfeasible. Not to mention, the larger settlements were populated by the kind of zealots who thought their way was the best way. No thank you. Faelan could imagine packing up his life in the city and living in some cabin in the woods, but he wouldn't trade one, perfectly fine, city for another.

*Frontier Lodge* wasn't exactly the kind of place he expected Anderson to be holed up in, but Clara had definitely made a big deal about it. He sniffed the air tentatively. The place smelled of old wood and sweaty socks, not unlike one artisan cheese he'd been forced to try back home. Astrid had some funny ideas about cuisine.

He smiled inwardly. He was softening; he could feel it. Ruhann had made his animosity melt away.

But for now, he needed to focus. Trying not to inhale too deeply, he swept the area for signs he was in the right place. There was a definite hint of Kirkhyrst about the threadbare rug.

The reception area was empty, so he trotted behind the counter, looking for the guest book. Luck was in his favour as it was laid out, open at the latest arrivals. Anderson, M, room 5. Hopefully he was in, and Faelan could get back to the scurry in time to polish off those chestnut buns. His mouth started to water, and he gulped it back. No one needed a drooling wolf appearing on their doorstep; one might mistake him as rabid.

Room 5 was at the end of the corridor on the ground floor. The familiar scents of the city grew stronger, a general whiff of life best left unexamined, and the sharp metallic tones of industry, mixed with something bitter. He couldn't quite place it. There were soft sounds coming from the other side of the wooden door. Someone was home.

Faelan considered his options. Would Anderson panic at the sight of a burly wolf on his doorstep? There was a rough peep hole carved into the door. If he could just angle it so the package addressed to Anderson was visible, that should do it. He jumped up, turning uncomfortably and rapped at the door with his claws, struggling to stay upright. He waited until he heard the click of the door handle being turned and slid down awkwardly.

He had just regained his composure when the door swung open, revealing a middle-aged man with a frown on his face, looking straight over Faelan's head. This better be

Anderson, he thought, and he attempted to clear his throat. It came out more like a growl.

The man jumped—his mouth falling open at the sight before him. Faelan quickly positioned himself so that the package was in his line of sight and prayed to Fenrir that the guy didn't carry a weapon. Who knew the types of people he was doing business with.

"Oh. Yes. I'm Anderson," the man stuttered, reaching out for the package, before thinking better of it and snatching his hand away. Faelan shuffled closer, hoping the look on his face was friendly and not menacing. Where was a mirror when you needed one?

Finally, Mr Anderson untied the package with shaking hands. Faelan stood patiently, trying to stay as still as possible. Beyond the open doorway, Anderson's room was full of metal boxes and coils of wire. Building supplies most likely. There wasn't access to anything more advanced than brick this far out. It was all wood and stone, woven fibre and rudimentary clay. He tried to recall what Anderson's business was, but he guessed it didn't matter, not if he got paid.

Seeing Faelan's gaze lingering on his belongings, Anderson moved to block his view. He huffed; he was a professional courier, not a thief casing the joint.

"Thank you, I'll confirm it as delivered," Anderson said, as he backed into his room and closed the door with a thud. Charming, Faelan thought, but he was mostly glad he'd found him so quickly. After all this running around, he was definitely in need of cake.

# Lailu

LAILU WAS STUDYING THE map of the Grid, trying to find a bearing to portal to. She wasn't one for jumping to random locations for fun, so most of her portals opened in places she had visited before. She had never had reason to go outside the borders of Ruhann and hoped she wouldn't mess up with passengers in tow. She traced her claw down the topological features, picturing the gentle valley where the hub sat. The river that ran through it started as a trickle, high up among the Eldurs. She'd tasted the water there, clear and fresh as a winter's day. She imagined the stream widening, welcoming fish and frogs to its water, watercress growing in the shallows. It left Ruhann and met iron, wires and levers, housed in a stout building. There, she had it.

"Right, I think we're ready," she said, calling Daisy and Lima over to an open clearing. "We should arrive within view of the hub at least—I don't want to open the portal inside since I don't know what we're dealing with."

"Fair enough," Daisy said, coming to stand next to Lailu.

Asha popped her head through the doorway.

"Is everything OK?" Lailu asked.

"Just so you know, that steamer's not heading anywhere today. And the only other scheduled boat is leaving about... now."

Lailu turned to the humans with inquiring eyes.

"It's up to you. Hub or dock?" she asked.

"Hub," Daisy answered without hesitation. "We'll sort out sleeping arrangements later."

With the three of them lined up, Lailu closed her eyes and willed the portal into existence, its pale blue light crackling into a circle. She linked hands with Daisy on her left and Lima on her right and pulled them through gently.

Lima's heart was racing. Lailu could feel the rapid pulse through her hand, and she gave the young human a reassuring squeeze. Lailu was sure the wardens had ushered them through the other portals in a polite but business-like manner; she preferred a more personal touch. She saw her portal as part of herself, just as much as her bushy tail or strong limbs. With human palms soft and warm against her paws, a soothing wave of energy flowed over her briefly before they stepped out into grassland, yellowed from the dry summer. A stark contrast to the lush greenery of home.

"Does this look right?" Lailu asked, letting their hands drop as Daisy looked around their new surroundings. There was a buzzing coming from the other side of a gentle hillock, and a line of cable snaked out across the landscape.

"That's it, I think. It's built into the ground—entrance must be on the other side." Daisy turned her map around several times and shrugged. "Let's go look."

Lima trotted behind, trying to keep up. Her shoes were black and smart, fine for walking around city streets or sitting at a desk, but they slipped against the smooth grass. Lailu had found a stack of fashion magazines in the library once and had grown fascinated with human shoes. They had so many types! She could see the value in some of them, but others made no sense. At least Lima wasn't wearing high heels, but they weren't like the other woman's practical running shoes either.

Daisy was marching off into the distance, but Lailu slowed to let Lima catch her breath.

"Have you worked for the Grid long?" she asked.

"Oh no. This is my first day," Lima replied. "I don't officially work for them. I'm an intern. I'm learning on the job, so to speak."

Lailu was astounded. Were they considered so unimportant to send a trainee?

"Daisy's been there forever though," Lima continued. "Not that I'm saying she's old... just experienced?"

The human was turning pink again.

"I heard that!" Daisy called from up ahead.

It took them around fifteen minutes to reach the heavy steel door, and by that time the humans were damp with sweat all over. Looking at them, Lailu was glad she only perspired from her feet.

"There should be a console in here that we can contact Kirkhyrst from, let Hari know what's going on. Do you need to let anyone know you won't be home tonight?" Daisy asked Lima. She shook her head, a fleeting look of sadness washing across her face.

"I don't think anyone will notice I'm gone. I don't spend much time outside my room." She shrugged.

While Lailu loved her nest, and sometimes craved privacy from prying eyes and ears, she wouldn't forgo meal times with the hustle and bustle of other Ratatoskr around her. And someone would always come find her if she hid in her shell too long. Lima seemed a little distant to Lailu, at least compared to Daisy, and she itched to bring a smile to her face once more. Everyone deserved to be missed by someone.

Lailu had transferred from another scurry when she'd chosen her path as Tree Keeper, leaving her family behind. Not that separation was ever truly an issue for Ratatoskr; she could visit at any time. She was looking forward to seeing them all on Tapping Day, when the scurries would come together to ensure the Eldurs were tapped in good time—she supposed that wouldn't be happening now.

If they didn't get to the bottom of the problem, there might never be another Tapping Day again. She gulped and turned her attention to the hub.

There was a strange, panel to the side of the door, with what Lailu had come to learn was the Grid's logo. Daisy placed a rectangle of plastic on it and pressed several buttons, entering some sort of code. The door opened with a click and a hiss, the stale air escaping from the bunker. Lailu wobbled slightly, a wave of anxiety coming out of nowhere.

"Are you OK?" Lima asked, her face creased in concern.

"I just came over a bit dizzy, ah..." Lailu slumped, and Lima grabbed her arm to steady her. "I may have to wait outside. If you don't mind?"

"Of course not. Shout if you need us," Daisy said passing a bottle of water to her. Lailu nodded weakly and went to settle herself on a tree stump a good distance from the door. This place did not feel right.

# Daisy

Pushing the door wider, Daisy entered the hub with Lima close behind. An automatic light switched on, casting them in a dull orange glow. Inside was a second door with another access panel. Overkill, Daisy thought. She knew security was important, but the systems were all password protected, with fail-safes built in, and barely anyone knew it was there. One solid door seemed enough to her.

The hubs were a relatively new project, designed to bring power to some of the outer farms and the settlements growing up around them. Farm workers wanted entertainment and transport too, and Grid powered machinery was increasing in popularity. Horses could only get so much done before they needed rest and food.

She hadn't had much to do with them. Either the novelty of the Grid in rural communities meant they were less likely to complain at the drop of the hat, or it just worked better on a smaller scale. The core inside this building would only be supplying a few thousand households, instead of millions.

The second door opened up into a sparse room with several consoles lined up on two desks. Boxes were littered around the floor, wires spilling out of them. No one was stationed here full time, and the space had that new furniture smell. Daisy nudged one of the consoles to life, tapping away at the logs and error reports.

"No surges. All the errors are run of the mill," she pointed some of them out to Lima. "The magic fluctuates, sometimes it will drop off briefly. See here. The Grid regulates all this, but you still get small outages."

"Like power cuts?" Lima asked.

"Lights will flicker a bit. You might lose connection to the Grid for a few minutes, not able to load a gridsite for instance. Power gets rerouted all the time to try and compensate. Out here, there's less to work with, so there are more drop outs."

"Is that what the leak is?"

"I don't think so. There's no lost magic as far as I can tell, but let's go look at the core. It won't be anywhere near as big as the one in Kirkhyrst, but it's still a sight to be seen." Daisy paused. "Just don't touch anything that looks, um, glowy?"

Lima nodded.

The hatch for the core was plastered with warning signs and yet another access panel, requiring multiple levels of authorisation.

"Curses, I'll need to contact Hari for a second code." Daisy sat down at one of the desks and started typing.

```
Hi Hari

We are up at hub ZETA003 investigating the
reports of the alleged leak into Ruhann. So
```

far there has been nothing to suggest that
the Grid is to blame, see attached logs. I
would like to inspect the core here for any
irregularities and need a temporary
authorisation code to access it.

We will be staying in Ruhann overnight, so
won't be in the office first thing. Please pass
the message on to whoever we have as Lima's
emergency contact.

Regards
Daisy


"Hopefully he's at his desk, I'm not sure we can video call from these things." Daisy twirled round in her chair while she waited.

"How far are we from Kirkhyrst out here?" Lima asked.

"Um... a hundred miles, maybe?"

"How does the Grid communicate then? If it needs wires?"

"They laid these huge cables underground, through fields and under rivers. It's quite impressive."

"How come I haven't heard about this?"

"They—the board—weren't convinced it would work. So, they kept it quiet. And the farmers whose land it is, were happy to agree to silence if it meant they got the Grid. If the project is a success, they'll be shouting about it from the rooftops in no time."

"But they don't use the same core? Sorry, I'm confused, I thought power was all generated in one place?"

"For Kirkhyrst, yes. But it's a risk, only having one. There's no contingency, and the city uses so much. I can see them building another core in the near future, somewhere closer to home. Though there're rumblings that small and many is a better strategy. Of course, all this is confidential."

Lima mimed zipping her lips. A few minutes later the console bleeped.

"Brilliant. He said he'll ping your dad too. Now let's get that hatch open."

After all the relevant codes were entered, the hatch swung open with a creak. Beyond the door was a circular space with a tall column of pulsing light in the centre. Raw magic raged in the confines of the core, crackling as it touched the invisible barrier keeping it caged.

The Grid didn't create magic, just gathered it from the air, or so she had been led to believe. She'd never stopped to think where the magic actually came from. There was plenty to go around so what did it matter?

Sylvain was adamant that the Grid had done something to set the fire burning, and Lailu had mentioned the trees contained their own magic. Daisy had a horrible feeling that they'd done something to disrupt the balance—expanded too fast, not sealed the cables. She didn't know what. Magic was mysterious, and the Grid was secrctive.

She was aware of magical beings, sure, but she hadn't connected the dots between the magic the Grid used and the magic out there in nature. Other resources weren't infinite; the Blackthorns ran quarries which scarred the landscape north of Kirkhyrst, each skyscraper taking something out of the land, twisting it into towers, leaving a hole behind. Out of sight, out of mind.

Magic was different though. Renewable. Not like every scoop they took left a scar on those who possessed it. Shifters and vampires benefitted from the Grid just as much as any human, and they would know if it was causing damage. Wouldn't they?

She busied herself checking the shielding and measuring ambient magic levels. Lower than Kirkhyrst's core, as they should be, but also lower than the readings she took in the forest. Cross-referencing against the logs, she worked out the average power levels for this hub since its installation. The numbers didn't lie, there was no way it had leaked in any significant manner.

What a waste of time. She slid down the wall and sat, staring into the core. Her workload had been growing and growing, and two days away was only going to add to the pile of tickets to go through. Oh, Hari would have sorted out Celia, but Daisy doubted he had picked up any more.

Every morning, she pasted on her happy-to-help face, did her work to the best of her ability, went home later than she should do. Eat, wash, sleep, repeat. She was exhausted, but it had taken a break in her routine to really acknowledge it. She'd told herself things would quieten down again eventually...

Eventually hadn't happened. When she got back, she would talk to Hari about hiring more analysts. And not just interns.

# Lima

"THIS PLACE IS MUCH bigger than it looks from the outside," Lima said, peering through the hatch. Tension in her head signalled a headache was on the horizon. It had started as soon as the hatch opened, and she was eager to get back out into the fresh air. The core was impressive yet compared to the gentle magic of the Ratatoskr, something felt off kilter.

"Do you ever think humans weren't meant to have magic?" The thought left Lima's lips before she'd stopped to think. This was Daisy's job, of course she believed in magic for everyone.

"If we were meant to have it, we wouldn't have to box it up and sell it for a monthly fee," Daisy said before Lima could take it back. "Don't look so surprised. What's done is done though, and a job's a job. I'm good at it, pays my bills... I can't say I want to live without magic, but we shouldn't take it for granted either. Oh, I'm rambling now."

"No, I get it. It'd just be terrible if we were hurting people."

"If it wasn't magic, it'd be something else. When people burned coal and wood in Kirkhyrst, the air was thick with smoke and made a lot of people ill. It's cleaner now, and magic gave us that."

Lima's heart sank, Sylvain was right, humans were destined to ruin things for someone. Her whole life the Grid had been there, making her life easier. Until today, she had never questioned it, never asked how it all worked.

During tiffin she'd been daydreaming of humans living like Ratatoskr did, but the scurry was a fraction of the size of Kirkhyrst. It was hard enough coordinating a sit-down family meal in her two-person household, let alone the kind of communal living the scurry promised. The city only succeeded thanks to its control of magic, creating wealth and jobs, so that everyone could seal themselves off in their own little boxes.

Yes, she needed a job, but beyond that, there was no responsibility sat on her shoulders. Lima appreciated that, but maybe if her life had more of an impact on society, she would relish the part she played. Sitting at a desk for eight hours a day, didn't seem like it benefitted anyone.

"If it helps," Daisy interrupted her thoughts. "I can't see how the fire is the Grid's fault, not directly. But if it is, we won't just brush it under the table, I promise."

"I know you wouldn't, but... would people like the Blackthorns care about some trees they've never even seen if we asked them to change their ways?"

"I see your point." Daisy sighed. "They do care about money though. And access to healthcare, so the loss of the Eldur crop is not nothing to them."

Daisy pushed herself off the floor and clambered out through the hatch, giving Lima a tired smile.

"There's no irregularities with the core, so let's get out of here, OK?"

They backtracked back through the office and made sure everything was secure, consoles turned off, doors closed tightly.

Lima took a great gulp of fresh air when she reached the outer door, pressing her fingers into her forehead in an attempt to release the tension. Glancing in Lailu's direction, she saw the Ratatoskr was entranced by a yellow and black butterfly which had settled on her nose. She wished she could capture the moment.

If only she had brought her camera, there were so many amazing things she could have photographed. She'd have to rely on her memory instead, or somehow convince her dad to take a holiday in Ruhann. Hah, fat chance of that.

"Did you find anything?" Lailu asked, disturbing the butterfly which flitted off into the sky.

"Not really," Daisy said. "Good news, there isn't a leak. Bad news, we still don't know what's going on. I'll do some data crunching when I get back to Kirkhyrst, see if I can find anything else like this, but… I'll be honest with you, it doesn't look like it's anything we've done."

Lima expected Lailu to protest, but she simply hopped up from her log and brushed herself off.

"This place is pretty. Different to home," Lailu said.

"Less trees?" Lima offered. Lailu smiled back at her, and for once Lima didn't turn red. This was definite progress.

"Definitely less trees. But so many grasses and insects, the way the wind blows through them makes a pleasant sound." They stood and listened for a few minutes. The grasses rustled as they swayed, and unseen crickets chirped. She was right; it was soothing.

"Our trees can be very noisy," Lailu broke the silence.

"What do you mean?" Lima asked.

"They creak and groan. At night, when all else is silent, I hear my oak burbling away. It is a reassuring reminder of life."

"I'd like to hear that," Lima said, and this time she did feel the heat flare up her neck and into her cheeks. Had she just invited herself into Lailu's nest for the night?

"Oh, that would be lovely! I haven't had a huddle in ages. Sometimes Hazel sleeps over, but I like having my own space. The curse of growing up in a big litter." Lailu beamed at her.

"I... er... OK?"

"As long as you don't mind sharing with a balurat?"

"A what?"

Lailu explained about the animals who lived the forest as they walked a distance from the hub, and she opened up the portal home with barely a pause in her enthusiastic chatter.

* * *

"I FELT AWFUL AROUND your hub," Lailu told her, now they were away from the others. They'd eaten a hearty vegetable stew for dinner, collected a fuzzy little creature with a swollen belly, and were now ready to settle down for the evening. Her host for the night had taken her hand and led her down beneath the roots of an ancient tree.

"I got a headache when I went in to see the core—it must give off something," Lima waved her fingers in the air to demonstrate. Balu watched her, having learned hands meant food and now alert to their every movement.

Lailu giggled and peered closely at Lima, whiskers tickling her face. Ratatoskr had different standards of personal space than Lima was used to, but she didn't mind.

"I don't suppose you have a touch of magic in you?"

"What, me? I'm human."

"Well sure, but maybe one of your grandparents was half human? Dallied with the fair folk?"

"I don't really know them," Lima mumbled. Her paternal grandparents showed up at Yule and birthdays, but they were the least adventurous people she had ever met, and that was saying something coming from her. And on her mother's side? A complete mystery.

"Hang on, did you say the fair folk? I thought fairies were made up?"

"Oh, they are, at least the kind with glittery wings and magic wands." Lailu laughed. "But the stories they're based on come from the Faidhean in the north."

Lima's mouth gaped open. "You mean there's a whole species of people we don't know about?"

"Ratatoskr know about them. And I'd imagine your wolf friend's pack does too. Humans have just chosen to forget them. Did you think Kirkhyrst was the centre of the world?"

"Well, yes, kinda," Lima said sheepishly.

"You are so very naïve, it's adorable."

"Kirkhyrstites would think that of you."

"Really?"

"All this living at one with nature, no consoles or machines, no glass or steel. That would seem... um... backwards, to some humans."

"We don't need it, do we?" Lailu gestured around her nest, which was indeed very cosy. "My oak will give me clean water and acorns if I ask. It might be a boring diet, but I'd survive. Can you say the same about your home?"

Lima shook her head. She could ask the intergrid for food, but that wasn't the same. It still came from the ground, needed someone to tend it and transport it to the city. If Kirkhyrst was cut off from the outside world, she wouldn't last very long at all.

"Ow!" Lailu squeaked, looking at her foot.

"What's wrong?"

"I think I burnt my pads. I can't really see." Lailu hopped on one foot, straining to see where the pain was coming from.

"Let me see," Lima offered. Lailu stuck her foot out and nearly fell over. "Stop hopping and sit down."

Lailu's paws were pink underneath, and several of her pads had blistered—one had recently burst. Lima tried not to grimace and gently blew the dirt from them.

"We should clean them. You could get an infection."

"Oh. I have some salve somewhere. Let me see..."

Lailu rummaged around, handing Lima a cloth, a small bowl of water, and a pot of something potent. Lima settled herself on the floor and started to softly tend to Lailu's feet. It most intimate thing she'd ever done.

"Would you like me to tell you a fairy story?" Lailu asked after several minutes of silence.

Lima nodded and Lailu launched into the story:

*Once upon a time, the universe was contained in a single tree and all the creatures of the world lived in its branches, trunk or roots. As the world grew larger and more populous, factions formed, and the tree stretched out its presence further and further.*

For those not wanting to lose touch with those they once called friends, they needed messengers. Ratatoskr were fast climbers and could scale the length and breadth of the tree in hours rather than days; they were the easy choice for the role.

Up and down the tree the Ratatoskr scurried, claws scraping the bark, digging in when they missed their footing. Not everyone appreciated the damage—others thought it was a price well paid for a speedy communication system.

One summer day, a magpie requested an urgent message to be delivered way deep down in the roots of the tree, where few dare to go. That would show those upstarts who dared hurt their home. Kai was a young and adventurous Ratatoskr who longed for a life of freedom. If he delivered this message, he would be the greatest messenger of all the tree and get all the best assignments. So, he took the rolled up leaf from the bird and set off down the trunk.

The lower he went, the darker it became, the light filtered out by the many layers of canopy above. A chill settled into his bones, but any good adventurer would not be perturbed by a little cold.

At the base of the trunk, he paused just a moment. There was a feeling he was being watched, but he shrugged it off. This was further than he'd ever been in his life! He was having fun. Or so he told himself.

Winding down under the roots, the sounds of life reverberated around him, muffled and strange. Insects scuttled past, and he thought for a moment a centipede had the teeth of a great cat, but he blinked the vision away. It really was so very cold, far too cold for a summer's day.

Frost lined the further reaches of chambers under the tree. Canopy dwellers often whispered about those who chose to live so far from the warmth of the sun. Oh, of course there were the moles, useful excavators, but the rest...

"So kind of you to deliver lunch," a voice spoke from the shadows. Kai froze—it was not the done thing to eat the messenger.

"I have a message from above," Kai blurted out.

He could not place the beast before him; it shifted from feline to boar to bird to something incomprehensible.

"How very quaint. Who would want to see you dead, I wonder?"

Kai thought about this a moment. It was odd that no one else wanted to take this message; the rewards for venturing so far would surely be great.

"It was a magpie," Kai told the ever-shifting shape below.

"I welcome your honesty. I would very much like roast magpie for dinner. Alas, I can't leave this place."

"Really? It's a bit of a wriggle, but I can show you the way."

The creature considered his offer.

"No one has ever offered to lead me out before. If it works, I shall grant you a wish. If not... Well, I shall feast on Ratatoskr tonight."

Kai gulped but agreed to this bargain. If he was going to be eaten anyway... He led the creature upwards, reaching the roots that lead out of the underworld. It would be a bit of a squeeze, but they appeared to Kai as if they could change shape.

"If you could be as slender as a snake, it would help."

"You think I haven't tried," the creature told him. "I slither and slide and slip straight back down."

Kai hoisted himself up on the roots and offered down a paw. The hand that took his was icy cold, and he held back *a shudder. With a heave and a grunt, Kai pulled the creature through, and they popped into the open air, the ground freezing around them.*

*A tremendous crack split the air, followed by squeals and caws from high above. The residents of the tree were falling, and the tree itself had opened up wide.*

*The creature smiled the smile of a predator, snatching a fallen magpie out of the sky, and crunched merrily on its bones. Kai trembled.*

*"I am a creature of my word. Your wish, Ratatoskr?"*

*Despite his fear, Kai knew what he wanted. To see if there was more to the world than this tree, to go on adventures and be free.*

*"I wish to be able to travel anywhere I please." Kai said.*

*"Done!" The creature clapped its hands, and a bright flow of magic left the tree, settling on Kai's shoulders. Around them saplings started to grow where the tree had split. A forest of many homes, instead of one.*

*Kai pictured a land beyond the tree, somewhere he could feel the ground between his toes and escape the chatter of noisy neighbours. A portal opened before him, and he stepped through.*

"The end," Lailu finished.

"Was the creature beneath the tree Faidhean?" Lima asked.

"Maybe, or the creature that gave birth to all magic-bearing species. We're not beholden to our myths; we know how stories get embellished with every telling."

Lima tried to stifle her yawn. The day had been very long, and she was too shy to ask where she would be sleeping. What she assumed to be Lailu's bed was covered in blankets, and Balu was splayed out across them, his dreaming actions mirrored in the dance of his paws. The floor was soft and spongy and would make an acceptable mattress for the night, if she could just free a blanket from under the balurat.

Lailu was right; Balu was very cute and had been happy to be petted by a strange human. He didn't seem much like a wild animal to her, but she hadn't spent much time with real animals to know the difference.

"Oh my, it's getting late." Lailu jumped up and pushed Balu over to one side of her bed. He grunted, eyes blinking open briefly before returning to his slumber. "I'll take the Balu side. His claws can be a bit scratchy, and well..." She poked Lima's pale, soft skin. "You're a bit delicate."

Something deep inside Lima lurched—she could do this. Having not planned to go anywhere other than a boring office today, she had no way to brush her teeth, and she hoped her mouth didn't smell too awful. She prayed she wouldn't drool. Or snore. Lailu was so casual about all this. Ratatoskr were happy sleeping in group bundles; it didn't occur to her that Lima might be nervous.

"Here, snuggle up. The nights are usually balmy, but it can get a bit nippy in the early hours." Lailu curled around Lima's body, fur so soft against her back. "Blow the candle out, won't you?"

Lima did as she asked and lay back in the darkness. Not a pinprick of light filtered through the roots, and as she lay there, listening to their breathing, she started to hear another sound. It was deep and rumbling but not altogether unpleasant.

"Is that the oak?" she whispered into Lailu's ear, but the Ratatoskr was already asleep.

# Daisy

THE WOOD BENEATH DAISY'S feet creaked ominously. Lima had been eager to join Lailu's huddle offer, and Daisy didn't want to be a third wheel—her intern was forever blushing in front of Lailu. She thought it was sweet. In all honesty, Daisy preferred to sleep by herself; it was what she was used to. Instead, she'd be allocated a treehouse at the top of a tall beech tree.

After returning from their excursion with Lailu, Faelan had reappeared sans-package. He'd taken one look at the rickety ladder leading to his room for the night and decided the ground was a safer bet. Tree climbing was not part of a wolf's skillset. He had taken up position at the base of Daisy's beech, curled up against the cooling night air, and she felt vaguely comforted by his presence.

Not that she thought anyone was out to get her, but she was a city girl and felt somewhat exposed up in a tree. The "house" was made from woven willow with a roughly thatched roof. One side had been patched with more substantial panels of wood, but it very much felt like sleeping outside. Every move she made came with a creaking sound, and she vowed to keep as still as possible.

What if she rolled over in her sleep and fell right out? She peered over the edge, eying up the distance to the ground. If she landed on Faelan, would he soften her fall, or would they both be squished into oblivion? She tried to cast her mind back to her brief lessons in physics... Something about terminal velocity?

Death by introversion would be her downfall; she should have just joined Lailu's huddle. After all, most Ratatoskr here slept under the trees, not in them, and they could climb with their bare paws! Even the big bad wolf had known better.

That was harsh, Faelan seemed nice enough. It's not exactly like they'd had a chance to get to know each other, but Daisy wondered if he'd decided to stay in lupine form to avoid small talk. She probably would too, given the choice.

She lay on her back staring up at the stars through the gaps in the thatch. Horrific wildfire aside, Ruhann really was beautiful. With a bit of modernisation, she could see this place being a luxury retreat. People would pay a fortune for the seclusion and novelty a tree house provided. Perhaps with slightly more luxurious bedding, she thought as she attempted to fluff up her pillows.

That the Ratatoskr shunned such capitalism was probably for the best. The soul of the place wouldn't survive the onslaught of humans.

An ensuite bathroom wouldn't have gone amiss though. All that rehydrating she'd been doing had made its way to her bladder. She weighed up her options. Climb back down, potentially fall and die. Wee herself up a tree and potentially die of embarrassment. Better the more noble death.

She somehow made it down with only minimal loss of skin. A chill in the night air raised goosebumps on her bare arms as she surveyed her surroundings. Weeing in the woods probably wasn't frowned upon, but Daisy was paranoid she'd go on someone's nest. A rude awakening for whoever lived below.

She would have to find her way to the latrines. Unlike the smothered skies of Kirkhyrst, starlight shone down from above, outlining the trees softly and providing enough light to not poke her eyes out.

Her feet took the path of least resistance, following a winding trail through the trees. A glow of candlelight flickered up ahead and voices drifted out into the night.

"We're not going to be able to deliver–"

"I'll handle it!" someone snapped. It sounded like Sylvain.

"Will you though?"

Daisy stumbled away from the hut, not wanting to be caught eavesdropping on an argument. Sylvain was a prickly sort of fellow, but she wouldn't want to be the one responsible for telling the pharmaceutical companies that their sap was delayed. Where the hell were those latrines? Thick bushes bordered the path on either side; they would have to do.

Crack! Daisy jumped, narrowly avoiding falling flat on her face. She quickly finished up, convincing herself it was nothing. Hundreds of animals lived out here, mostly harmless. It was probably a badger. Yes, that was it, a badger, hunting down big, fat, slimy slugs.

Wetness slapped against her face. She shrieked, flailing with her hands. Just wet leaves. But as she steadied herself, she heard the faint sound of breathing on the other side of the bushes.

"Who's there?" she whispered and received a whine in response. Poking her head above the bushes, she was met with the reflection of moonlight in two golden eyes.

"Oh, my giddy aunt!" Daisy let out a breath. "You scared the wee out of me. Literally."

Faelan huffed at her and turned to leave.

"Hang on a sec," she called after him, and he paused in his tracks. "If you know where you're going, can you take me back to my tree?"

Another huff. She hoped that meant yes. His dark fur was hard to make out in the dim light, and she was tempted to reach out and grab a tuft. Propriety held her back. Instead, she walked close to him, his body giving off a pleasant warmth. Did shifters run hotter than humans? There were so many things she wanted to ask him.

They turned a right where Daisy was convinced she would have turned left by herself and arrived at the clearing with the treehouses clustered around it. A bundle of blankets and pillows had been left on the ground, but Faelan circled a patch of grass and curled up into a ball once more.

Daisy looked up at the ladder, then back down at the not-yet-sleeping wolf.

"Err... Do you mind if I just kip down here?"

Not bothering to open his eyes, Faelan huffed again.

"Are you this chatty in your human form?" she mumbled under her breath, forgetting about his keen hearing. He grumbled a little and exhaled a long sigh. She interpreted that as "if you must sleep here, please shut up" and laid a blanket out on the grass beside him.

With the shifter's warm presence providing the sense of safety the treehouse lacked, tiredness soon took over, and she quickly fell asleep.

# Lima

LIMA WOKE TO A tickle in her nose, and warm fur enveloping her. She snuggled in closer, her half-conscious brain failing to process where she was. It took her a moment to realise the tickling was being done by a tail. A tail attached to an awake Lailu, who was now watching her carefully. Lima froze.

"You're cute when you sleep," Lailu said, her nose inches away from Lima's. "You mumble."

Lima hoped she hadn't been mumbling anything embarrassing.

"Hello," Lima said, words failing her. Before the silence could grow awkward, a wriggling bundle of grey fur appeared from beneath the blankets and licked Lima's face. She burst into giggles, and Lailu followed suit.

"And hello to you too Balu," Lima said and rubbed the balurat under his chin.

"I bet he wants breakfast," Lailu said. Balu's ears perked up at the word. "I can't believe he's learned the word breakfast already."

She repeated the word over and over, the balurat's head tilting a little further with each repetition. Considering he'd been rescued from a burning forest only days early, he was adapting to his new, domesticated life with ease.

Lima would miss this. The easy companionship, the wildlife, and people who cared about the same things she did. It had only been one day, but a sense of belonging had set in. Which was ridiculous, she was a human among Ratatoskr.

"Do you see humans very often? Out here I mean?" she asked.

"Oh, they don't come to the scurry at all. The wardens will meet the sap traders down at The Hart. That's a tavern near where your boat came in," Lailu said.

"The wardens?"

"Like Sylvain and Asha. They sort of organise the scurry, make sure jobs are allocated and interact with outsiders. Not just humans, but the other scurries too. We don't farm much here, so we need to bring food in. Things like grain for those lovely pastries you were scoffing down at tiffin."

Lailu poked Lima playfully in the stomach.

"So, Sylvain's like your boss?"

"Boss?"

"In charge of you?"

Lailu laughed. "Oh, I suppose so. But he doesn't order us around, just makes sure the things that need doing get done. As long as I tend to the trees..."

"Oh Lailu. I'm sorry, your poor trees."

"I shall ask the clouds for rain. Maybe nature's water will quench the fire more than our buckets do."

Lima patted Lailu awkwardly on her shoulder, unsure how best to comfort her. Despite everything, Lailu had approached them with a kind smile and taken time to welcome them into her home. Literally, in Lima's case.

She knew what it was like to hide your true feelings behind a mask and thought Lailu's might be starting to slip.

"I have a question for you," Lailu said, getting out of bed, with Balu in hot pursuit. He dragged the blankets with him, pulling them off Lima and into a tangled pile on the floor.

"Sure."

"Why do humans turn pink sometimes?" Lailu asked as she folded the blankets, back turned to Lima.

Lima felt the rush of blood immediately rise to her cheeks. "Um. It's a physiological response to... stuff."

"Stuff?"

"Yeah... erm... like awkward situations?" The moment the words came out she wished she could take them back.

"I make you feel awkward?"

"No, no, I didn't mean—see I'm not good in social situations. I worry I'll say something stupid, and then I get embarrassed and go red. And... and... sometimes blushing means someone likes someone."

"Ohhhhh. You like me?" Lailu asked, the smile returning to her face.

"Um. Yeah? You're interesting and kind." Her face really was on fire now.

"Well thank you. Interesting and kind are two things I aspire to be. I like you too, Lima."

* * *

THE JOURNEY BACK TO Kirkhyrst was mainly uneventful. Lailu sent them on their way with a picnic fit for a vegan king and explained how to send a message by bird. Lima wasn't convinced that the pigeons of Kirkhyrst would cooperate, but Daisy assured her that a few older people kept messenger birds in the city for emergencies. As would the university if she was ever in a pickle. Lima wasn't sure what kind of pickle would involve her needing to send bird mail, but she liked the idea of being able to write to Lailu.

Adam had greeted them in a tired but cheerful manner. Selene was still running with no signs of any other anomalies, and he was keen to get home to his family.

"I'll put her in the shop when I get back," he said. "I 'aven't taken holiday in so long, the kids will appreciate me taking a bit of time off."

Lima spied a crate of halo rings loaded on board, all neatly packaged in a rustic sort of fashion. Clearly some in Ruhann were not shy of a bit of commerce. She thought happily of the halo rings wrapped in leaves, tucked away in their picnic hamper. They also had chestnut buns for Faelan, who'd missed out on yesterday's batch, flapjacks dotted with seeds, and freshly baked bread slathered in sorrel pesto. She couldn't wait to dig in.

There weren't many people returning to the city. This departure was not scheduled for starters, and it was late in the season for holidaymakers, with the nights drawing in already. It seemed only last week that they were celebrating summer solstice, but they were well into autumn already.

Soon it would be time to make a decision about her future. Lima kept putting it off. Putting off even thinking about it. The thought of all the resources the university could offer made her wonder if she should just suck up her dad's demands and do a course he approved of. Would it be so bad?

If she impressed Daisy maybe she could get a job at the Grid. Would she even have a say in hiring decisions or did she have to impress Hari too? She had barely seen the man, eager as he had been to offload her onto someone else.

She tried to push the thoughts from her mind and enjoy her last view of Ruhann as the steamer set sail homewards.

# Lailu

THE SOUND OF THUNDER rumbled in the distance. That was odd, the air had been fresh and clear for days, a storm wasn't to be expected. However, she'd asked for rain and would welcome it in whatever form. Lailu scaled her oak for a better look at the skies, and Balu scampered up after her. She was an agile climber, and the balurat struggled to keep up. Lailu thought about picking him up, but he looked like he was having fun, so she left him to it. He didn't have to follow her around if he didn't want to.

The skies around the scurry were full of fluffy white clouds, no tell-tale thunderhead in sight. She needed to get back to the Great Forest to check on the Eldurs. Their excursion out to the hub hadn't been fruitful, and she needed to face the damage. She took a moment for Balu to reach her. He chirped as she ruffled his fur. He was so soft, and while it was wrong of her to wish it, she hoped he'd stay with her forever. She was growing quite fond of the greedy bundle of fluff.

She'd enjoyed her time with the humans, and her nest was oddly silent without Lima in it. She'd been so interested in the nature around them, it was charming. The artificialness of the Grid was concerning, but it didn't need to get between them. She'd been brought up to believe in interspecies cooperation, and humans were just another species. A deer might eat the bark off a tree, scarring or killing it, but that did not mean the deer was not permitted its place in the forest.

Humans appeared to be plagued by injuries and illnesses, all requiring Eldur sap to treat in some way. Recalling Lima's soft, fragile skin, she could easily see why. It would be cruel to deny them nature's bounty, and in return they received whatever the wardens requested. Food to carry them through a harsh season, knowledge in the form of books, fabrics finer than they could weave themselves, but never money. The humans loved money, but Lailu couldn't see the point of it. They could only use it to trade with humans, who were happy to trade for sap anyway.

She imagined Lima injured, unable to access the sap that would provide her comfort, and a strange feeling fluttered through her chest. Of course she wouldn't want Daisy, or any of the countless humans she hadn't met, to suffer either, but... She hoped she would get a chance to see Lima again; to discover if they could be friends despite their differences.

For a moment, she considered opening a portal right there, up in the canopy of the oak. It was something they'd done as kits, falling backwards and hoping they'd be cushioned on the other side. Kits were indestructible, or at least bruised less than older Ratatoskr. Hah, she was starting to sound like Sylvain; she was barely one and twenty years, and she knew how to land safely. The secret was to relax, let everything go loose and floppy, and the ground wouldn't shear off any bones that way.

As much as she'd like to, the risk of landing in a raging inferno right now was too high. She didn't want Balu to follow her back there either. She slithered back down the trunk, calling Balu to follow. She had a few spare nuts stashed away and used them to convince him to stay put in her nest. She wouldn't be long.

She stepped out of her portal into a deluge and was almost pushed back through by the force. Rain soaked through her fur in seconds. She blinked the water from her eyes, fumbling around for a leaf large enough to shield herself with, but every sign of life had been burned away, a swirling torrent of grey water left in its stead.

As the rain beat against the skeletal remains of the Eldurs, what was left of the blue fire sparked into the surrounding air, threads of magic flying high into the clouds. In other circumstances it might have been a beautiful sight, like fireflies flitting off into the night. Had it not been daytime, had the magic not been swirling in the clouds above rather than dissipating into the ether.

The thunderhead was laced with blue veins, glimmering against the dark vapour. The trees here were long silenced, and instead of their screams a dread settled into her bones. Lightning flashed bright blue, and static built up around her, causing her hair to stand on end. The drumbeat of rain drowned out any other sounds, but she knew there was nothing left living to make them. No rustle of balurats, no chattering birds, no deer nibbling on saplings. The magic of living things was leaving this place, and settling high above, out of their reach. And, without their magic, the pines could not regenerate.

The forest was dead. She was a Tree Keeper who had failed in the worst possible way. Scrabbling at what remained of a nearby tree, the charcoal flaked away beneath her paws. There must be roots, a germ, a tendril of something to regrow next year. Anything. But the further she dug, the more her heart tightened in her chest. She sat in the mud, a hole two feet deep before her. There was nothing left.

Above, the sky crackled ominously. The storm was on the move, heading southwards towards the scurry. There was no reason to think the Ruhannian Oaks were at risk; they had stood centuries without catching the burn. Otso had shown her the beech branch, shown her it could be extinguished. Yet, she couldn't risk that the storm was something else entirely. She had to warn the wardens.

Levelling her breathing, she opened up her portal and stepped backwards, letting its light envelop her. She didn't notice the flash of red as she vanished into thin air.

# Daisy

As SOON AS SHE got home, Daisy flopped into her comfy chair and logged onto kirkhyrst.social. She couldn't remember the last time she'd been offgrid so long. Her usual morning routine was to get a coffee, check there was no urgent, actual work awaiting her, then scroll through her timeline. She told Hari it was to get her brain going so she didn't make mistakes on the important stuff, but she'd seen him posting during work hours too. @hari@grid.official had even liked some of her posts. Was it better or worse to be using a work account?

Daisy had resisted attaching her ongrid persona to her job. She technically had an @grid.official account for if she needed to contact people for work purposes, but she preferred to use gridmail. She thought of Faelan, delivering packages far and wide and wondered if her comms allowance would stretch to a courier now and then.

Think of the devil. A notification popped up:

`@faelan@alder.pack:`
`@daisychain@kirkhyrst.social te`
`k4bavuyeehyrfk`

Of course, his pack had their own server. They were very organised, if somewhat insular creatures. Daisy's hopes that Faelan had returned to human form were dashed. Unless he'd dropped something on his keyboard, that seemed like the combination of letters a large, unwieldy paw might hit. She was impressed that it had reached her and not another Daisy. She pressed follow anyway.

Flower names were less common than they once were. They weren't considered very modern, and people tended to assume her parents were of the nature loving, technology denying variety. Well, they did love nature, but they also had a television and a car and all sorts of mod cons to tend their lovely garden with. They were also avid social media users, for better or for worse, and she had a message waiting for her from her mum:

```
@marthainthegarden@kirkhyrst.social:
@daisychain@kirkhyrst.social the lawn is
full of daisies right now, thought of you,
kiss kiss
```

She clicked the like button, not having the mental capacity to reply in words. At least it was an acknowledgement she was still alive. She promised herself that she'd talk to her parents at the weekend and scanned through the rest of her notifications.

There was a new follow from @notalimabean @kirkhyrst.social. No message, but she could guess it was Lima. Her profile picture was a white cat wearing a witch's hat. Daisy just had an awkward snapshot; she was laid on her parents lawn with her hair fanned out... and yes, there were some actual daisies in shot. She was such a cliché.

Had she actually made some new friends, or were they just being polite? She had her book club who met once a month, but she was generally content socialising ongrid. Friends like they portrayed on television dramas seemed like hard work. As much as she enjoyed her own company, at times she thought it would be nice to have someone she could just hang out with at a moment's notice.

Oh, she was always welcome at the vamp bar downstairs. Etienne had made a special badge for her that read *No Snacking Here* to ensure she returned with all her blood left in her veins. Some vamps came in for a moan about the state of vampirity these days, and she was happy to sit there and be a sounding board, but without partaking in the bar's main activity, she never fully belonged. At least they served cocktails.

Not that Faelan had spoken to her; maybe he was one of those arrogant, alpha knows best type shifters. Though she was pretty sure the alphas of the Alder pack were a lawyer and a council member, neither of which involved running around delivering packages in Ruhann. She tried to resist the urge to search ongrid for him but failed.

There wasn't much. He was listed in an old puff piece about up-and-coming future alpha prospects, but nothing since, his name fading into obscurity. There were a few public photos from pack socials—his golden stare directed at the camera in disdain. She went back to Faelan's profile, scanning over his recent activity. It was all pretty standard stuff, a bit boring to be honest.

Further back in his timeline, there was a back and forth between him and someone called AstroWolf, filled with in-jokes and the sort of teasing that would get you blocked by a stranger. That had stopped about six months ago. Huh, a break-up maybe. She couldn't tell if AstroWolf was male or female or none of the above. She clicked away, disappointed in herself for looking.

It wasn't unusual for her to work from home on a Friday, and she saw little point in showing her face in the office for the few remaining hours of the week. She just couldn't handle dealing with the mountain of work awaiting her, even if avoidance was only making it worse. No one would notice if she slipped downstairs for a drink, and the bustle of the bar would crowd out any lingering loneliness.

She returned to her gridmail and quickly rattled off a message to Hari, keys click-clacking beneath her fingers as she filled him in on the lack of substantiating evidence that the Grid was at fault. That was what he wanted to hear after all. She paused before sending it, then added a suggestion that the Grid could be disturbing natural magic and further research would be beneficial. She worded it in a way that hinted at a lawsuit in waiting; that would get their attention.

The other anomalies were worth looking into, if only to further their knowledge of how magic worked. She made a mental note to raise these investigations on their system before she signed out for the weekend.

Reaching for the door, she paused. The smell of wood smoke still clung to her hair, and she became acutely aware that she was still in yesterday's clothes. Clothes that had spent the night under a tree next to a faintly musky wolf. Hari might not notice she was slacking off, but she would certainly turn heads downstairs. And not for the right reasons.

First, she needed a shower. Her bathroom was tiny but functional. She had to practically stand in the shower to close the door behind her, so most the time she left it open. One benefit to living alone, even if two incomes would cover a slightly bigger bathroom. As she rinsed her hair, fragments of Ruhann washed away down the drain. Ash and soil, a small twig. She half expected a beetle to come crawling out.

She wasn't a vain person, but she liked to think she had minimum standards for herself. Rocking up at a bar with half a forest in her hair would certainly spark Etienne's interest. Interest in her non-existent love-life, no doubt.

Freshly scrubbed, she selected a clean pair of jeans and a plain black t-shirt. Nothing that screamed bite me. She would have preferred to have put her damp hair up but didn't want to taunt Etienne's patrons. Although, at this time of day, it was unlikely to be busy, let alone crowded with vampires. Navigating in daylight was just too much of a hassle when the sun could burn you to a very literal crisp.

As expected, the ground floor level of the bar was deserted, and Daisy padded down the spiral staircase into the basement. Multi-coloured fairy lights were strung across the bar, at odds with the candlelit ambiance of the rest of the room. Leather-clad booths lined the walls, offering a sense of privacy while still in hearing distance. Etienne didn't put up with anyone taking advantage of humans here.

Behind the bar, a tall, dark-haired figure was polishing glasses, wearing a suit that looked like it might have been made from Daisy's nan's curtains. A sort of velvet with large red roses blooming across its shimmery surface. He spun around at the sound of Daisy's footsteps and grinned a lop-sided grin.

Daisy couldn't help but grin back. She gestured at his outfit. "What's with the couture?"

"This? You like it?" He twirled with a flourish.

"Not my cup of tea."

"Ah but it is the latest from Flora, a promising young team at the Arts Institute! One of a kind."

"It's very you, Etienne. But you know me. When it comes to fashion, I like comfort over style." She pointed at her clothes.

"You have never said a more truthful word, my darling. Now what can I get you?"

Daisy peered over the bar, scanning the bottles for anything new or interesting. Blood was not the only thing drunk at *Etienne's* by a long shot. A hazelnut liqueur caught her attention.

"Can you make me something with that? Something reminiscent of the great forests out west?"

Etienne raised an eyebrow at her request but got to work on her drink without question. He was a good bartender, not one to pry, but there if you needed to vent. Oh, and he made awesome cocktails.

"So, what brings you here in the middle of the day?" OK, maybe he did pry, a little.

"You'll never guess where I just got back from."

Etienne looked her up and down.

"Did you finally discover Dawn?" Etienne asked, referring to the hottest night spot in town. It didn't open its doors until well past Daisy's bedtime.

"No, a bit further afield." She paused a moment, before adding "Ruhann."

The vampire gasped dramatically.

"I must admit, the vast wilds of Ruhann seem more your style than Dawn. What on earth are the Grid doing out there? They haven't finally come to their senses and signed up for power, have they?"

Daisy filled him in as best as she could, skimming over the details. There didn't seem any harm in sharing, not when it looked like the Grid wasn't at fault, and he might appreciate the magical mystery.

"Ooh, the Alder pack. They're some sexy beasts, the lot of them." Etienne whistled when she got to the part where they discovered Faelan's identity.

"That's what you're taking away from this?" Daisy laughed. "He was mostly in lupine form anyway. That would be weird."

"Pah. He'd be all man when you needed him to be."

"Stop it Etienne," Daisy swiped at him. Any chance to try and set her up, he would take it. She wasn't sure celibacy existed as a concept to vampires; they all seemed to be horny all the time and were happy to act on it. "Anyway. I think he was stuck. Maybe still is."

Etienne frowned at this.

"His pack, it's a powerful one. Magic that old and strong can't just glitch out." He looked serious all of a sudden. "No. He must have had his reasons for not shifting back."

The vampire appeared to be talking more to himself than Daisy.

"Ets, what would happen if... um... your magic faltered?" She hoped she hadn't overstepped; the vampire's face was more ashen than usual.

"Oh, I imagine I'd wither away into a pile of dust and blow away into the wind." His flippant tone did not match his expression. Not one bit.

# Faelan

The Alder pack lived in a big rambling house on the north side of the river, its once grand proportions hidden behind years of extensions and adaptations. Ivy crawled over the brick, tracing the lumps and cracks of a house well lived in. An imposing ash stood sentry beside the front door, sweeping branches reaching out towards the upper windows. Perfect for a teenage rendezvous, or sneaky getaway.

A worn path wove through rosemary bushes to the left of the building, leading to a small wooden door. Faelan crouched down and pushed through, flapping the door open, thankful to whichever former resident had installed it. He padded along the corridor, pausing by the kitchen door. His hunger warred with his need for peace; he didn't have the energy for a confrontation.

Astrid and Kane were sat at the kitchen table, a newspaper spread out at the crossword, a large bag of cheese puffs and several bottles of cider beside it. He had forgotten it was Friday, their day off from pack duties. He felt a pang for the easiness of their companionship. Their knees touched under the table, as if they couldn't bear to be parted by mere inches of air.

"Ten down, a heavenly bite from afar, eight letters, ends in G?" Astrid read out the clue, and Faelan took the opportunity to tip toe past the open doorway, praying they wouldn't hear the tap of his claws on the wooden floorboards. He made it to the staircase, and the safety of carpet, and padded up to his room at the top of the house.

He could move out of course, and he'd been saving his earnings in case it came to that. No one expected him to stay, but this had been his home for thirty-six years; it smelled like home, of the pups they'd once been back when they hadn't a care in the world. The banister still bore the toothmarks of Kane's teething.

None of it was anyone's fault. Deep down he knew that.

He sighed wearily and went to prod his console on with his nose. None of the shifter packs had had the foresight to invent a paw friendly keyboard, but with a bit of care he could still navigate around the intergrid. The trackpad was at least sensitive to his claws; the problem was they were attached to his big, oafish paws. He clumsily navigated to kirkhyrst.social and stared at the feed. Aimlessly scrolling and not taking much in was par for the course. Daisy's bright smile floated into his mind. He could have a quick look at her profile, see if she'd posted anything about yesterday.

Several Daisies later, he was staring at her picture. It wasn't posed or edited like so many photos these days. She was just... her.

"Faelan," a voice sounded from his open doorway. He jerked, accidentally hitting his keyboard with his paws. He turned to face Astrid, her pale hair pulled away from her face in a messy bun, a look of concern wrinkling her otherwise perfect face. Faelan tensed.

"It's not like you..." She gestured towards him. Not like him to be a wolf, she was just too polite to say it. Maybe that's why they hadn't bonded; he was too human for her.

"This might be a good time to talk." She paused. "Since you can't talk over me."

He could howl over her, though. That was petty—he would sit and listen like a good wolf.

"You know I love you, so does Kane. You're our pack mate, as good as any sibling. No, better. We didn't want to hurt you but... ARGH! I can't describe it—this pull." She waved her hands around, pacing back and forth.

"I want to be there for you, but I don't need to be there with you. You know? When Kane leaves without me I feel this thing deep inside. Like I might break if I don't see him again. I mean, I could do without that part, I didn't ask to be bonded to anyone. I am a strong, independent female wolf. But it happened, so here we are." She reached out to Faelan, but he flinched away from her touch. Not now, not yet.

"I don't make the rules, you know? The pack must be led by a bonded pair, blah blah, blah. It was unfair of anyone to expect you to be alpha. Not when we didn't know." Astrid fell silent.

Fenrir, he couldn't stand this. She looked so sad. Stupid wolf traditions. They would have made great alphas together, as friends. But no, some mystical phooey needed to take place. Think human politics were mad? They didn't have a patch on the pack.

"And... things weren't working, were they? Between us?"

She was right. They'd dated on and off for years, but the pressure for something to happen was always there. In bed, it was hard for Faelan to shake the though of the alphas hovering over them, waiting for something to happen. It really put a dampener on his arousal.

They'd had fun at the start. Their pack wasn't so backwards that they'd forced them together; if they were destined to be together in the end, it didn't matter if they played the field first. Once they were bonded, they wouldn't be interested in anyone else, they knew that. The problem was, as the years wore on, the bond never emerged, and they kept on being interested in other people.

Faelan couldn't help but wonder if things would've been different if Kane had been around more. The day Kane returned from Samaz, the younger shifter walked through the door, and something changed in Astrid's eyes. He saw the very moment the bond took hold and could do nothing to stop it.

"We didn't fall in love on purpose," Astrid said in the tiniest of voices. Faelan's heart broke in that instant. She should be happy at being in love, not grieving for the loser wolf who couldn't even bond with the most beautiful person he knew, inside and out. Being alpha wasn't everything, despite what Mother thought. He would drag himself out of his self-pity eventually, and work at being their beta. The best beta a wolf could hope for.

Head down, ears laid flat, tail tucked neatly between his legs, Faelan offered his future alpha female an apology.

"Oh, don't start with that submissive crap." She laughed. "You need to tell me when I'm being stupid or getting a big head, right?"

Astrid launched herself at Faelan, enveloping him in a hug, and he let her cling on for a minute. He wasn't going to give her the satisfaction of leaning into it.

"So… Why are you slinking round in lupine form, my dear little wolf?"

Faelan cocked his head to one side, wondering how to convey the weirdness of yesterday with body language alone. The pack had ways to communicate, but for things that were generally relevant to being a wolf: rabbits this way, sniff this interesting smell, a sore paw, sexy times brewing. That kind of thing. As adolescent pups they'd worked out a secret code to pass on messages without the grown-ups catching on, but it was too limited. That must have been the last time any of them were stuck, their hormones running rampant.

The workings of the Grid were so far from wolf life, he had no idea where to start. He turned to his console, where Daisy's profile was staring right back at him.

"A lady friend?!" Astrid squealed before he could close the tab. "Here I was, worrying about you being alone, and you're off seducing lovely ladies already!"

Faelan shook his head frantically and somehow managed to land on the Grid's website. He widened his eyes at Astrid who had gone from glum to delighted at the speed of light. He could already feel the tension between them easing away. Maybe he should just pretend it's all about a woman. Daisy had slept by his side last night; there would be traces of her on him.

"I don't understand? Twenty questions time?" This was going to take forever, but he capitulated.

"Are you stuck?"

Faelan nodded. He didn't know how Astrid cottoned on so quick. Some of that mystical alpha phooey at work? She thought carefully about her next question.

"Have you been anywhere unusual lately?"

Nod. There was no way she would even think to ask about Ruhann. He didn't even think the problem *was* Ruhannian in origin.

"Was it the glass factories?"

What a random suggestion—no one went to the industrial quarter if they could help it. Not unless you worked there. Perplexed at her questioning, he shook his head.

"Steelworks?"

He shook his head again. If she was just going through every location in the city, this would take forever.

"Did you eat a whole mega meat feast pizza by yourself again? You know it gave you tummy trouble for days."

He rolled his eyes and answered no. She wasn't even taking this seriously. Which would be fine, but he would quite like to return to his human form before the month was out and might need some help. He had things to do, money to make, mysteries he wouldn't mind knowing the answers to. The pizza had been worth it though. Thinking about it made saliva pool in his mouth. He could really do with a proper meal.

Astrid leaned in to sniff him, inhaling the last two days' worth of scents.

"Interesting. Faelan, why do you smell of Eldur Pines?"

Faelan's ears perked up instantly.

"Sorry, wrong wording. Were you near Eldur Pines recently?"

A nod.

"I can't believe you've been off having adventures without me." She pouted. "You didn't get caught up in a burn, did you? No, the timing's not right."

Faelan paused a moment and waggled his head in a gesture he hoped was understood as yes and no.

"The burn's early?"

Another nod. How did she know about this stuff? The documentary channel? Had she been enrolled in a secret alpha training school he wasn't privy to?

"Did you get stuck after coming into contact with the trees?"

A shake.

"So before?"

A nod.

"This isn't helping. So, you've had two separate interesting things happen since I last saw you?"

He wasn't so sure about interesting, but he nodded anyway.

"I wonder if something's disrupting natural magic—"

He yipped loudly, jumping up before remembering to nod in answer. Astrid glanced at the screen, the Grid's website declaring magic for all.

"Has the Grid been meddling in Ruhann?"

He shrugged; he wasn't sure. Daisy seemed just as surprised by it all, but she was only an employee. Her bosses could be hiding something.

"Hang on a minute, that woman." Astrid strode over to his console pushing him out the way, alpha mode kicking in. He would have liked to have told her she wasn't alpha yet, but let it go. After a bit of clicking, she brought up Daisy's profile again.

"Ah ha! She works for the Grid!"

He already knew that, although at least it might stop her prying into his non-existent love life. He was investigating a lead, not grid-stalking a woman.

"Little wolf, I don't know what you've stumbled upon but colour me intrigued."

# Lima

MANY UP-AND-COMING Kirkhysrtites could be found in the Glassmarket district, where the former glassblowing workshops had been converted into sleek apartments, mixed in with smart townhouses and shops selling glittering trinkets. Beyond a small museum, visitors would be hard pressed to find anyone making glass there now. That industry, along with steel, was the realm of the Blackthorns who had transformed the world of construction with their machines, taking raw resources and spinning them into girders and panes.

Go back a hundred years and the air would have been choked with soot, workers coughing up their lungs after only a few months on the job. The Blackthorn Process had been warmly welcomed, only to push everyone who wasn't a Blackthorn out of business. Except for a few hobbyists, all glass and metal came from a single source.

Lima trudged up the cobbled street, reluctant to return home. She wondered if they had even noticed she was gone. The door to their townhouse was a deep red, with a large knocker in the shape of a lion, mostly ornamental since a small console was discreetly installed to one side. Their housekeeper would have a conniption if anyone actually knocked. Think of the paint, she'd screech, like paint was a rare commodity. She came very well recommended, according to her dad, but Lima often wished for staff she could get along with. Like Mary at number eleven, who always had a smile and kind word for her. Or that they were poor and just cleaned the house themselves. She was imaging her dad in a pair of pink rubber gloves as she entered her passcode into the console. The door beeped open, and she stepped through into the echoing foyer.

This house really was too big for the two of them, but it meant she had her privacy. She could go days without bumping into her dad, especially with his long working hours. She knew he did something to do with trading resources but didn't care to learn more. That was one of the reasons she was interning at the Grid, it was that or learn the family business.

Lima trailed upstairs to her room. She had her own ensuite bathroom and a view of the park from her bay window. She knew she was privileged to have this, but she yearned for her own place at times, to not have to feel like a guest in her own home. It was a silly fantasy, being able to run home and chuck her dirty shoes into a corner, to lounge around and eat whatever junk she felt like. A place where she could invite people, someone like Daisy, who would laugh and fill the room with cheer.

Not that Daisy would want to hang out with her weird intern anyway. She would have a proper adult life, filled with friends and places to be.

She sat down at her desk and switched on her console. This was her lifeline to a different world, a place where she could chat as an equal about photosynthesis and ocean currents and live vicariously through other people's pets.

She would love to have a cat, or a dog, or even a spider. But no, her dad said that the only place for animals in the home was on his dinner plate.

She knew from kirkhyrst.social that things could be so much worse. No one was hurting her. Her dad wasn't a bully. More like incapable of being a single parent, and his views and values were so completely unaligned with hers. She thought wistfully about life in Ruhann, living at one with nature, no one forcing you into a box. No one forcing magic into a box either.

Out of interest she searched for Daisy. She had her work gridmail, but it'd nice be stay in touch after her internship. Daisy's timeline was a mix of topics; books, animal photos, the latest research into energy production, jokes Lima didn't quite get. She saw that Daisy chatted away with strangers about anything and everything. Before she could second guess herself, she pressed follow. There, it was done.

She stared out of the window a while, watching a family with a tiny dog run around in the grass. The dog yapped at butterflies before spotting a squirrel. The squirrel froze for a second before darting towards a tree, dog in hot pursuit. In a few bounds, the squirrel was safely sheltered in the branches, the dog left at ground level, barking. Come down, I won't eat you, promise.

She enjoyed coming up with the inner dialogue of animals. She was glad she didn't try it with Faelan, who obviously had his own inner dialogue, being a shifter and all. Probably lamenting having to follow them around. She hoped his pack would help him shift back, even though the idea of being stuck as a wolf for the rest of her life didn't bother her as much as being stuck here.

Her thoughts drifted back to Lailu. Sleeping with Lailu curled around her had felt so comfortable. Comforting. Back in Ruhann it had felt so right, but in the harsh, artificial light of Kirkhyrst, she realised they were too different. A human and a Ratatoskr? What a joke.

Did people even do interspecies relationships; was there some law about it? The intergrid would tell her. She scrolled through search results, clicking on potential answers, twice landing on sites she wanted to scrub from memory. One dating site promising "furry fun" was full of photos of scantily clad women astride feline shifters like it was the most normal thing in the world. She didn't want to do sex stuff, she just... she didn't know. She had a hankering for close friendship and good hugs, that was all.

Several wrong turns later, she stumbled upon a forum where humans were discussing their relationships with shifters and vampires. It was no surprise that no one was contemplating a relationship with a Ratatoskr within the reaches of the Grid, but the existence of these people gave her hope.

**//InterspeciesRelate**

**Yanni123**
Hi folks, new here and looking for some advice. FH(21) dating MV(27) going on 2 years. My parents just found out my boyfriend is a vampire. He is super sweet and monogamous, but they have told me it's too dangerous and I have to end it if I want to live under their roof. To top it off they've demanded I show them a negative VTD test before I can come home!

I don't have savings and only work part time, so moving out right now isn't an option. I don't want to end it, but I love my parents, even if they are bigots.

**D0bb1n**
Can you move in with BF?

**GrumpySunshine**
You have my sympathies. Been with my vampire partner for 9 years (she's *much* older than yours) and my family never speaks to me. Screw them!

**VampLoverNo1**
You should both get VTD tests, whatever you decide with your family. Clinic down on Tanner Street will sort you out, no questions asked. Stay safe xxx

**mstoothy**
Go to Talia's Tea Rooms on Seventh. She will give you a bed for a few nights till you get yourself sorted. So sorry you're going through this, just know you're not alone.

**WoofMe**
Urgh. Shifter happily married to human here, my mum was adamant I'd screw up any chances of being alpha. Like there was any chance of that! Pack is actually really cool with it, invites both of us to all the social things. Even the naked night runs, though my spouse politely declines those!

I'm guessing the fact you're asking means his housing situation isn't an option for you. As mstoothy said above, reach out to Talia, she's good people.

**Deleted Account**
You're all disgusting and deserve VTD rot

**WoofMe**
I've reported dan783445, ignore them.

**KaitlinKat**
You don't know me and I know it's hard trusting people ongrid... but I'm part of a commune of lone shifters, if that's not an oxymoron! We all left our packs for various reasons, nothing bad I promise. If you need a place to stay, we have room on the sofa. DM me.

**Yanni123**
Thank you for all your kind words, it means a lot to me. My boyfriend lives with other vampires and I just feel weird about staying there. Will get the VTD test done, I'm just worried what I'll do if it's positive.

**mstoothy**
One step at a time Yanni. We're here for you whatever the results! Xxx

**KaitlinKat**
Hey Yanni, is everything OK? Been a few days of silence. We're all wishing you the best.

**Yanni123**

KaitlinKat so kind of you to check in! VTDs were negative, phew. Been a whirlwind since I last updated. Went to Talia and she put me in touch with a mixed shifter couple who are happy for me and boyfriend to rent their spare room for a very reduced amount! So... had another huge argument with fam, but I'm an adult and they can't stop me living my life. Hoping in time they will come round but ready to start a new chapter.

**mstoothy**
So relieved to hear you sorted something out. Don't forget to check out the <u>ISA events</u> pages. Lots of meetups with like-minded people. Maybe you'll see one of us there.

Reading through the stories, she found those who had found love and acceptance. Many who'd been disinherited by their families had been welcomed into a new community with open arms and were happier for it. Lima thought of her dad, the awkward "birds and the bees" talk she'd endured. From what she'd garnered from the euphemisms, her dad expected her to be having sex with human boys; he'd rather she didn't but that's what girls did. Luckily for her, school had explained that some girls like girls, and some boys like boys, and some people like both, or neither. None of them had mentioned that some girls like vampires.

There were several references to ISA events, so she clicked around until she found their listings.

**Interspecies Alliance Presents**...
Harvest Festival Ball @ The Old Corn Exchange
18th September, 8 till late!

All species welcome, leave your prejudice at
the door.
Grab your coloured coded badges at
registration.
Under no circumstances proposition anyone
with a red badge. No means no.

Lima was pretty sure she'd be one of those wearing a red badge. Closing the browser, she leaned back in her chair. Humans just needed to adopt the huddle, a platonic pile of snuggling for those who felt alone, without any expectations of something more. Lima, naïve human that she was, had just misinterpreted the signals.

# Lailu

Lailu emerged from her portal and tripped straight over a thick, twisted vine. She let out a gasp as she landed on the ground, which was oddly moist beneath her. She lifted her head from the moss, taking in the sight before her. Unusually smooth trunks stretched up into the canopy high above, where masses of glossy green leaves blocked out the sky. The air caught in her throat, dense and soupy, and her heartbeat thudded in her chest as realisation dawned.

Obviously not the scurry. Had she been too distracted when she opened the portal? These things happened, and it had been a stressful couple of days. She rubbed her ankle and tried to orientate herself, gazing around at the unfamiliar forest.

One plant that she recognised, that was all she needed to ground herself. While Hazel was a walking encyclopaedia on animal life, plants were Lailu's forte, and her curiosity won over from her shock. Testing her ankle, she found she could still put weight on it, nothing broken or sprained.

The trees were too tall and broad to get a good look at, yet she was certain they were nothing that grew in

Ruhann. Her beloved trees had more character in their bark—rough to the touch or peeling like paper. She pressed a paw to one trunk, feeling the hum of life. A row of ants wove skywards up the silvery bark, carrying a variety of debris from the forest floor, bark, circles of leaves, a twig, sometimes another ant. They were several times the size of Ruhann's ants, with an oily hue. Staring at them wasn't helping.

A bush to her right had finger-like holes in its waxy leaves. Another had vivid red flowers with protruding yellow tongues, and the whole forest hissed with some unseen life. Not a single living organism was known to Lailu. She knew regions of the world had different climates, and the ecosystem evolved to adapt, but she wasn't aware it could be quite so different.

Further west of Ruhann, the land got scrubbier as the forests lessened, and Kirkhyrst was surrounded by grassland. Keep going east and the coast was next, the islands of Samaz hotter and drier than the mainland. The north was mountainous but otherwise forested much like Ruhann. South of the Tarac was more of the same, trees giving way to rocky beaches at the southern edges.

Knowing this was different to experiencing it. Maybe the books were wrong. She thought of the throngs of humans who travelled into the edges of Ruhann each summer, their thirst for adventure only taking them so far. But at least they were discovering new places, trying new things.

For a species with the unique ability to travel great distances at the flick of a tail, Ratatoskr sure liked to stay in their place. She sighed, one thing at a time. First priority was the storm, alert the scurry, and then come up with a plan to resurrect the Great Forest. She had panicked, only checked one tree. A team of Ratatoskr could help her look for signs of life once the land was safe; the wardens would grant her that.

Her fur was already soaked through to the skin, and the clammy air was making her uncomfortable. She would go home, dry off, and come back with someone able to point out something to anchor herself with. New discoveries were exciting, nothing to be afraid of. She thought of home, with a focused mind this time, and turned around.

It wasn't there. She scrunched her nose up, pushed at the part of her deep within that had never failed before. Never failed until this day, in an unknown land. Her portal refused to form.

"Deep breaths," she muttered to herself, trying to stay composed. The anxiety she had kept at bay was threatening to take control, sending her pulse racing. A tremble worked its way up her tail. She slumped against a trunk, feeling the welcoming murmur of magic greet her. These trees weren't so different, and the thought soothed her somewhat. Maybe she'd just weakened herself portalling Daisy and Lima around. She would rest here, then try again. And if it still failed, a refreshed mind would be better equipped to come up with a plan.

She curled up into the crook of a tree and let the exhaustion of the last two days settle over her. It was a lot. The fire, the worry. Even the good parts—like meeting Lima—it all used up energy.

She thought she'd be too scared to fall asleep fully, but she woke up to find an offering of strange looking nuts laid by her paws, with no memory of how they got there. She sniffed and nibbled delicately, the taste quite unlike the hazelnuts, acorns, and chestnuts she was used to. They seemed edible, and she was too famished to worry if they would poison her.

She thanked the unseen bearer of gifts, perhaps too shy to disturb the strange creature asleep in their forest. If all the plants were different, there was a good chance the animals were too. She'd dreamed of smoke and blurred faces and was glad she hadn't woken to alien eyes staring at her. She knew she should try her portal again, but a dread had taken root in her. What if her magic was gone for good? Burned away like the Great Forest. Not even the eldest, most frail Ratatoskr lost their portals. In fact, many opened their portal as their last living act, stepping through into the afterlife. Sometimes Lailu had the morbid thought that their bodies were all just piling up in some faraway location, sight unseen.

She recalled the comfort of the huddle with Lima and Balu curled up beside her. The knowledge that there was someone there in the dark to hold your hand was something she hadn't realised she needed. Not until a strange little human slept in her nest, adding her mumbles to the oak's familiar sounds. Just because she didn't want to live under the crush of her siblings, didn't mean she wanted to live alone for the rest of her life. She needed contact. Laughter. Love.

She looked around for signs of whoever left her food. Would they take her in, and treat her as one of their own? The nuts hadn't been a trap, and she felt perfectly fine after eating them. Someone cared enough to feed her. She held onto that thought.

A single tear rolled down her cheek. She would allow herself that, a single tear of self-pity, then open her portal and go home. Her confidence would fuel her magic, and all would be well.

"Home sweet home," she whispered, and squeezed her eyes shut.

# Faelan

FAELAN WAS HEADED TO the kitchen for breakfast when an arm darted out of the storage cupboard under the stairs and pulled him inside by the scruff of his neck.

"Astrid what exactly are we doing in here?" Kane mumbled through a mouthful of toast. "We're a tad old for sardines."

"Shush, we're never too old to play" she said, cuffing her mate. "But no. Faelan discovered something."

"That he actually likes being a wolf?"

Faelan huffed. He had softened towards Astrid the other night, but it was a bit much being jammed inside such an enclosed space with the two of them. He'd spent a large chunk of the weekend sleeping, interspersed with attempts to shift. Being cooped up was starting to make his pelt itch with pent up energy, but Kirkhyrst wasn't designed for free-running wolves. Astrid had suggested yoga, but downward dog was the only position he could realistically attain in this form.

"Children. Play nicely." Astrid went on to relay the snippets of info she'd teased out of Faelan. Why she'd waited so long to inform her mate was a mystery, but she was very independently minded and didn't need his input on everything. He wouldn't put it past her to dream up a scheme without either of them.

"We should take this to Luna and Jacob." Kane was quick to turn to the alphas. That answered the why.

"You know what they'll say. It's not pack business, don't interfere with the humans. Like we don't all share our world with them."

"Luna would be plenty pissed off if the Grid went down. It would seriously hamper her garden gnome addiction. I can't see her going to a shop. Who even sells those things?"

"We'll work out what's going on. If they need to be involved, then fine, we'll tell them. If not, no harm in them not knowing." She glared pointedly. "We'll show everyone what competent alphas we will be."

"Oh, sweetheart. Everyone understands. You don't need to prove yourself."

Faelan was starting to feel hot in this airless, cramped cupboard. He didn't need to be witness to their love right now.

"Right." Astrid turned awkwardly in the small space, brushing against his fur. "We'll need to speak to your lady friend." OK. Getting even hotter now. Who knew wolves could blush?

Kane laughed. "Now this I need to hear."

Faelan tried to turn around to suitably glare at Kane, but knocked over a mop and bucket, making a loud clattering noise.

"Shhhhh!" Astrid hissed as Faelan tried to untangled himself.

"You know, my love, it's highly suspicious the three of us hiding in a cupboard. We could just, you know, have this conversation in the garden. Like normal people." Kane was finally talking sense.

Astrid glared at both males, before shoving the doors open with a huff. Kane looked down at Faelan with a conspiratorial wink. It was almost like old times between them.

"Now my wolf, tell me more about this lady friend." Kane used air quotes behind Astrid's head. "Wolf? Human? Vampiiiiiire? You need your wing-man to translate while you're all wolfy?"

"She seems human," Astrid said turning to Faelan. "But more importantly, she works at the Grid."

"I see." Kane paused. "Actually, I don't. If Faelan is stuck this way, that's pack business. What does the Grid know about shifting?"

"Did you miss the stuff about the Grid poking around in Ruhann? Maybe it's all connected."

"Maybe Faelan ate a bad pork chop."

"Oh, come on, he's been stuck like this for days now. And I know he misses his hands."

Kane snickered.

"Not like that!" Astrid smacked her mate's arm. Faelan was ready for this impromptu meeting to be over already. Mystery be damned. "Anyway. I want to speak to this Daisy person. Please?"

No one could resist those puppy dog eyes.

"OK. But later, I have stuff to do."

Astrid bounced on her heels and leaned over to give Kane a kiss. Faelan turned to get out of there pronto.

"Five o'clock little wolf, no excuses!" Astrid called after him.

He wished had had work to distract himself with, but he could hardly tender for new jobs in his lupine form.

His regulars he could deal with, but they'd been quiet since his return to the city. Usually, he'd try his chances around the Gridiron, chatting up receptionists in the hope they had some urgent deliveries lined up and oh, how wasn't it convenient that he was a courier. Or they'd take his name and promise to contact him for future work.

Lots of documents were sent by gridmail now, but there were still plenty who didn't quite trust it. Paranoia was a good earner for him. Luna was always on at him to set up a legitimate business with an office and gridsite, but something told him he made more money by being the sort of guy anyone could approach.

It's not like he was untrustworthy. He always gave his real name, his association with the Alder pack meaning something in this city. But he didn't keep records; if the council came chasing him for information, well what a shame, he didn't have it.

He found himself pining for the wild country out west where he could spend his time running freely. If Travis had more deliveries for Anderson, he'd be first to volunteer. For now, he'd have to make do with the parks of Kirkhyrst.

Someone in the pack had at least taken to leaving food out for him, things that were easy to eat in lupine form. He scoffed down a tepid bacon sandwich before returning to his room. No point in running on a full stomach, he'd go out later. And then he would go along with Astrid's plan, as always.

# Lailu

RELIEF WASHED OVER LAILU as she stepped out of her portal and into a long stretch of Eldur Pines, their sweet scent steadying her senses. It took a moment for her brain to catch up. These trees were alive, growing, not a sign of the burn among them. The wardens had done a sweep of the Great Forest and determined the fire was widespread, so how...

The trees whispered a song she could not decipher. Oh no. Was she destined to hop from forest to forest, alone for all eternity? She concentrated on her nest, Hazel, Balu, her family, even Sylvain, but no fizzle of connection stirred.

She sniffled.

"Do not cry little Ratatoskr," a melodic voice boomed from beyond the trees. She didn't see the figure at first, so shrouded in mosses and lichen it was. Long, gnarled antlers stood high above an angular face; its teeth far too jagged to belong in any herbivore's mouth. They stood with an unnatural stillness that filled Lailu with an urge to flee.

"You are far from home, yet the craobhan na beatha sing you are friend not foe." They tipped their head to one side, shedding shards of green with the movement.

"Faidhean," Lailu's whisper was little more than a breath on the wind, carried away by the trees.

"Ah so the Ratatoskr have not forsaken our memory."

Lailu attempted to push all thoughts of fairy stories from her head. Told to scare silly kits into behaving, to not venture too far into unknown wilds. So embellished by humans, that they didn't even realise they were based on anyone real. No, no use dwelling on stories when she couldn't untwine fact from fiction. She straightened her spine and addressed the being before her.

"Forgive me for trespassing. I did not mean to venture into your lands. It was an accident... with my... um portal." She wasn't sure how much the Faidhean knew about her people and made a vague circling motion with her paws.

"Your draoidheachd dorais."

Lailu had no idea what they'd just said, her confusion must have played across her features, and something shifted in the being's face. What was once terrifying became more like a wild creature, and wild things, Lailu could handle.

"Your kind's brand of magic is to open doors is it not?" And after a drawn-out pause, they added, "You may call me Ramus."

"Ramus—yes, doors. I'm Lailu."

"Be wary who you give your true name to, little Ratatoskr."

Oh wonderful, she thought. She should have taken heed of those fairy stories, after all. She was too polite for her own good, introducing herself without a second thought. Ramus beckoned her into the dark woods, and throwing caution to the wind, Lailu followed.

The shadows cast by Ramus's antlers reached towards Lailu, and she flinched away, not certain what she was seeing. The trees sang out to her, a breeze caressing her fur, comforting her, or distracting her. Distraction was a comfort of sorts, she supposed. Out of the corner of her eye, she could sense movement, but when she turned her gaze in its direction there was nothing.

Ramus took great strides ahead of her, untroubled by the undergrowth as if the forest flora were yielding to his path. Lailu took great pride in being able to navigate the Great Forest with ease but here she stumbled trying to match his pace. His movements weren't rushed; they were elegant but appeared to defy basic anatomy. It was unnerving to watch the Faidhean for long, so Lailu concentrated on her paws.

He walked down a shallow incline, and as Lailu followed in his footsteps, the trees became more layered with life. Lichens hung like curtains, with mosses carpeting the trunks. Fungi sprouted from beneath bark, and ivy tangled its way up to light. Deep ovals of hollowed out darkness sheltered curious eyes. They blinked at Lailu, and her eyes skittered away from their gaze.

At the bottom of the hill was a gentle river, where insects with bejewelled wings dipped and dived above the water's surface. Lailu yearned to dip her tired paws into the inviting water, unaware of the shadows passing beneath. Instead, Ramus guided her to where a roaring waterfall plunged into inky darkness. She hesitated at the opaque pool, but the Faidhean splashed straight through it, heading through the curtain of water.

It was as if he'd vanished into the rockface. Lailu glanced back at the stream in longing. A bird fluttering down to take a drink, a pretty little thing with streaks of pink in its feathers. As its head dipped down to scoop up mouthfuls of water, a shape loomed beneath it. It breached the water, its mouth all teeth, and in a flash, the bird was gone.

Lailu stumbled backwards. At least Ramus hadn't shown any signs of wanting to eat her, despite his terrifying appearance. She would call this place the Land of Teeth until she knew otherwise. Perhaps Ratatoskr's blunt teeth were just as horrifying to these toothy inhabitants.

So, she braced herself and darted through the water after Ramus. There she found a deep cavern carved into the rock, disappearing into darkness. Their footsteps echoed as they ventured deeper underground; the light from the entrance replaced by the soft glow of luminescence from the walls. The rock was coated in an unusual moss, each flower a globe of pale green light that pulsed slightly as if in time to a heartbeat.

She held out a paw, allowing the soft light to illuminate her claws in the gloom. She would very much like to study it, to learn how it thrived so far from sunlight. Everything in Ruhann would shrivel and die if left in the dark too long. Herself included.

Ratatoskr were known as an adventurous species, often mistaken for brave. The truth was their portals meant they could easily escape trouble in an instant. Lailu had lost that safety blanket, unsure if she'd be able to portal out of these caves if the need arose. She would just have to be the brave Ratatoskr from the stories, wandering into the underworld to claim her freedom.

It was actually pleasantly warm down below the surface, the droplets of water swiftly drying from her fur. The echoes of their footsteps soon mingled with the murmur of voices. They emerged into a cavern, the ceiling domed high above and a pool of pale water at the centre. Around the pool sat three Faidhean.

The one on the left reminded Lailu of a badger, short and rounded with black and white stripes down their face, but very decidedly not a badger. On the right was a smaller version of Ramus. Yet, it was the being in the centre who demanded her full attention.

She was tall and almost human in appearance, yet with a distinct lupine edge to her face which suggested a shifter on the edge of change. Her skin shimmered underneath her dress of furs, and her eyes were a piercing gold. Lailu tried not think of the dead animals she was wearing; it was unwise to criticise the customs of others, but they made her skin crawl.

"We have a visitor from Ruhann," Ramus announced her without sharing her name.

Lailu bowed low, recognising some sort of respect was required. She did not want to be skinned alive. Nor dead. And if she were to perish here, she would very much like her pelt to return to Ruhann, not turned into some sort of fashion statement.

Three pairs of eyes stared at her in the soft light, assessing.

"You come to tell us why the magic pulls?" the lupine Faidhean said, her words taking on a strange lilt.

Lailu looked back blankly.

"Pulls?"

"A feeling. As if it wishes to pull itself from beneath our skin, to depart our bodies for the ether," Ramus added. "Your door has led you here, has it not?"

Lailu considered this. She hadn't felt any such sensation, instead her magic wasn't doing what she wished, went on and off at a whim. If it had brought her here, this Land of Teeth must be the source of the pull, not the other way around.

She took a deep breath—nothing ventured, nothing gained.

"Our Eldur Pines are burning too soon. And the fire, it's not normal. It looks like pure magic, and I think it was dissipating into the clouds... could that be this pull you talk of?" Lailu asked tentatively.

She was met with silence, their gazes boring deep into her soul. Her mind was whirring, she suspected she was north of the Arran Plateau, a very long distance for it to be the same problem plaguing the Great Forest. If it was, the whole world was in trouble. So many species relied on stable magic to survive, and if this week was anything to go by, she only knew about a fraction of them.

"Um... if you don't mind me asking, where am I?"

"Tionnfell," Ramus responded this time. "Nine hundred miles north of Ruhann's border."

Lailu gasped. She needed her magic back, there was no way she could travel that far without it.

"My portal magic has been failing me. I was trying to go home, and this is the second land I have been delivered to instead. There was this awful storm, like the magic was fuelling it. Or it was stealing it, I don't know! Our trees are sick. And Kirkhyrst has been having problems too."

The Faidhean tensed at the mention of Kirkhyrst, and the lupine one hissed something unintelligible under her breath.

"The humans should not have magic," Ramus said without emotion, a statement of fact. Lailu thought that was a bit unfair. It wasn't humans' fault they were born without it, and they had been so creative in making it work for them.

"Well, they do, and it's going wrong for them too. They're trying to help." Lailu resisted stamping her paw, just. She might not know many humans, but the ones she did were not at fault, she was sure of it. "The Grid sent their people to Ruhann, and they couldn't find anything wrong. It's not them!"

The thought of Lima being scrutinised by these beings made her heart hitch. It was a good thing she were so far away, back in Kirkhyrst and shielded by the solid walls of the city. Lailu would trade these dank, oppressive caves for the city in a heartbeat. Her portal was already broken; the humans could hardly make it worse.

"And you trust these humans?" the badger-like Faidhean asked.

"I... er... yes. They care about the natural world." Lailu didn't repeat Sylvain's words about profits, but in a way, she understood. There were more things at stake than the trees, and the humans had a vested interest in making things right.

The Faidhean talked among themselves, Lailu failing to catch any familiar words. She supposed she wasn't meant to hear whatever was being said. She hoped it wasn't how best to eat her.

"We cannot permit you to wander freely. Not with your tainted magic," the lupine one said at last.

And with that the conversation was ended, the three Faidhean turning away from her. At least she hadn't blurted out her name this time, but she bristled at the word tainted. At least that's what she thought she heard; their accents were strange, and her brain struggled to keep up with their words.

Ramus tugged her away, leading her deeper into the cave structure, where she lost track of the forks in the path. If she couldn't rely on her portal, she was not getting out without a guide. There were doors set back into the rock down here, some adorned with decorations, others nothing more than a scratched word in an unfamiliar script. Ramus came to a halt outside a door of ash, the wood knotted and scarred.

"You may rest here. No one will bother you." He opened the door revealing a bed of furs and a ball of moss lighting the small room. She sat gingerly on the side of the bed, disturbed by how much the pelts felt like Faelan's beautiful fur. Without another word, door swung shut, and she was alone once more.

# Daisy

"THERE'S A MOUSE IN your fuse box Ms Reid," Daisy emerged from out of the basement dangling a confused looking mouse from its tail.

"Oh dear." The elderly woman covered her face with her hands.

"Yes, she's been building a little nest in there by the look of it. Gnawed through some wires." Daisy was just relieved this was a normal case, with an obvious fix. "I'll schedule in an engineer to come round and replace it."

"Should I put out poison in future?"

Daisy looked aghast. "No! Just keep the area around it clear. Don't leave any food lying around." She didn't like to judge their customers, but Ms Reid's house was so cluttered she couldn't move without bumping into something.

She had barely sat down at her desk before Hari had ordered her out on the rounds today. The cases were piling up, and since they had found no evidence of leaks or tampering in Ruhann, the case of the burning trees was closed. Daisy had wanted to do some more research, but she guessed she was going to have to do it on her own time. She hoped Hari had given Lima something more interesting than filing to do while Daisy was out of the office.

The last three homes Daisy had visited had all had occurrences of intermittent power loss, no rhyme nor reason as to why. She'd reset their systems in every case and asked them to report back if it happened again. She hated those types of problems. An overzealous mouse, she could deal with.

Outside, she lifted the mouse up to her face and gave it a stern look.

"Please, behave yourself, and go nest somewhere less dangerous," she told it, before letting it free on the street. It scampered off, disappearing into the bushes. She was not going to start killing innocent animals just because some people thought they were pests; it's not like the mouse knew any better. She guessed the Ratatoskr had rubbed off on her.

There had barely been any coverage of the forest fires in the news. Presumably the whole of Ruhann hadn't burned to a cinder, or she'd have heard something by now. Wouldn't she?

Last week had really zapped her energy levels, dealing with so many new people was hard, though no one would guess from her sunny demeanour. That outward appearance took work and she wanted to spend the day slumped at her desk, not trotting around town speaking to strangers.

Stifling a yawn, she checked the next job on her list: a commercial property down in the Glassmarket registered to Blackthorn Industries. Not one of their factory sites, those were all on the outskirts these days—the city's northern perimeter fortified by a wall of industry.

Their offices on the other hand, were situated in a high-profile district with links to their legacy; this was where deals were made. Daisy had forgotten to ask Hari how things went with Celia Blackthorn. If they were all experiencing power problems, the Grid would be in trouble. Blackthorn Industries were their number one customer, using vast quantities of magic to power their machines.

Celia wasn't involved in the business so much but benefitted from its profits. She had a minor role, some concocted position to allow her to draw a wage without doing much work. Instead, she spent her time being seen. At parties, at charity events, making sure to be at the scene of anything her family thought might be of benefit to their behemoth of a company. The Grid might be the ones controlling the power, but the Blackthorns had Power with a capital P.

Daisy noticed all her callouts were to affluent parts of town, and she found it hard to believe no one in the rookeries had issues. Sure, the industries vital to keeping the city running were important, but people like Ms Reid had other options if their power failed. She made a mental note to compile her own list of cases for tomorrow—it was probably just Hari running the query wrong, filtering by geography rather than priority. He might be the boss of her, but she wasn't scared to tell him when he was wrong. Which was worryingly often, since the Grid didn't spend much time training management on the day-to-day systems.

The Blackthorn Industries office was a modern amalgamation of old, sooty brick bolstered by steel girders and vast plate glass windows, showcasing what their machines could achieve. No need to throw out all the old with the new, it announced, we can preserve our heritage while modernising. Just let's not think about all those glassblowers and blacksmiths who lost their livelihoods. Daisy wasn't in a position to lecture on monopolies; it's not like power could be bought from anyone who wasn't the Grid, and she was fine with that. So why were the Blackthorns any different? She composed herself before pressing the intercom button.

She was quickly buzzed into to the spacious foyer, where the structure of the building was on show to the world. A young man touched elbows with her, thanking her profusely for coming so quickly. Little did he know, she'd purposefully done the residential visits first, but what harm did it do to give the impression that the Grid was busy and didn't bend to privilege. Even if it did.

Daisy checked her notes. Some sort of display issue on the building's consoles, which sounded to her like a software problem, not a Grid problem. The receptionist unlocked one of the rooms, filled with desks and consoles. They flickered on and off in the dimly lit room. That was odd.

"They just show some sort of gibberish," the receptionist informed her, pulling out a chair at the nearest console. "They're all the same, the whole building. We've sent everyone home for the day—didn't seem much point in trying to work. Except for muggins here."

Daisy smiled and turned her attention to the console. The display darkened before refreshing to show a screen full of symbols that looked like words yet weren't. Not to her eyes anyway. Historians had found texts in the old temples that couldn't be read by anyone alive today and had hypothesised that they were dead languages, impossible for modern humans to comprehend. Visitors to the history museum were invited to try their hand at translating one passage etched into a stone tablet, in a vague hope that one day a genius would waltz through the doors and declare the mystery solved. These symbols reminded her of those etchings in the museum, but they had no place on a console in an office specialising in sand, silicon, and glass.

"Erm. These symbols? Are they part of the security here?" She thought she better check; Blackthorn Industries must encrypt everything when not in use.

"Not that I know of. I've never seen anything like them before. Janice said it gave her a headache. I guess it's all the flashing. Come to think of it, I'm feeling a bit off myself."

"Have you installed any new software lately." Daisy decided to ask the usual questions, since she did not expect to be able to fix this. After the receptionist answered all her questions with predictable, if unhelpful, answers, she decided to take a different tack.

"How familiar are you with the power usage across Blackthorn Industries?"

"I see the bills—they're mahoosive. I could pull them up for you but..." He waved his hand vaguely at the consoles.

"Any recent increase you can recall?"

"Oh no. We've been requesting an increase in our quota for months, but the Grid keeps pushing back. We can't hog all the power, apparently."

Hari hadn't told Daisy any of this. She would be having words later. The consoles kept on flashing, and she peered at the strange symbols looking for anything familiar. The ways in which the magic was malfunctioning were getting weirder and weirder, and nothing in her training had prepared her for weirdness.

"Do you mind if I take a few photos?" She wanted to study the symbols further, but not if it got her into trouble. The Blackthorns were famously close-handed when it came to how their business worked. The receptionist gestured for her to go ahead.

Were her eyes deceiving her or was there a blue halo around the screens? She blinked to clear her eyes and was greeted with a moment of darkness. It was just the flashing light; it was messing with her already tired eyes. The whole place felt eerie though, like something might jump out at her at any moment. She told herself she wasn't used to all this open space—agoraphobia, that was it.

"We should turn it all off to be safe; we don't want any accidents. I'll file an urgent incident report, and we'll get someone round to reinstall all the wiring." Nine times out of ten, a fault in the wiring was the root cause: magic shorting out on a breakage or a loss of power somewhere along the way. This wouldn't be a quick job, but the building was clearly unusable in its current state.

Daisy's mind flashed to the burning forest. She did not need to see Kirkhyrst burned to the ground too. As much as she'd like to move Blackthorn Industries to the bottom of the pile, it wasn't worth the risk. "I should take some readings before I go."

The meters were bland, black rectangles with a small screen that was inert for most of the time. They had no power of their own, so were useful in finding leaks of magic, which would briefly power them to give readings. Daisy looked down at hers in horror. It was off the charts high. The only time she'd seen higher levels were in Ruhann the week before.

"Turn it off. Now!"

# Lima

SAT IN A QUIET corner in the basement of the Grid, Lima clicked her way through the backlog of cases. Hari had thought better of assigning her coffee duty and instead asked her to go through any cases without any activity in the last three months and close them off.

"If the problem's still happening, they'll tell us about it," Hari had told her. Lima thought that rewarded pushiness, and she imagined all the patient people waiting for their case to be dealt with but too polite to chase it. Maybe that was just her. Her dad would certainly be on the phone every day until a problem was fixed.

Most of the cases were simple power outages, and she was surprised at how frequent these were. The Grid was supposed to be a robust system that could be relied on. The other reports were of unusual glitches; over the last few days she'd learned that Daisy loved solving puzzles, so she was surprised they hadn't been picked up. She jotted the ticket numbers down in her notepad with the intention of passing them on. The Grid had a massive backlog right now, and maybe the policy of closing cases without investigating made more sense when everything was business as usual.

She didn't think Hari would appreciate an intern telling him how to do things, so she kept quiet and returned to her task. It was almost therapeutic, the repetitive nature of opening each case on her list, checking for any red flags and closing them down, her list getting steadily shorter as the day went on.

She must have been through at least thirty before she started to notice a pattern. She'd been creating a mental map of the locations as she went and while she didn't know every address, those she did were all down in the rookeries. She went back through the cases, scouring for any hint of an upmarket address, or a commercial property, left unattended.

No one was paying her any attention, so she brought up the search function on the system, pausing to work out what to search for. Then a phrase caught her eye: recently updated. She clicked, her screen filling up with cases. Lima looked surreptitiously over her shoulder. She felt so paranoid that someone would catch her, but Hari hadn't exactly told her not to go poking beyond her assignment.

There were familiar names and addresses at the top of the list. She clicked on Celia Blackthorn. The heiress had reported some malfunctioning lights the morning Lima had started her internship, and had received a visit from the Grid—Hari of all people—on the very same day. She was under the impression Hari never left his desk.

Lima compared the case notes with those of the rookeries. Perhaps the lights were strobing and were a health risk. As she read, it became clear that Celia's case was merely an annoyance while families in the rookeries were left without power for days, and no one bothered to check on them.

Blackthorn Industries was the second only to the Grid in terms of power in this city, it made sense that they would take higher priority... but it wasn't like Celia actually did anything at the business, unless you counted promoting the lifestyle of a Blackthorn heir as work. She closed Celia's case and opened the next one, bristling at the injustice of the world.

Had she been assigned this task on purpose? Hari wouldn't have guessed a kid from the Glassmarket district would recognise the street names of the rookeries. However, Lima absorbed information like sponge, and after watching a, somewhat patronising, documentary on the rise and fall of the rookeries, she had decided to walk the streets herself. Everyone was so friendly, nods and good mornings coming from all directions. Doors were propped open, and children played in the streets free of cars. Not a soul singled her out as not belonging.

Her view of the place was seen through rose-tinted glasses. Intellectually she knew some people had things tougher than herself, but she struggled to see past the friendly veneer to the poverty lurking in the forgotten corners of Kirkhyrst. It was naïve of her to think that they would display their hardship outwardly, and she'd sort of had faith in the system. You didn't leave your neighbours flailing. Nevertheless, people were often too caught up in their own lives, their own problems, to see that others were struggling. The council had initiatives to help those who needed helping, as long as they had the will to help themselves. But if you had the will and were still ignored, what then?

Her indignation fuelled her desire to sort out this— this inequality of service. The Grid was supposed to benefit everyone, rich or poor, born in Kirkhyrst or from lands beyond the sea. That was its whole reason for being.

Lima went back through the cases she'd already closed and scribbled down a quick map of the residences. She briefly considered that she was breaching the terms of her internship, but she didn't plan to give the information to anyone outside the Grid. She slid the folded map into her bag. If anything came of it, she would speak to Daisy.

After she'd finished sifting through all her cases, Hari was too busy to find any further work for her, and Daisy was still out on her rounds. She was given the choice to wait or take the rest of the day off. She hastily wrote a note for Daisy and left in on her desk. If she hurried, she could reach the rookeries and be back in time to have dinner with her dad.

* * *

THE AIR OUTSIDE WAS cloying, Lima could almost feel the static of a thunderstorm building up around her. She didn't mind the rain so much, and she'd dressed much more casually today, in sturdy laced boots, skinny jeans and a loose t-shirt, all black of course. She pondered adding a second colour to her wardrobe as she strode towards the tram stop. Perhaps purple or a deep green. She didn't want to be a walking cliché, but black made it easy to get dressed every day.

Sometimes just existing was hard. She knew she should be grateful for the comforts her dad provided for her. A safe home, food on the table, access to the Grid, an allowance for black clothing. If there was something concrete wrong in her life, she felt she could rally round and get past it. This was just… inertia.

In Ruhann, she had briefly felt alive. She could breathe, in spite of the smoke in the air. Life was simpler. The Grid had done so much to further civilisation, but it also added to the things to worry about. Was she spending enough time networking ongrid, or too much time frittering her time away scrolling? There were so many new occupations being created every day, thanks to the marvels of the Grid, but magic was taking away jobs from people too.

Sometimes she wanted nothing to do with it, but she didn't want to be left behind either. Left alone. If she had to add the destruction of nature onto her worry list, her head would implode.

Not that she could do a single thing about any of it. She felt helpless, but she had seen a glimpse of a simpler life, where nature was important, and no one knew how many followers you had. She imagined trying to explain kirkhyrst.social to Lailu and smiled. It seemed a bit redundant when you had the ability to portal yourself anywhere. The Ratatoskr must have a better sense of personal boundaries than humans though. She shuddered at the thought of trolls being able to magically turn up at her door day or night. Most of them were too lazy to do anything in real life, but portals would change that.

The Ratatoskr could choose to portal into strangers' houses, but they chose not to. That was the kind of people Lima wanted to be around.

Were trolls real too? Not the kind lurking in the bowels of the intergrid but the kind that live under bridges. Or in caves. She wasn't sure which stories would be the most accurate. She really needed to find a bird friend to carry her questions to Lailu. She would feel silly asking ongrid about trolls, but Lailu wouldn't mind, she was sure of it.

The tram took her over the Tarac, its water brown and murky today. She tried not to think what was making it that colour and focused instead on Iron Bridge. It wasn't the prettiest of the city's bridges, the oldest Kirkhyrst Bridge was made from hand carved stone and the Blackthorn Suspension Bridge was sleek and ultramodern, but Iron Bridge was of a sturdy construction and linked the rookeries with the south bank.

The buildings closest to the river had been converted of course; the rookeries were pushed further north with each passing year, closer to the factories where many of the occupants worked. The Blackthorns said it was good to live so close to your workplace, short commute after all, but really it was just pushing the great unwashed further out of their line of sight.

The oldest part of the rookeries was all stone tenements, packed together but spacious inside with large windows overlooking the streets. Further out, the buildings were more modern, but stingier with dimensions. More people stuffed into less space.

The tram slowed as it approached a street market, and Lima pressed the button to get off. She thanked the driver and hopped off, out into the market's hustle and bustle. The wares on offer were an odd mix of fresh produce and random items of unknown origin. Shapeless t-shirts and loudly patterned leggings swayed in the breeze. Traders shouted out their deals, this day only, you'll never find a better price. One stall was demonstrating a device to peel boiled eggs, the audience enrapt as if the one thing holding them back in life was eggshells in their lunch.

Crunching into an eggshell was annoying, Lima supposed. She peered round the stalls looking for house numbers; her first address was somewhere around here. The door to number 31 Hedge Row was painted black, chipped and peeling after years of neglect. The building was divided into flats, and the buzzers were covered with a scrappy piece of card: *Not working, come in and knock.*

Lima pushed tentatively at the door which swung open. A chunk of wood had been wedged in the doorway to prevent the lock catching. The hallway was dark and cool—a faint smell of decay in the air. The bare wood stairs were well worn, and lead upwards to 31D, who had reported power failures last month.

The building was still; no buzz of power emanating from any of the flats. Lima trudged upwards, raising a hand to rap lightly on the 31D's door. A teenage boy opened the door, scowling at her presence. Lima cleared her throat.

"Hi. I'm here from the Grid. An incident was reported at this address?"

"Took you long enough," the kid replied. "Muuuum! Those worthless turds at the Grid have graced us with their presence!"

Lima's mouth fell open. She had thought using the Grid's employment as cover would gain her some respect. Still, a woman in overalls appeared at the door, her face a picture of cautious hope.

"Ignore my son. He gets his manners from his dad." She smiled at Lima, opening the door wider and beckoning her inside. "I'm Fiona, thank you for coming. I know you must be busy. So many of us have problems these days. Technology, eh?"

Now she was inside, Lima wasn't sure what her plan was. She didn't have Daisy's toolkit, or really any knowledge of what she was looking for. She'd just followed her heart and indignation. She mentally shook herself. She was here now, the least she could do was try and help this family.

"Is the whole building out?" Lima asked. "The report is just for this unit."

"Oh, it comes and goes. No one else bothered reporting it, but I said to our Terry, you won't know it needs fixing if no one tells you. The Grid're not mind readers, just magic!" Fiona chuckled. "I'd offer you tea, but I don't have the fire going yet."

"You've been cooking over the fire?" Lima was surprised people still had real fires inside the city. At home they had installed Grid powered fake fireplaces for ambiance, but they wouldn't boil a kettle.

"Oh yes, much more reliable. Though it's hard getting the fuel now—you have to get down to the river as soon as the boats come in. And it's expensive, especially on top of the Grid fees. So, we try and have pre-cooked food when we can. It would be such a relief to get the power back."

"I should look at your wiring," Lima jumped up suddenly feeling rather embarrassed about coming here, bringing false hope. She didn't even have the authorisation to offer the woman a discount, which she felt was the least the Grid could do. Imagine charging for a product they weren't even supplying.

Fiona led her over to the meter and fuse box. The meter's display was blank, but it all looked in good condition. Lima made a few notes—made up nonsense she hoped looked official. She could feel the tears building up behind her eyes.

"I'm so sorry it's taken so long to get to you," Lima started but Fiona brushed her off.

"Oh, bless you, you're only young. We all know it's not you making those decisions."

Lima smiled weakly.

"I'll flag this for an engineer. But... I, er... have others I have to get to today. If you'll excuse me," Lima muttered her goodbyes and fled down the stairs.

# Lailu

THE WALLS OF THE cave pressed in around her, damp and oppressive. Lailu had never considered herself claustrophobic, but the thought of being trapped underground forever sent her pulse racing. The space was not much smaller than her nest, but the stone was cold and unfeeling. Not like her beloved oak.

She swore she could hear scratching and the faint flutter of wings. What could birds be doing this far underground—no, please not bats. She loved all living things, she really did, but bats tested her resolve. They were leathery with sharp teeth and flapped around in incomprehensible movements. She had yet to meet one who made her feel warm and fuzzy. She was Ratatoskr; she should be permanently warm and fuzzy.

She willed away her tears, focusing once more on her magic. She only needed it once, to take her away, anywhere but here. There was magic here—she could sense it in her bones. Something ancient and earthy, so far from her bright portal magic, but she would take it if she could.

She visualised grabbing hold of that tendril of foreign magic, wrapping it around her paws, letting in sink beneath her fur. She tried wiggling her toes, her tail, jumping on the spot, and twirling round, trying to knock the magic loose.

Alas the darkness remained, and Lailu growled in frustration, smacking her paws against the wall. Why did this have to happen so far from home? If it had failed when she had just been too lazy to walk from one side of the scurry to another, she would have had support and sympathy in abundance. Maybe she was ill? Had the humans carried something with them from their city?

No, she wouldn't be dragged into that way of thinking. It was all too easy to blame humans for everything. Sylvain was so sure the Grid was responsible for the fire that they hadn't even started investigating other causes. If only she'd been more assertive. They portalled to the Great Forest over and over. A stray bit of their own magic could have ignited it for all they knew. There was something up with magic, the Faidhean had said as much; she just needed to find out the cause.

The flapping of wings intensified, followed by a thump at the door, and she cowered against her bed. Were the bats trying to get in?

She was about to apologise to the bats for thinking ill of them when the door swung open. She covered her face, expecting an onslaught of wings and teeth... but nothing happened. In the doorway stood a small girl with raven black hair. She might have been a younger version of Lima if it wasn't for her eyes. They were an oily black from lid to lid. The girl tilted her head to one side, inspecting Lailu while a feather drifted down from the ceiling, landing on her shoulder. It settled a moment before melting into her skin.

"I heard you crying," the girl croaked, her voice at odds with her appearance. "What is wrong?"

"I'm trapped down here, that's what wrong. All the while my home is probably on fire!"

The girl ruffled feathers that weren't there.

"Probably? Don't you know?"

"Well, no, because I'm here."

"You are Ratatoskr are you not?"

"Yes."

"Use your door."

"It's not working!" Lailu shouted, flinching at her own voice. It echoed in the confined space. "I'm sorry... I don't mean to..."

The girl made a clicking noise in the back of her throat. Lailu was sure she would leave now, but she carried on standing there, staring intently.

"If one day you open a door for me, I will go find news of your home," the girl offered.

"A door where?"

"That would be telling. I can say it will be no burden to you when the day comes."

Lailu weighed up her options. She didn't think sending a strange Faidhean girl through a portal at some unknown point in the future was too much to promise. What harm would it do? And she so wanted to know if the scurry was safe.

"There was a storm above the Great Eldur Forest of Ruhann. Do you know it?" Lailu asked.

"The forest or the storm? I know of many storms; they blow me off course—"

"The forest!"

The girl blinked and nodded, unperturbed by Lailu's uncharacteristic anger.

"My scurry is south from there, Warden Syl—" She stopped herself before she gave Sylvain's name. "There is a black furred warden there. The storm, it destroyed the forest, burned it to the ground. I just want to know my scurry is safe."

And with that, the girl exploded into a ball of feathers. In her place a large raven hovered in the air. It croaked once and flew away into the dark.

* * *

A SHADOW APPEARED AT the doorway to what she had come to think of as her cell. If the girl was back already, she could hardly have made it to Ruhann. But what did she know about bird shifter magic? If that's what she was. For all Lailu knew, the girl had decided the bargain wasn't worth it. What need did a being who could fly great distances have of a portal anyway?

As the shadow came into focus, she recognised the antlers of Ramus. If this was a prison, visitors roamed freely. She supposed her door was never locked; she had only chosen not to get lost in the tunnels.

She wanted to ask about the girl, but something held her back. Ramus loomed over her small form, breathing hot air against her fur.

"Come with me," he commanded.

Lailu wobbled to her feet and followed him out.

# Daisy

GRID HEADQUARTERS WERE ABUZZ with activity, engineers and analysts flocking to and fro. The central atrium was home to the iconic glass lifts, a gift from the Blackthorns to symbolise their working partnership. Daisy had never trusted them, preferring an opaque floor under her feet, and took the stairs whenever she ventured to the upper echelons of the building. Her office was located in the basement, down a short flight of steps hidden from view, exactly how she liked it.

She had been repeatedly invited to move to an office with a view, but she like the peace and quiet of the lower levels, and the server room was just a hop and skip away. Not that she went around the office hopping and skipping, at least not until after her second coffee.

"Hari, are you still here?" Daisy called, heading toward her boss's office. He was on the phone, bleary eyed and unshaven, but waved her over to the chair by his desk. She slumped into it gratefully and pulled out the readings from the Blackthorn offices.

"Take a look at this." She handed the paper over to Hari as soon as he was off the phone.

"No rest for the wicked," Hari replied with a wink. "What am I looking at exactly? Did you leave your meter on test mode again?"

"No, Hari. I've just come from the Blackthorn Glassmarket office. All their consoles are unreadable, flashing on and off, and the text is illegible. And *that* is the atmospheric magic level in the building." She nodded at the readouts.

"A leak?"

"Not unless every device in that building is leaking. The main power supply was stable. I turned it all off of course."

Hari dragged his hands down his face.

"It doesn't make sense. We've had some issues with flow rates these last few weeks, but I'd expect less atmospheric magic, not more," he said.

"Blackthorn have been requesting more allowance?"

"I've heard rumours of some friction there, but we've been resisting upping anyone's allowance precisely because of the low flow."

"Hari, do you mean to tell me we've been running around trying to solve minor issues all over the place, and it's actually all because we're running out of power?"

"No, no, nothing like that." He stood up and closed the door. "Don't let the board hear you say things like that."

"What's going on? You know I told the Ratatoskr that the fire wasn't our fault—don't make me a liar."

"You think they tell me everything? I'm as much in the dark as you," Hari sighed. "For what it's worth, I looked over the data from Ruhann. If anything, the power's going in the wrong direction. They have more, we have less."

"Maybe we accidentally left the core on reverse?" Daisy attempted to joke. Hari did not look amused.

Nothing made any sense. If the Ratatoskr were somehow secretly stealing magic from Kirkhyrst they would have hardly called in the Grid in to investigate. She imagined them opening a giant portal inside the core. No, that was ridiculous, they wouldn't put their precious ecosystem at risk like that. They distrusted the Grid's technology, that was clear.

There was no other way for the city's magic to reach that far, not without being purposefully channelled through wires, and big ones at that. And it wouldn't explain the excess magic in the Blackthorn offices, not if magic was leaving the city.

Maybe nature had finally got fed up of humans meddling in magic. Time to get revenge.

"I'll need to call this in upstairs," Hari's voice interrupted her train of thought.

As he reached towards the receiver, the overhead lights flickered. Two pairs of eyes turned upwards, watching, waiting.

"That's not good," Daisy said, stating the obvious. If there was one place guaranteed to have a reliable, steady flow of power, it was Grid HQ. "Hypothetically, if we did run out, what would we do?"

"That's not going to happen."

Exactly at that moment, the lights went out and Hari and Daisy were plunged into darkness.

"Shit," they said in unison.

# Lima

LIMA HAD WANDERED THE streets of the rookeries until the light started to dim. She had walked to each of the addresses on her list but hadn't gone inside. Hadn't wanted to speak to anyone else. Raise their hopes. She did try and detect signs of power, a light or appliance, the hum of everyday Grid-powered life, but the buildings were still. Each and every one.

As twilight descended, she expected to see more lights appearing in windows, but most remained dark. The streetlights flickered dimly, not the full brightness she was used to. It was as if she'd been cast back in time, to a time and place where magic was the preserve of shifters and vampires.

She knew she should get back. Tonight was one of the rare occasions her dad wanted to dine with her. Wanted an update on her internship no doubt. The food would be exquisite, the finest ingredients money could buy, prepared in a kitchen with no expense spared. There was no way her dad would go without power for weeks, not even a day. If power hadn't been restored in an hour, he'd likely be storming the Grid offices demanding answers.

Lima wanted to go back to Fiona, tell her they shouldn't take no for an answer. If the whole rookery turned up at their doorstep, the Grid would have to take notice.

Ahead of her, a group of tired but cheerful workers returning from their dayshift tumbled into a pub lit up by magic. It looked inviting, but more importantly, people talked in pubs. She could spare a few minutes to soak in the sentiment of those who lived here without exposing herself. Rest her tired feet and grab a drink before heading home.

She hung back at the bar, waiting for the regulars to be served their pints. Lima didn't much like the taste of beer and wanted to keep her head about her, so she quietly asked for a glass of water, pushing some coins across the counter.

"Water is free, sweetheart," the kindly bartender told her.

"Take it, please, a tip," Lima responded. She felt awkward not paying for a drink, and it was still cheaper than a bottle of fancy water in downtown cafes. She found herself a seat in a corner, sinking down into the soft padding, and took out her notebook. While she was here, she could compose a letter to Lailu.

*Dear Lailu,*
*~~Was lovely to meet you~~ I'm so ~~glad~~ happy we got to meet each other. I hope the fire is under control, and Balu has not eaten everything in sight. ~~Everything is normal and boring in Kirkhyrst.~~ Can I ask you if trolls are real?*

She couldn't think of anything write that didn't sound totally inane. She wanted Lailu to tell her stories, like the one about Kai and the tree, but didn't know how to ask without sounding needy. She chewed on her pen, listening to the hubbub of the pub.

"I swear, if I have to work one more evening, I'm going to murder Carly," someone said at the next table.

"Things still bad?" their companion asked.

"We're still three people down on what we need. Blackthorn won't raise salaries. Their name is muck around here—I'd quit if I thought I could last long enough. Don't blame people for not applying."

"Yeah, I'm feeling ya."

"How're things going with Sam then?"

The conversation quickly veered away from work and onto the various merits of Sam, who could do amazing things with his toes. Lima, hurriedly looked around for anyone else to listen in to. This is what she deserved for eavesdropping.

A pale, slight woman with cropped purple hair wandered into the bar.

"Sorry Bels," the bartender called over. "Nowt for you here tonight."

"Never mind." The woman's shoulders sagged. "I'll take a house red, if I may. I'll just pretend it's O-Poz."

As she walked across the pub, eyes tracked her. Lima was surprised to see such wariness in their faces; vampires didn't go around eating people uninvited. Lima caught the vampire's eye and smiled.

"Mind if I sit with you?" the vampire asked.

"Go ahead. I was just resting my feet before heading home." She reached out an elbow. "Lima."

"Belinda," the vampire responded with a light elbow bump. "The crowd here isn't usually so dour. I swear there's something in the air this week."

Lima perked up and opened her mouth to find out more, but the pub was plunged into sudden darkness.

"Vampire attack!" someone yelled.

Belinda burst out laughing. "Yup, you got me. I'm here to suck you all dry. Just let me find you first."

"I knew it!" another voice called out.

Beside her, Lima could feel Belinda grab her arm. A soft light appeared by the bar as someone started to light candles, passing them around. Lima looked over to her new companion. The vampire was doubled over with mirth.

"Can you believe these guys?"

Lima shook her head not sure what to say but could feel her lips turning upwards at the corners. She accepted the proffered candle and placed it between them, the light casting ghoulish shadows across their faces.

"Should someone report this to the Grid?" Lima asked.

Belinda laughed, but not unkindly.

"Not from round here are ya?"

"No. I was... erm... following up some things for... um... work?" She hated how her sentence turned into a question. Knew her dad would call her out on her lack of assertiveness.

"Power's always going off. You just wait it out, comes back eventually."

Lima peered out the windows. It looked awfully dark out there, like someone had snuffed out all the lights of Kirkhyrst.

# Daisy

Night had descended while Daisy manned panic stations at the office. Eventually they all agreed they needed food and sleep if they were to be in any fit state to solve the mess they were in.

They filed out of Grid HQ in worried silence. The moon was a sliver of a crescent, and the streets were shrouded in an inky darkness where the high buildings blocked out what little natural light there was. Daisy had taken the streetlights for granted all these years, happily traversing the city at night without a care for her personal safety. Some primal instinct surfaced in the dark—a dark she really needed to walk through to get home.

At the thought of home, she realised her neighbours would be in their element, their eyesight acclimatised to the shadows from a lifetime of shunning the sun. She wished Etienne was here now, a friendly face to chat away the fear pooling in her stomach. There was nothing to be scared of, she told herself. These were the same streets she'd walked a thousand times.

Gathering up her courage, she stepped down the street, feeling the familiar cobbles under her feet. The pavements were crowded with all sorts of obstacles, and she supposed the middle of the road would be a safer bet. If cars were still running, they'd be seen a mile away with their magic powered headlights.

The darkness wasn't quiet. There were concerned murmurings. A muffled melody of shrieks, laughs, and sobs. Loud bangs and the smash of dropped items or damaged property. Sound amplified by the loss of sight. This was the soundtrack of a city adjusting to a darkness it hadn't seen in decades.

The absolute darkness was disconcerting. If the lights had come back on this instant, they would have exposed numerous individuals flailing around with their arms out, shuffling one inch at a time or walking as if on ice. Daisy could just about hear the presence of others in the nothingness, cursing her lack of preparedness. She briefly wondered if Lima carried around candles and matches in that bag of hers.

*One step after another*, she told herself, *you can do this.*

The sound of brash words and unkind laughter drifted out of the darkness. A group of men were ahead of her, somewhere. She paused, considering her options. This was the most direct way home, and she had no reason to think they wished her ill, just because no one could see. Kirkhyrst was a safe city... or it was under the glare of the magic they usually lived under. She'd just read too many horror books, that was all. She squared her shoulders and carried on.

A crash of glass sounded from her right, and Daisy leapt out of her skin, slipping on the damp cobbles. An involuntary sound escaped her.

"Who's there?" a voice asked out of the gloom.

She took off at a run, not caring where she was going. She just wanted to be out in the open. There—she could see a glimmer of light. Turning a corner, she crashed straight into a solid body. A pair of hands grabbed her arms roughly.

"Hello there," a gravelly voice said, their hands roaming her body. She tried to wriggle free. "Oh, come on now. Don't you want a bit of company on this cold, dark night?"

"N-n-n-no," she stammered. "I just want to get by. Please?"

"Don't keep her to yourself," another voice joined in. Daisy's heart felt like it was going to burst out her chest; perhaps she would die of a heart attack before they had a chance to do anything to her. That was her preferred option. She knew no self-defence—had nothing on her that could be a weapon.

The owner of the first voice shoved her roughly against a wall, broken glass crunching under their shoes. Daisy squeezed her eyes shut, not that she could see much anyway, but it made her feel an iota better.

Then another sound made its way past the pounding of the pulse in her head. A car? No, it was something that sent a chill up her spine, some remainder from ancestors who knew to be scared of what came out at night. The sound coalesced into a growl—make that many growls, getting louder and closer. Could this night get any worse? Assaulted, heart attack, and eaten by wild animals was not how she expected to leave this world.

Her attackers had gone still; they sensed the danger too.

"Ow!" one yelled out, letting go of Daisy. She scrambled away. Feeling out in the dark, she collided with thick fur. She pulled her hand away quickly but could feel the beast turning towards her. Hot breath on her face, and the scent of animal mixed with... rosemary? Maybe she was having a stroke—she'd heard they triggered phantom smells.

Her thoughts were spiralling out of control. She needed to move, very slowly and quietly, but away from whatever was happening here. Were her eyes adjusting to the dark? She swore she could make out shapes in the shadows but nothing that made any sense. She crouched and moved in what she hoped was the opposite direction of her attackers. Man and beast alike.

Someone was keeping pace with her; she could feel a presence. Something hot, damp, and rough dragged across her cheek. She fell back, her muscled tense and ready for the bite she was sure was next.

"Something fucking bit me!" was followed by another scream, and then the thud of retreating boots, with the sound of claws scrambling in pursuit. A howl filled the air, chilling Daisy to the core.

She sat on the cobbles, bracing herself for her fate. Her whole world was the sound of her pulse and the gasp of her burning lungs as she gulped down air. She could sense a change in the air beside her, and she dared not move.

"Well, that was fun," a posh female voice said. "We should scare off hideous men every night. Are you OK sweetie?"

"I... er... what?" Daisy looked around uselessly. Her eyes picked out a faint pale shape.

"Hang on. Let me grab my clothes."

Daisy was struggling to process thoughts and wondered if she'd hit her head.

"Introductions may be in order," a different, male voice said. A warm mass of fur pushed up against her side and huffed. Hang on—she recognised that huff.

"Faelan?" Daisy ventured, and the wolf nudged her gently.

"Bingo!" the female voice answered on his behalf. "And I'm Astrid, and this is Kane. We're Faelan's pack."

"You saved me," Daisy whispered.

"The least we could do. We should get you home, then we can talk."

Daisy walked the way home with one hand laid against Faelan's broad back. He didn't seem to mind offering this small comfort. Once she knew she wasn't going to die, she'd burst into tears, the adrenaline leaving her body swiftly. Away from downtown, more natural light filtered down to street level, and Daisy's breathing slowly evened out.

As the streets reached more residential districts, they grew lighter; candles were placed on doorsteps, and portable lights shined out from windows. Even the clouds had parted, letting starlight shine down—a rare sight in Kirkhyrst.

She risked a peek at the shifters who had come to her rescue. The female was stunning, with high cheekbones, grey eyes, and an athletic build. Her hair was paler than the two males and appeared to glow in the limited light. The male was broad shouldered but not much taller than the female, olive skinned with golden eyes like Faelan. Daisy wondered if they were related, not really understanding how pack dynamics worked. Perhaps Astrid was his mate.

She quickly moved her hand away from Faelan, not wanting to risk the wrath of a jealous shifter. She'd kind of got used to him following her around, and she hadn't stopped to ask questions. Well, she couldn't exactly expect answers, not when he was always a wolf.

Everyone they passed was in a hurry, scurrying from the darkness to the safety of their homes. Daisy couldn't blame them—she couldn't wait to sink into the softness of her battered sofa herself.

"Damn, I need a drink," she muttered.

"Want us to detour to a bar?" Kane asked.

"Oh, no. I live above a bar anyway. If I don't have a bottle of something at home, Etienne can always provide." Daisy omitted the vamp bar part, not knowing how shifters felt about vampires. In the books she read, they were always mortal enemies, but they weren't the most serious of stories. She doubted Etienne was capable of being anyone's mortal enemy anyway; the worst he would do is create a particularly potent cocktail in their honour.

For one horrible moment she thought of Etienne as a pile of ash, the magic failing him as well as the city. She looked at the shifters beside her. They hadn't had any trouble switching between human and lupine form earlier. She coughed, not sure how to bring it up.

"So, your shifting magic is OK? I mean..." She pointed at Faelan in explanation.

"Oh yes," Astrid replied. "It's just old grumpy pants here. And that's what I wanted to talk to you about."

Daisy furrowed her brow. Could they smell her on Faelan? Or was there some sort of pack telepathy going on...

"I didn't do anything to him, if that's what you mean. I don't know much about shifters. Or magic. Just the kind that runs through the Grid. Even then, it's not like I can do anything with it," Daisy rambled.

Fatigue finally caught up with her, and she didn't have the energy to deal with anything else today. Whatever the pack wanted with her, she hoped it could wait, but she could hardly turn them away after saving her. The timing was impeccable... she stopped in her tracks.

"Were you following me?"

Faelan huffed and tipped his head to one side.

"Faelan was following your scent," Astrid informed her.

"That could be construed as creepy."

Astrid shrugged. "We didn't know where you lived—your boss wouldn't tell us, so we used our noses. Well Faelan did, human noses are a bit rubbish." She wrinkled hers in demonstration.

They rounded the corner onto her street, the sign to *Etienne's* dim without its power. It wasn't quite bereft of life; the sweet sound of a violin floated up the stairway from the basement bar, and the burble of conversation could be heard within. Thick red candles illuminated the way inside. Still open for business then.

Kane was sniffing the air, suddenly more wolflike than human.

"Wait. I can smell blood." He held the group back.

"That would be Etienne's." Daisy pointed to the stairs. "Vamp bar?"

"Ohhhh, cool. I've always wanted to go to a real-life vamp bar." Kane's face relaxed back to human, cheerful and friendly. Astrid swatted him gently on the arm.

"Another time? Blackout? Magical weirdness? Remember?"

Kane pouted at her. Daisy fumbled with her keys and, with a shaking hand, let the three shifters into the cramped hallway of her flat. Shoes were discarded haphazardly on the floor, and she tried to push the mess out of sight. Candles were stashed next to her fuse box—

she knew better than anyone that magic wasn't infallible. She lit three of them, handing them out to each pair of hands, though she was probably the only one that needed the extra light.

"Sorry, there's not much space," she said, as she led the way into her living room and spied an unopened bottle of red wine on the sideboard. "Just let me... uh... open this. Anyone else want some?" Three heads shook in unison. Right, just her. In the kitchen, she dripped a lump of wax into a mostly clean jam jar and jammed her candle in to secure it while she rummaged in the draw for a corkscrew. She fought with the wine's cork for several minutes, her limbs weak from shock. She was muttering all sorts of curse words under her breath, when a large hand appeared and took the bottle gently from her. Kane prised the cork out with a load pop.

"Thanks," Daisy said.

"No problem. Astrid's always too rough with them and snaps the cork," Kane said, rolling his eyes.

"I heard that," Astrid called from the living room. Daisy was not surprised; the kitchen was directly off the main room, only a few metres for the shifter's keen hearing to pick up on every hiccup. Astrid had made herself at home of the sofa, with Faelan at her feet. Daisy sunk into the cushions, clutching her wine glass, and Kane perched on the arm next to Astrid.

"So Faelan's stuck?" Daisy got the ball rolling. The quicker they got to the point, the sooner she could go to bed.

"I haven't seen him spend so much time as wolf in years," Astrid said. "You work at the Grid, right?"

"Um yes, I'm a support analyst—I try and work out what's gone wrong, make sure someone's assigned to fix things... that sort of thing. But we've never had stuck shifters reported to us before."

"So, you weren't experimenting with anything when he shifted?"

"What? No!" Daisy was affronted.

"Sorry, gotta ask." Astrid didn't look sorry, but Daisy let her continue. "You were out in Ruhann with him?"

"How did you know?"

"He smells of Eldur Pines," Astrid answered. "It's quite pleasant if you can get past the whiff of burnt magic."

"We were on the steamer together, and we passed through some sort of magical anomaly. At least I think it was." Daisy went on to explain her theory, that whatever affected the steamer, also made Faelan shift.

# Faelan

FAELAN HAD ALREADY SAT through several iterations of this conversation, and it wasn't like they were making any progress each time. He took in Daisy's flat instead. It was cosy, and she sure had a lot of stuff. Several bookcases were jam-packed with books, stuffed in whatever space they fitted—no attempt at any logical order. A dusty houseplant sat near the bay window, where a low bench served as additional storage. It was currently piled with more books, a blanket, and a bowl encrusted with whatever Daisy had eaten for breakfast that morning. He resisted the urge to sniff it.

Instead, he studied the titles on her shelves: *The Were and the Witch*, *The Forbidden Pack*, *The Blood and the Shift*. There was a definite theme going on. There were some human romances too, with pastel spines and punny titles. He missed reading already. He preferred mysteries, but mostly he just wanted a good story and characters he could root for; words to occupy his mind.

His fifth day in lupine form, and he was starting to consider the possibility he really was stuck as a wolf. He was lucky to have his pack—they'd make sure he didn't lack for anything—and his trip to Ruhann proved he could still do his job to some extent. If this had happened to anyone else, a lone shifter, someone whose pack's ideals didn't sit right with them, well they were screwed. Kirkhyrst wasn't set up for anyone other than humans. The vamps and shifters were welcome because, for the most part, they passed as human, but Faelan well knew there were others out there who hadn't chosen the city as home for a reason.

No one would say it outright though. People called the Ratatoskr squirrels, a slur they would argue as harmless, but it concealed a deeper concern. They were animals, not humans. If the Eldur sap wasn't such an essential commodity, one with no other source, the Ratatoskr would not be given the time of day. If Faelan snarled at the wrong person, unable to shift back and apologise, he'd be rounded up in no time. Despite his recent behaviour, he knew his pack always had his back and would come for him, but if any of them could be stuck in animal form, what would become of them?

He was getting ahead of himself. It had only been a few days, and with the power out, it wasn't like no one would be looking into the whole wonky magic thing, right? Unless the power cut was some normal equipment failure, and they were barking up the wrong tree.

As Astrid interrogated Daisy, Faelan let his ears pick up sounds from downstairs. Laughter and music filtered up through the floorboards; the vampires and their companions seemed to be taking the blackout in their stride. He could tell Kane's attention was divided too, the lure of the bar snatching his attention away from his mate. He would have to get better at masking his thoughts when they became alphas. It was as much a political position as anything.

He had a sudden urge to reach out to Kane and ask him if he was alright. Stuck in his own head, Faelan hadn't paused to consider what the bonding meant for Kane, a male who had grown up with zero expectations of alphadom upon his shoulders. The three of them used to be as thick as thieves, and he'd let his pride drive a wedge between them.

"Do you have much to do with Blackthorn Industries?" Astrid asked and Faelan zoned back into the conversation at hand. He'd have time to fix things with his packmates later.

"They're a major client—they use so much power, but we don't get involved in their day-to-day stuff. Why?"

"It might be unconnected, but there's a leopard shifter who has difficulty with her change. She works at the glass factory."

Faelan's ear's pricked up. He hadn't known about this.

"Oh, you mean Kaitlin?" Kane asked and Astrid nodded. Faelan was so out of the loop. When was the last time he had hung out with shifters, not just the wolves, but anyone from their wider community?

"It's not quite the same as Faelan..." Astrid glanced towards him. "She's just changed a few times without really meaning it and then struggles to get back. But as far as I know she's always unstuck herself within a few minutes. We all just assumed it was some sort of hormonal imbalance."

"She works in their R and D department." Kane rolled his Rs making it growl-like. The argh and dee deparrrtment.

"I almost forgot." Daisy sat upright. "What with everything going on today. I was at their Glassmarket office. They had some weird stuff going on with their consoles and huge amount of energy levels. Mad levels."

"Are they being careless?" Astrid asked.

"Astrid, this is big. If they're a threat to shifters, we have to get the alphas involved. The Blackthorns—they're not people we can mess with." Kane interrupted. "Whatever this little investigation is, enough is enough."

Faelan studied Astrid's face. She didn't look like she would acquiesce that easily. If she were in lupine form, her hackles would be raised. Daisy's face creased in confusion as she looked back and forth between the shifters.

"The Blackthorns have nothing to do with Ruhann or even the steamer we were on. I doubt they ever leave the city," Daisy said. "Even if this Kaitlin's magic is being affected by her work, and I agree that's worrying, how did the effects reach so far?"

"They're experimenting with some new process, and they're doing it out of town?"

"In Ruhann?" Daisy laughed. "The Blackthorn Process requires its own Grid substation to run. There's just not the infrastructure to support their kind of experiments out there."

"Plausible deniability," Astrid said, not giving in. Faelan loved her for having his back, but they weren't getting anywhere, and he thought Daisy made a fair point.

"We should go," Kane said, sensing the stalemate. "Leave Daisy to recover without us hovering over her."

Daisy seemed relieved. They weren't going to find answers here, and she looked ready to drop. They said their goodbyes and slunk out into the dark of night.

# Lima

AFTER AN HOUR MAKING small talk and playing cards with Belinda, Lima had given up hope of the power coming back on. She was surely late for dinner and wasn't keen on the lecture about timekeeping she would receive. Still, she should try and get home.

Belinda flashed her a smile as she got up to leave.

"Need an escort? I don't fancy sticking around here." Belinda gestured to the remaining patrons nursing their drinks in the dimly lit pub.

"Oh gods, yes!" Lima let out a sigh of relief. She didn't relish walking through the rookeries in the pitch black and had no idea how far-reaching the blackout was. A friendly vampire was better than nothing.

They walked towards the Glassmarket in an easy silence, their footsteps echoing in the empty night. Only a touch of ambient light lined the streets, so Lima kept her hand on Belinda's arm to guide her through the dark.

"Um. Do you mind me asking a question?" Lima asked.

"One, that was a question," Belinda replied with a grin. "Two, sure go ahead. Though if you're going to ask me if I'm dead, I'll be disappointed."

"No. Gosh. Do people really ask that?"

Belinda nodded. "On a regular basis. I'd be angrier, but no one teaches humans the basics so it's not really their fault. The old guard don't help; they do nothing to quash rumours. It adds to their mystique. And no, I wasn't turned either—I was just born this way."

"I was just wondering... Well, you didn't get served blood in the pub. Are you hungry?" Lima stared off into the distance as her question left her lips.

"A tad," Belinda said. "I'm not going to become ravenous and attack you if that's what you're thinking."

"No, no. I just thought, maybe you're feeling weak? Like, do we need to go somewhere to get you blood?"

"Oh bless, aren't you sweet? Nah, I'm fine. I ate at lunch, and contrary to what people believe, we need a lot less food that you humans."

As they approached the Tarac, Belinda paused.

"Huh, that's odd," she said.

"What is?" Lima looked around, realising what indeed was odd. The banks of the river were shrouded in darkness, more so than the rookeries, where flickering candles had signalled life. South of the river appeared dead.

* * *

"DON'T WORRY, YOU DON'T need to invite me in," Belinda winked. "But I'll take your socials if you don't mind? It's not that often I meet charming, open-minded ladies."

Heat rushed to Lima's cheeks. She fumbled around in her bag for a pen and paper, handing over her details to

Belinda. The vampire left with a skip in her step, leaving Lima facing her locked front door.

A locked door with no working console. Briefly, she considered shimmying up the drainpipe just to avoid a confrontation. She was extremely late, and she knew it. She could only hope that the blackout meant dinner had been abandoned. She raised her hand to knock on the door and stood back.

After a few minutes, which felt like hours, the door opened a fraction, a worried face peeking through.

"Oh Miss Lima! Your father was so worried!" Angela exclaimed, opening the door to usher her through. Lima very much doubted that her father was anything but annoyed. She followed the housekeeper into the kitchen.

Angela had somehow salvaged dinner from disaster. A salad of crunchy raw vegetables had been whipped up instead of roast potatoes, and the mutton had been slow cooking long enough before the power went out to be edible. Now wasn't the time to point out that she was considering vegetarianism.

Someone, probably Angela, had the foresight to stock the cupboard with candles at some point, and the kitchen looked almost romantic. Lima helped herself to a drink from the silent fridge and perched at the island—anything to delay facing her dad.

"Angela?" Lima ventured.

"Hm?" Angela didn't lift her eyes from the roast.

"Do you remember the power ever going out before? Like across the whole city?"

"Not the whole city, no. A house or a block might go down, but the Grid always fixes it. That's what you should be learning at your job."

"It's only an internship."

"For now, but you work hard, make your father proud. OK?"

She nodded feebly and helped Angela carry the dishes through to the dining room.

"Lima." Her father was seated at the long dining table, face lit by flickering candlelight. He put down the book he was reading.

"Dad," Lima responded, bracing herself for his ire.

"Can you believe this?" he asked, gesturing to the room.

She mumbled a noncommittal response.

"They didn't let you loose on the core, did they?" he joked, but his laugh was empty.

"Hah hah. No. I left before this happened. I was just getting a drink, with a friend. Got caught up." The thought of her actually socialising might distract him. He nodded, staring at his barely touched drink.

"You know, the Grid won't be in dominance forever," he said.

"Erm."

"Kirkhyrst won't be either. There are opportunities out west—one day someone will be the one to raise a city just like this. Kirkhyrst started from nowhere too."

Lima wasn't sure what to say. Her dad's faith in Kirkhyrst had always seemed unshakable.

"The Grid. They've had a monopoly on power for far too long. Something like this was bound to happen. We need competition, consumer choice!" He bashed his fist against the table, and Lima shrunk back. "The Blackthorns are no better. How can industry thrive when they're the only suppliers of the goods we need to flourish?"

"Er. Dad? Is everything OK?" Lima asked. She'd seen her dad go off on rants before, but she thought he admired the Blackthorns. The Grid. Why the hell was she interning there if not?

"We've lost a few contracts lately. Nothing for you to worry about."

"Oh." Lima wasn't used to any sort of vulnerability from him. This was odd.

"So, tell me about your day. Have they got you pushing paper around?"

"It's a paper free office Dad." She paused, not knowing how much to tell him. "I've been going through old cases. Just admin stuff. Daisy—that's my supervisor—took me out on a call last week. That was interesting."

She resisted saying where it was. If he hadn't noticed she was missing overnight, she wasn't sharing her tales of Ruhann with him. Belinda had distracted her a short while, but her thoughts soon returned to Lailu. She could only hope that whatever was going on in the city hadn't reached Ruhann; that the Ratatoskr were all safe and sound in their nests, Lailu included.

# Lailu

LAILU'S PAWS ACHED—SHE hadn't walked so much in all her life, certainly not since she came into her magic. She enjoyed scaling trees and taking a stroll through the woods, but she had become so reliant on portal travel. Lazy perhaps. She vowed to walk more when she returned to her old life. She must be missing out on so much. Still, she could do with a sit down.

Instead of being led to her doom, Ramus had ushered her out of the cave system and back into fresh air. He'd said they were going to somewhere more suitable for Ratatoskr. She very much thought Ruhann was a more suitable place, but it would take weeks to walk home, especially at her current pace.

If she was lucky, there were some kindly, tree-dwelling Faidhean in the area. She would be quite content being taken in by a rookery at this point. Birds would not confine her to a cave. Bats on the other hand... she shuddered. *Think kind thoughts*, she repeated in her head, a mantra to keep the dark thoughts at bay.

Ramus had been silent for hours. Lailu didn't know how to start a conversation with a Faidhean, and he didn't seem inclined to start it himself. Nightfall would soon be upon them, and she was worried about where they'd spend the night. She had slept in many a tree, but this land was unsettling. The trees themselves looked like her trees, yet everything was just a little bit off.

They stopped periodically to sip cool water off the proffered leaves of scraggly bushes. Lailu was careful to thank them for their service. No reason to upset the local flora.

After what felt like a whole day of walking, the landscape started to change; the trees petered out into a pale and rocky scene, with shards of stone jutting out of the ground at gravity defying angles. Certainly not a more welcoming place for Ratatoskr. Fatigued and anxious, Lailu wasn't paying attention to where she was walking.

"Look out!" Ramus warned her a moment too late. The ground crumbled away from under her, and she scrabbled for purchase against the loose rocks. Gravity had other ideas, and she slid down the scree, limbs flailing. A scraggly tree grew out from the cliffside, and its branches reached out for her. Lailu stretched out, her claws brushing the first branch, not finding purchase.

Her tail lashed out and curled around a lower, thinner branch—not enough to hold her weight but enough to swing her round, and as the branch snapped, she grabbed hold of the trunk, her breath uneven. She couldn't bring herself to look down.

Several pebbles rolled past, and she screwed up the courage to look upwards towards their source. Ramus was at the edge, peering down at her.

"The ground before was solid," he said unhelpfully.

"Well, it's not now," Lailu muttered.

"My apologies. I did not consider this path would be unsafe." Ramus went quiet, his gaze unfocused. Lailu was confident in her grip on the tree, but she wasn't confident in the tree's grip on the cliff. It bowed downwards with every movement.

"Hold in there little tree," she whispered. A portal would be the answer, but she didn't want to be stranded in yet another unknown location. At least here she had Ramus. She hadn't decided yet if he was a friend, since he barely talked to her. He hadn't eaten her, and that was always a good start. She was grateful he hadn't abandoned her in the caves forever. Hanging off a cliff in the open air was infinitely better than rotting underground.

Above her Ramus said something indecipherable, speaking in his own language. Then she became aware of voices coming from below, not so far away to be a fatal distance if she fell. She risked a peek and let out a gasp at what she saw in the distance. Towers rising up out of the valley. A city.

Two women, almost human in appearance, stood at the base of the cliff, which she could see was more of a steep slope interrupted by sharp boulders. It wouldn't have been a pleasant freefall, but a controlled descent wasn't impossible.

"If you can hang on, they will fetch a rope," Ramus said at last. Lailu took a steadying breath and focused on the city in the distance, rather than on the rocky ground below. The five towers were of a pale stone, which glittered in the sun. The rest of the buildings circled them, thinning out into single story dwellings on the outskirts. It was nothing like the organic and rambling settlements of Ruhann. If she wasn't dangling halfway down a cliff, Lailu would have appreciated the strange beauty of it all. As it was, she considered the city a sign of safety, of people who could help her if she fell and broke something.

There was a saying that Ratatoskr always landed on their feet, and of course they were no stranger to falls. However, Lailu was used to forests and cushioned landings, friendly trees who would do their best to soften her fall, and even then, she didn't always land on her feet. She'd once landed badly on her tail, bending it the wrong way, and she couldn't climb for a whole lunar after. She certainly wasn't prepared for this land of harsh rock, all angles and sharp ends.

If she survived this, she was going to have so much to tell Sylvain. Not to mention the scholars! She would be the centre of attention for days with all the strange and wonderful things she'd seen. She was sure she'd be able to laugh about it all from a distance.

The tree creaked ominously. Lailu concentrated on the features at the base of the cliff, the pale rocks and silvered trees giving it a ghostly feel. She readied her mind, envisioning solid ground beneath her paws, and her portal opened up below her. Relief rushed through her; it had worked! She heard startled cries from below, briefly glimpsing a gathered crowd, before she closed her eyes and fell backward.

# Daisy

THERE WAS A SHARP tapping at the window—it filtered through to Daisy's dream state as a hammer hitting her desk. Why was Hari hitting her desk, they had so much work to do... Oh. She awoke, groggy, and tried to place the noise. She remembered the blackout; it so didn't take much for humans to revert to hostile animals. No, not animals, animals were nice.

She staggered over to the window. If some brat broke it, there would be hell to pay. A jay was perched on her windowsill, its curious eyes staring back at her. Daisy wiped sleep from her own eyes and focused on the bird. Attached to its leg was a slim wooden tube. As she came to her senses, she yanked open the window, careful not to disturb her messenger.

"Hello. Wow. Bird mail! Whatever next." The Grid's flock of messenger pigeons had dwindled over the years; there wasn't much use for them besides sending an occasional message out to Ruhann. She thought the dove-keeper had retired long ago, but maybe emergency measures meant they'd dusted off any birds they could find.

The jay held out its leg and let Daisy take the tube, letting out a loud *kschaach* and hopping from foot to foot. Was she supposed to pay it?

"Hang on, hang on. Will water and peanuts suffice?" The bird bobbed its head and quietened down. Daisy went to get the offering and unfurled the message, the paper coarse and lumpy. It was not from the Grid.

*Dear Daisy,*

*After your departure, Lailu went to check on the Eldur Pines and did not return. We sent out a search party into the Great Forest to no avail. It is unlike her to be absent from the scurry for so long, and so we are concerned for her welfare. I'm hoping that her inexperience may have driven her to seek you out in Kirkhyrst.*

*Please respond with haste. Attach your message to the bird who delivered this, they will know what to do. Refreshments for our messenger would be appreciated.*

*Regards*
*Sylvain*

The jay had made itself at home on her coffee table, staring at the wine glass she had abandoned the night before. She replaced it with a shallow bowl of water and a packet of nuts, the scent of stale wine making her feel a little queasy.

Daisy found her notepad and ripped out a sheet. The paper was much smoother than Sylvain's handcrafted sheet, a sign of machinery versus craftsmanship. On another day, she would have appreciated the work that had gone into it more. Today, she was filled with concern for Lailu. She had been so friendly and helpful to them, an invasive species in their home, she hated to think of her lost in that burning forest.

*Dear Sylvain,*

*I am sorry to report that Lailu is not with us. I will of course ensure she contacts you post haste if she does turn up. If there is anything we can do to help, please do not hesitate to ask.*

*Kind regards*
*Daisy*

Quick and to the point. She stared at the bird, deep in thought. How had the bird known to come here and not to the Grid? She assumed previous messages from the Ratatoskr went to the main office, and not to an employee's home. She couldn't imagine Hari having his breakfast interrupted by an insistent jay.

Daisy went to use her console, forgetting the power was out for a moment. She was so used to having magic there at her fingertips, she felt a bit lost. She was sure Lima would want to know about Lailu, since the two had bonded over the course of their visit. Checking the time, she realised she could meet Lima at her home and walk her to work. Hari had handed her Lima's paperwork at some point, and Daisy tried to remember where she'd stashed it. She wasn't designed for a world without the Grid.

Eventually she found the papers crumpled up at the bottom of her work bag. Smoothing out the paper, she found Lima's address and worked out roughly where it was. It didn't seem too far out of her way. She thought about getting coffee and pastries to soften the news with, but nowhere would be open with the power out.

Coffee! She was not going to get through the day without it. Why didn't she think to start a cold brew the night before? The memory of her fear drifted back. Oh yes, that. Kirkhyrst was not supposed to be like that; it was a safe place for a woman—for anyone—to walk at night, as she had done so many times before. Any concerns she had about taking magic away from its natural source paled at the good it had done. If magic was gone for good, then what?

She couldn't believe how quickly people changed when the world wasn't looking. She was so naïve in thinking the city was full of decent people. It all fell apart after only a few hours without magic—a magic they had no natural right to.

The jay had polished off the nuts and resumed its hopping.

"I guess you want to get on your way," Daisy said and rolled up the note tight enough to fit into the tube. She fumbled a bit with the attachment, but when she gave it a gentle tug, it stayed in place.

"Good enough?" she asked the jay, who responded with a croak and flew off out the open window.

"You're welcome," she called out after it and went to get ready for work. She reached for her *She Boobed Boobily* t-shirt before coming to her senses. She might be called upstairs to talk about the problems at Blackthorn Industries and wanted to be taken seriously. Rummaging around in her wardrobe, she managed to find a top without any writing on it: a plain green thing she hadn't seen in months. Hopefully it still fit her.

The cold shower did a poor job as caffeine replacement, but at least Daisy was awake. The walk to Lima's would give her time to get her brain functioning. The Glassmarket was almost an hour away at a brisk pace.

Holden Hill had become a fashionable place to be seen in recent years. When Daisy chose her flat, it was more about what she could afford within walking distance of the Grid. Back then it was home to those on the edge of society—not as poor as those in the rookeries but a little less human. Its affordability had of course attracted artists and start-ups, those who traded a good address for a better standard of living, and as they became successful, the district sprouted cafes and bars, a theatre, and weird little shops selling niche items.

Etienne had been around since the olden days. He spun yarns about how he started the bar when Holden Hill was still farmland. No one believed him. What kind of trade would a vamp bar do amongst farmers? They were just as likely to skewer him with a pitchfork as drink at his bar, but they made for good stories.

And stories fuelled the myth of the vampire, after all. Even Daisy's parents had baulked at the idea of their dearest daughter living above such a place, and they weren't exactly bigots. The day she'd moved in, Etienne had welcomed her with a hamper full of local delicacies and never once brought up the idea that she might share her blood. After ten years of their somewhat friendship, she felt less weird about it. If he was starving, Daisy liked to think she'd offer her arm.

Not her neck; she had her limits.

Today the streets were subdued. After last night's roaring trade, *Etienne's* doors were closed, and the usual hustle and bustle of cafes trying to catch commuters was missing. The aroma of freshly ground coffee was absent from the air too. She was obsessed. If luck was in her favour the office would have rigged up some sort of emergency back-up to provide her the sweet nectar she was craving. A bitter black espresso would be fine too.

As Daisy strode down the hill, the yeasty scent of freshly baked bread hit her. The Holden Hill Baking Company's wood fuelled ovens burned away throughout the night, serving the best sourdough in town. With Kirkhyrst's clean air regulations, you had to be exceptional to get special dispensation to use such artisan methods. There was quite a queue forming, and Daisy walked past with regret, catching snippets of conversation as she went.

"Remember when—"

"—hope we get a discount—"

"—and I grabbed her breast!"

"Noooo."

"I couldn't see!"

"—hold his horses—"

"Unconnected, it's all safe—"

"—point in going to work."

"We'll see—"

"—soooo hungry!"

The sounds of life continuing as normal washed over her. Turning into Lima's street, Daisy double checked she had the right address. The stately townhouses were the kind of thing she drooled over in glossy magazines. She smoothed down her rumpled clothes and tried to make her damp hair respectable before someone reported a ruffian loitering on their street.

Daisy admired people who looked effortlessly smart, but she just didn't have it in her. The moment she put clothes on they instantly became Daisyfied: creased, stained, too baggy, or too tight, in all the wrong places. It was one of the reasons she was so grateful to have her job at the Grid. No one cared if the person fixing their power problem was scruffy as long as they fixed it.

These houses looked like they contained the effortlessly smart *and* fashionable sort of people. Daisy found Lima's house; its modern console was dead to the world. She stared at the lion. It was ostentatious and probably not intended for actual use. She took hold of the heavy metal ring held in its mouth and knocked twice. It felt rude to be hammering on a door before nine in the morning.

The door cracked open an inch.

"Yes, the Samson residence?" a woman's voice called out.

"Hi. Er, I'm Daisy." Silence followed. She belatedly realised the person on the other side was coached to not let any old cold-caller cross the threshold. "I work at the Grid—I'm supervising Lima? I've come to collect her."

Daisy held up her Grid pass for good measure. It generally opened doors for her wherever she went.

"Oh, thank the heavens!" The door swung open, and Daisy was faced with a woman in her fifties, dressed in uniform. Not Lima's mother, unless she enjoyed early morning role-playing. "The power has been out all night. The phones won't work—Mr Samson has important work to do."

"There's a city wide blackout." Daisy gestured outside. "Everyone is working on it as fast as they can, but that's not why I'm here."

The woman's face fell. Daisy stood awkwardly in the hallway until the thunder of feet came crashing down the stairs.

"Daisy!" Lima said breathlessly. "What are you doing here?"

"I ran into some trouble last night... Thought you might like an escort to work. What with the blackout and everything."

"Dad is fuming. I think he left already, hoping his office would have power. Is your place out too?"

"Yep."

"Angela." Lima turned to the housekeeper. "You should go home for the day; there's nothing you can do here."

The woman looked conflicted, but Lima was right. The whole building was reliant on power, from water for cleaning to ovens for cooking. All Angela could do was hover and wring her hands. Lima dismissing her for a few hours was the least she could do.

"OK, Miss Lima. As soon as the power is fixed, I'll be right back. You need to eat," Angela said pointedly.

Daisy was sure Lima was capable enough to find a meal herself, but she kept quiet. This was not her world. The door clicked shut behind the housekeeper, leaving Lima and Daisy alone in the echoing hallway.

"Nice house you have here," Daisy said.

Lima rolled her eyes. "I would much rather live above a vamp bar and eat pizza every night."

"I don't eat pizza every night. But I see your point. This is... um... a bit sterile?" Daisy hoped she hadn't overstepped.

"Definitely. The moment a spot of dirt appears, Angela swoops in to clean it."

Daisy stopped herself just as she was about to ask after Lima's mum. She hadn't mentioned anyone other than her dad in small talk, and it was wrong to presume. This house was so big and empty. Was it just two people rattling around with an overzealous housekeeper? She had to stop being so nosy.

"Before we set off, I received this from Ruhann." Daisy handed Sylvain's note to Lima, who smiled at the sight of the rough paper. As she read, her face fell.

"Oh Lailu," Lima whispered. "She wouldn't just leave without telling someone."

Daisy agreed. She didn't voice the most likely scenario—that Lailu had got caught in the fire.

"What can we do?" Lima asked.

"She could be anywhere, you saw how her portal works."

Lima's lip wobbled. Daisy couldn't stand it—her intern had been nothing but good-natured, and she didn't want to crush her spirit.

"Let's go get the power back, and then we'll see what can be done?"

"Can you fix it?"

Daisy laughed somewhat hysterically.

"You think I'm some kind of magician?"

* * *

OUTSIDE THE GRID HEADQUARTERS, a crowd had gathered to shout at staff going into the building. People were desperate for answers. Daisy shook her head; it had only been one night without power and already people were champing at the bit. They should have been happy to have the day off. A security guard was stationed at the doors, turning away anyone without a pass.

Inside someone had set up back-up power units, dotted around the building, providing limited power to those trying to fix the problem. The lighting was dim, and they couldn't access their basement desks. At least Hari agreed that Daisy and Lima could share a console to add extra pairs of eyes to finding the solution. Not that anyone had the faintest idea of what the problem was.

On the walk over, Lima had shared her misgivings with Daisy, who was sure she didn't just overlook all those cases in the rookeries. Surely yesterday was an anomaly, and before that? She couldn't remember going out to the rookeries in forever, but she wasn't meant to be doing house calls either. She was meant to be analysing stuff from the comforts of her desk and sending engineers out.

She agreed to follow up with her team once the power was restored. The rookeries were low priority right now, along with everyone else's minor grievances.

"The core's just dead," Hari whispered to Daisy, checking over his shoulder for eavesdroppers. "Ops tried rebooting it several times, but zilch."

Lima stayed quiet, and Daisy didn't draw attention to her, knowing she shouldn't really be privy to this conversation. Lima had a habit of blending into the furniture, an admirable skill in a world where everyone was clamouring for attention. If the power sector didn't work out for her, she could easily become a spy.

"We've got a few more hours before the hospitals run out of power, but then... we're going to be looking at deaths. There's people hooked up to machines, keeping them alive. Oh gods, I knew we should have fast-tracked the mini-core initiative."

"Breathe, Hari. One step at a time. Can we round up more back-up units from anywhere?"

"I don't know how we're meant to get hold of anyone, not without gridmail and phones."

"Birds," Lima whispered.

"Oh my gods, you're a genius," Daisy said, turning to Hari. "Do we still have the carrier pigeons? Whatsisname used to feed them."

"Burt? Is he even still alive?"

"I'm sure I've seen him about in the Meadows. He feeds anything with wings; if anyone knows how to round up a bunch of messenger birds, it's him. You write the requests for help, and he'll get them to where they need to go. Well, his birds will."

Hari looked slightly dazzled—Daisy doubted he'd slept at all last night. He nodded a few times, seeming to come to some conclusion in his head.

"OK, birds, worth a try. And you two… just look for anything that might be a clue, alright? We've had so many weird things going on, we should have seen them as a warning," he said, shaking his head. "Engineers are all ring-fenced—no sending them anywhere, for anyone."

"Not even Blackthorns?" Daisy asked cheekily.

"No. Not even if ancient fire gods knock on your door demanding we fix their lights. If you must, send yourself."

"I don't suppose we have coffee in the building?" Daisy asked hopefully.

"Nils!" Hari called out, flagging down a passing assistant. "Can you get these two some caffeine?"

Nils nodded and scurried off in the search for coffee.

"It's the second question of the day, right after have you fixed it yet?" Hari sighed. "I'll let you two get on. Don't leave the console on standby when you're done with it. We have to conserve every drop."

Hari walked off, yelling at people to find the bird guy.

"What about all those power outages in the rookeries?" Lima asked once Hari was out of earshot. "That's a clue, right?"

"Give your list here." Daisy took Lima's notes and started searching through them. The more she read, the more her brow furrowed. Once the last case was reached, she pulled up the query tool use and started typing faster than Lima could keep up with.

"What are you looking for?"

"Cross-referencing power outages and response times with geographical areas. It'll take a few minutes to run." Daisy sat back in her chair.

"Do you think the blackout is connected to the Eldur Pines?" Lima asked after a moment lost in thought. Daisy didn't respond at first, then opened her gridmail. As she was searching through her saved messages, Nils came by and deposited two mugs of black coffee on the desk.

"Sorry, no milk," he apologised.

"No worries. Thanks for getting it so quick," Daisy said to him before turning back to her screen.

"Here. I got a request from the university a few weeks ago—they were doing research into the effects of magic draw on the ecosystem. I guess at the time I just dismissed it, but maybe they have ideas? Can't be any more a waste of time than sat around here looking for a needle in a haystack."

The console blipped to alert Daisy that her query had finished. The two women stared at the screen. It was hard to deny that the rookeries had a problem, and one that was being ignored.

# Faelan

THE URGE TO RUN was back. Not to run away from his pack, just to run freely, like he had done through the forests of Ruhann. The best Faelan could do within the confines of Kirkhyrst was the Meadows, a long strip of parkland left wild for the benefit of residents, since it was considered good for human mental health to have contact with nature. If that were the case, Faelan didn't understand why they kept themselves cooped up in this city. The world was a big place; they didn't have to live stacked on top of each other. Now he was free of responsibility, he didn't have to either.

His pack was family, and while he didn't choose them, he did love them. Leaving them was a huge decision—one he wasn't sure he was capable of making. One day, in the not-too-distant future, he would run with them again, with Astrid and Kane, with the next generation of pups. For now, his own company was all he needed.

The air was warm and dry against his nose, with the lingering promise of rain. He looked up at the sky, where clouds gathered on the horizon in ominous shades of yellow and slate grey. All the more reason to run fast. He took off, weaving between the trees, leaping over bracken, and kicking up clouds of dust and debris.

"Oi wolf!" a man shouted and stepped in his path. Faelan skidded to a halt, his claws scraping the sun-baked soil. He caught the scent of Travis before his face: sweat mixed with machine oil and metal, and a subtle waft of snuffed out candles.

"I have another delivery for you," Travis sneered. Faelan didn't remember him being so odious, but a job was a job. "Anderson's still out the in the wilds—can hardly send a human. Not one with any sense."

He threw a hefty package at Faelan, who caught it in his jaws, eyes narrowed. This blackout was bringing out all the nasties. Normally he would refuse such rudeness, but the scent of Ruhann spread through his memory, the feel of the forest rushing past him at a gallop. Just this once. Well second time. He nodded his head at the man.

"Good boy," Travis went to pat his head, and Faelan growled in warning.

"OK, no touchy. I get it. Now shoo, time's a ticking."

* * *

THE HOUSE WAS HEAVING with bodies. Without the Grid, work was out of the question, and with few options for fun, the pack had congregated in the place they knew best. Faelan pushed his way through, and surprised greetings met his ears as his extended family caught sight of him. Theoretically the house belonged to the pack, but everyone knew it was the domain of the alphas; not everyone wanted to live in their shadow, and that was fine. When Luna and Jacob stepped down, this place would become Astrid and Kane's. A week ago, he'd rather cut his own tail off than live here under their rule, but he was starting to soften towards them as a couple.

He couldn't stay angry at Astrid for long, and Kane was as far from the popular image of an alpha as you could get. Oh, he looked the part, but he was a big softy at heart. Perhaps that's why the bond had gone to him—Fenrir knew that the world didn't need more macho males in charge of things. They needed lawyers and smart-talkers, kindness and compassion.

Some days Faelan felt too old-school for the modern world. Even though he was barely older than Astrid. They had waited so long for the bond to show itself, and he felt like life had passed him by already. Everyone kept waiting for the signs, pushing the two most likely candidates together at every opportunity. No wonder he felt lost; he'd spent his whole life preparing for alphadom, and out of nowhere, it was taken away.

No, Kane didn't take anything from him. It wasn't Faelan's to start with. The fault should lie with Luna and Jacob; they should have known it wasn't going to be him when he passed his thirtieth. The bond needed time to know what was right, but it had never taken so long before. At least not for an alpha pair.

Astrid was sure something nefarious was afoot, but Faelan thought maybe being stuck was his punishment. Fenrir judged him and found him lacking, so he'd be better off as a wolf. He supposed there were worse punishments.

He paused to watch the pups playing, a blur of fur and joy. One pup split from the group and came to a halt before Faelan. Bracken was the most serious of the younger generation, though that didn't mean she never had time for play. She had a permanent frown between her eyebrows—a quirk of nature. To Faelan, it seemed her personality had grown to match her appearance.

The small pack of adolescents had stampeded out of sight when the pale grey wolf booped Faelan's nose in greeting, jostling the package in his mouth. An invite to join. Playing with the pups was something he should do more often, and he sorely wished he had time to join Bracken and her friends in a game of tag or tug, or whatever was the game of the moment.

Alas he needed to find Astrid; she'd help him attach the package securely and without questions and provide assistance on finding passage to Ruhann. The steamers must be one of the last remaining vestiges of power in the city, and he hoped they were still running. There wasn't a system for wolves to buy tickets, and the intergrid, when it was working, wasn't easily accessible with paws. Last time he used it, he'd accidentally messaged Daisy, like a creepy creeper looking her up the moment he got home.

And then they'd followed her. In the dark. Fenrir, what must she think of him? While she'd been polite to them the night before, she was clearly rattled by her experience. Humans could be arseholes, but was he any better?

Faelan raised his eyes in the direction of Astrid's room, and Bracken whined for a moment, before bounding off in the direction of the others. He circled around the ground floor, finding Astrid and Kane lounging on a sofa in the den, content in their own company. He dropped his package and prodded his damp nose against Astrid's leg. She yelped in surprise.

A gap appeared between them, and he took the opportunity to leap up on the sofa, pushing between the couple. No ignoring him now.

"What do you want?" Kane asked with a mouthful of fur. He pushed Faelan out the way, launching him into Astrid's lap.

"If you wanted snuggles, all you had to do was ask." Astrid laughed, ruffling Faelan's fur. He huffed in irritation and looked back and forth between the package and Astrid pointedly. "Back at work already, little wolf?"

Faelan nodded, and Astrid reached down for the package. This time the address of *Frontier Lodge* had been scribbled on the front, its recipient there for the long haul now. It didn't take Astrid long to catch on. She sighed and stood up, Faelan falling from her lap.

"So much for my relaxing day off. I gotta get this," she said to Kane and headed off upstairs in the direction of her room.

Behind closed doors Astrid crouched down and stared into Faelan's eyes.

"What's this about? You don't need the money that bad, do you, to go running off again when..." She waved a hand at him. Faelan shook his head; it wasn't about the money. He just needed space and fresh air. And Fenrir the air was fresh in Ruhann, even with the Great Forest ablaze, which was odd when he stopped to think about it.

During the hottest, driest years, the forests north of Kirkhyrst caught fire and the mild hint of smoke tinged the air of the city. Perhaps Ruhann's winds were blowing in the opposite direction. Travelling by portal was thrilling, but he hadn't been able to fully ground himself the in the land's geography, not without traversing it by foot.

But also, magic was weird. From a human's point of view, how did you even start to explain shapeshifting? Or portal wielding Sciuridae? That the same magic powered their city was astonishing. And weird.

"Do you think going there will help you find answers?"

Again, Faelan answered no, even though a part of him wanted to know what was going on. He scrunched up his face.

"Oh. You don't really know, but you feel like you want to go?"

Yes, he bounced up, nodding as he remembered to answer. They might not be bonded, but she still knew him deep down. When he could speak again, he had to tell her how much she meant to him, and that he would support her, and Kane. He just needed a bit of time to be a grump about it all.

"Let's rig up some kind of harness for you." She rummaged around in a cupboard, holding up various bits of fabric to Faelan before finding the right combination. Nothing too sparkly, he hoped. Why did she have so many straps lurking in there? He quickly shook the thought from his head—anything that might have been, was long in the past now. It had to be.

With some heaving and shoving, the package was tightly secured to his back. Faelan circled around a few times to check his mobility. He would have to remember not to squeeze through any small spaces, but he should be good to go.

"Hang on a minute," Astrid said and returned with a small pouch. "We can put your ID and some basic supplies in here. Just in case. Try not to lose it."

She fastened the pouch around Faelan's neck and held his head in her hands, studying him for a moment, then bent forward to place a kiss on his forehead.

"Don't do anything I wouldn't do!"

# Daisy

LIKE MUCH OF KIRKHYRST, the university was a mix of old and new, tradition sitting next to displays of the progress they had made. The campus sprawled over several acres, offering room, board, and entertainment to the students, in addition to the education they expected. Daisy squinted at the map in the main courtyard, looking for the science building. She suspected the job of designing it had been given to a new student, and they had gone with a small, handwritten font that didn't have the best visibility. At least it looked pretty.

"Is it that blue building?" Lima suggested, pointing at an L-shaped box on the map. Daisy guessed the word did start with an S. It was either going to be science or a social venue.

"If it's not the science building, hopefully someone will be around who can point us in the right direction."

They set off down the winding paths, through landscaped gardens full of mature trees. Someone had done a good job in the past, had the forethought to plant for the future. It did make the campus hard to navigate though, and they had to backtrack twice when they came across a dead-end.

"Did we accidentally walk into a maze?" Daisy said.

"All these nooks and crannies are very private," Lima responded, hoping they wouldn't stumble upon any trysts. Daisy waggled her eyebrows.

"Come on, I think the S building is just behind that hedge. Shall we find science or a drinking hole?"

"I wouldn't mind either."

The path opened up in front of a round glass building, where a metal sign shaped like a double helix indicated they were in the right place. Inside, the corridors echoed— the hustle and bustle of university life absent. Fortunately, there was still someone sat at reception, a young man deeply engrossed in a paperback book. A mystery from the look of the cover. Daisy cleared her throat, making him jump.

"I'm sorry. I was at a really tense bit. How can I help?"

"We're here from the Grid, responding to a student's request for information."

"Really? I thought you'd be busy trying to fix all this."

"We're doing what we can with limited power." Daisy hoped she wasn't going to be judged everywhere she went. It's not like they could just flick a switch and get the power running. The problem with no one knowing how magic worked was everyone thought it was easy. She wished she'd said she was here to investigate the blackout, but she was worried about getting caught in a lie and it spiralling out of control.

"Clarissa Redmond and Lyle Stewart," Daisy prompted.

"Ah. They're here as always. Up the stairs, last door on the right."

The receptionist went back to his book, and Daisy ushered Lima towards the stairs, which were also modelled on the double helix, two intertwining spiral staircases. They really were going for a theme here. While the corridors were quiet, signs of activity could be heard behind the doors—metal clinking against glass and murmured conversations in soft tones. At the end of the corridor, a door was propped open with a shard of rock.

Daisy knocked on the door and stuck her head around the frame. The room had the benefit of tall windows, the natural light more than making up for the lack of power. Benches lined the walls, full of microscopes, jars and boxes. In the centre sat a dark-skinned young woman, her hair tied up in a bun, and a freckly, red-headed, bespectacled man who looked no older than Lima.

"Hello, I've come about your gridmail." Daisy did the introductions, and Clarissa's eyes lit up.

"How wonderful. I thought I'd just been ignored. No one wants to talk about environmental science. It's all magic this, magic that. But magic *is* the environment." Clarissa said animatedly.

"We were in Ruhann last week," Daisy said and was greeted with matching ooohs from Clarissa and Lyle. "The Eldur Pines are burning early. I assume you're familiar with the species?"

"Of course. Fascinating lifecycle. To create such a useful substance, and so much of it, only to burn away and start again—" Lyle started.

"Anyway. The Ratatoskr said the trees don't have enough anaesthetic sap yet; they're in pain, and the burn started anyway. Can you think of anything that might disrupt the natural magic in this way?" Daisy interrupted him before he could start monologuing.

"Other than you?" Lyle said.

"Me?" Daisy squeaked.

"Not you personally. The Grid."

"It does seem a bit of a coincidence," Clarissa added.

"Well, yes. That's why we're here. To see if it is."

"Where does all the magic come from?" Lima spoke at last.

"Nature!" Clarissa stood up and went over to the whiteboard covered in flowcharts. "We have a theory that all living things contain magic. Even humans, to some extent. Of course, Ruhann contains so many more obviously magical species than Kirkhyrst, which is ironic considering how much magic we suck out."

"Excuse me? Did you say suck out?" Lima asked.

"Yes. The air doesn't really have much ambient magic, except around disturbances. Say we cut open this leaf here—" Clarissa pointed to a potted plant. "We would briefly see a rise in atmospheric magic before it dissipated."

"So, you're saying we could harvest magic? Like potatoes?" Daisy was flabbergasted. It couldn't be so easy; someone would have done it already.

"Theoretically. But we know how hard it is to cultivate high magic species. A whole sack of potatoes would barely power one lightbulb for an hour."

"This doesn't make any sense. The Grid pulls magic from the air and transforms it. We've seen high atmospheric magic in Kirkhyrst just this week, and we barely have any regular plant life to kill off, let alone high magic ones."

"Living things die all the time," Lima said quietly. They all looked at her, and the conversation tailed off. Had the magic they all relied on been pulled from the normal lifecycle of the city? If so, why had it stopped all of a sudden?

"Could the Grid be pulling magic out of living things?" Lyle asked.

"Would that explain the Eldur Pines? We're so far away," Daisy said.

"The pines burn when they're ready for regrowth. If their magic was depleted, perhaps that would trigger a burn. Cut their losses so to speak."

Clarissa got up and busied herself opening and closing drawers. She grabbed a small vial of what looked like lichen and emptied it out onto a slide. She pushed it under a device Daisy couldn't identify and flicked some levers. A fizzle of static burst in the air. The lichen curled and browned. When Clarissa gave it a poke, it dissolved into dust.

She opened up the device and took out a small crystal, a pinprick of blue light held inside.

"What was that?" Daisy asked, entranced.

"We use this device to make batteries. Little storage units for power. We usually just run it in the background processing ambient magic. As you can see, if we remove the magic directly from this lichen, it dies," Clarissa said, distracted by her findings. Daisy and Lima stared at her in horror. "I don't want to draw conclusions without thorough research, but it could be excess power draw is killing the Eldur Pines, and because of their unique biology, they are trying to regenerate. That would not explain why the Grid has no power though, it should have more."

"Lailu!" Lima blurted out.

"What about her?" Daisy asked.

"Her portal. It's magic. If she was far from home and we—we drained her! We must go find her Daisy!"

"Breathe, Lima, breathe. We don't know anything. It's just a theory. The other Ratatoskr are fine—we wouldn't be pulling it from a single person." Though as Daisy said this, she realised she had no idea, only that Lailu was missing. Sylvain had no reason to keep her updated on the state of the whole scurry. He hadn't even mentioned the fire.

Clarissa grabbed a chair and steered the shaking Lima into it.

"This Lailu, she's Ratatoskr?" Clarissa asked gently, and Lima nodded. Daisy filled the two researchers in on everything they knew.

"This will make quite the paper." Lyle whistled.

"Lyle, this is not the time," Clarissa scolded him.

"Plus, what I've told you is confidential. I could lose my job." Daisy added. She didn't need it published all over the city. Hari would understand she was just trying to solve the blackout, but he wasn't where the buck stopped.

"Sorry. It's just. This could be a massive breakthrough."

Daisy wasn't sure she wanted everyone knowing what the source of magic was. Not out of any gatekeeping loyalty to the Grid, but there were those who wouldn't think twice about exploiting it. Then what would happen to the Great Forest and the Ratatoskr—and the shifters? She'd forgotten all about Faelan.

"What do you know about shifter magic?" she asked.

"Very little, they don't tend to discuss it outside their packs. If we found a lone wolf, so to speak, they might be more amenable to questions, but we haven't found one yet." Lyle shrugged. "Why do you ask?"

"I was wondering about how this might affect them. That's all. Like a loss of magic wouldn't cause them to shift..."

"I would think not. They'd more likely to be weakened, left in one form or another. It's not really my subject area."

"And vampires?"

"Now that is an area of special interest to Clarissa," Lyle said, brightening.

"Shush." Clarissa glared at her colleague. "It was one time. We do have some studies going on into the nature of vampires though. Is the need for blood genetic or viral? That sort of thing."

"But the longevity, that must be magic?" Daisy asked and Clarissa laughed.

"That's just a myth!"

"Etienne has had his bar for decades and looks not a day older than me. Explain that."

Clarissa and Lyle exchanged a look.

"Is there any magical creature you haven't met?"

"Fairies?" Daisy joked, and the researchers burst into laughter.

# Lailu

LAILU OPENED HER EYES. The trees towering over her were white, the wind whispering through their heart-shaped leaves, and the ground beneath was littered with shards of rock. She looked around; she had done it. The scree slope stood before her, less intimidating from the bottom, and the little tree that had saved her hung on, its branches swaying as if in a wave. She wiggled her claws at it in thanks.

"That was quite a trick," Ramus called from above. He was working his way down a steep, winding path, his cloven feet unsuited to the task.

Lailu picked herself up, inspecting herself for wounds. A few scratches, and she'd be sore tomorrow, but she was all in one piece.

"What is this place?"

"Did you think all Faidhean live in caves?" Ramus asked, amusement in his voice.

*Well, yes,* Lailu thought, but didn't speak out loud.

"Some prefer light to dark, company to solitude. We are many and varied. Welcome to Baile Reulta"

As they ventured into the city, she discovered the Faidhean were just as varied in form. While those in the caves had been unsettling, many here looked much more human than their subterranean counterparts. More solid. There were hints here and there that they were something other: unusual coloured eyes, furry ears, or horns emerging from their hair. No one was in the slightest bit Ratatoskran though.

They didn't stop and stare, but Lailu received some curious glances as she walked through the streets behind Ramus. Some of the glances were directed at her companion, his moss and lichen encrusted visage standing out against the clean lines of the city.

She would've loved to spend time exploring, but she was oh-so tired. Taking in the position of the sun, it was well past tiffin and heading towards dinner. Lailu hadn't eaten since breakfast. She was famished.

She balked at the outline of a spit-roast boar outside a drinking house. She wasn't quite so famished to eat meat. Silently blessing the boar for its sacrifice, she hurried past, and followed Ramus to a tall wooden building. A sign at the door proclaimed *The Thirsty Squirrel*.

"Very funny," she said, but she was thirsty and hoped such a place would be welcoming to her kind. Lima had told her that people in Kirkhyrst called them squirrels in a bad way, but she had no issue with being compared to such spritely creatures. They were quite similar in many ways, agile climbers, fond of nuts. Lailu didn't go around burying nuts though—that's how trees were made. Squirrels were as important to the forests as any Tree Keeper.

Ramus ducked, his antlers not quite fitting through the low doorway. Lailu blinked as Ramus blurred in front of her very eyes and transformed into a more human form.

He still had antlers, only smaller and unencumbered with plant life. His skin was iridescent, like oil on water.

"You're a shifter?" Lailu asked.

"Merely a glamour—a shift in perspective. If I were to die now, I would return to my natural form."

"But you fit through the door now?" Laili didn't really understand.

"The door is also a matter of perspective" Ramus disappeared inside the tavern.

Lailu instantly felt more at home the moment she stepped beyond the threshold of *The Thirsty Squirrel*. Everything was made of wood, planed and polished, but wood all the same. Behind a long bar, there was a vast assortment of bottles in all shapes and colours, and a russet furred face turned to greet her.

"Oh my! What a surprise!" The Ratatoskr clapped her paws.

"Cashe, this is Lailu. She became lost and... the caves are no place for her." Ramus introduced her.

"Oh, your poor thing." Cashe rushed around the bar and enveloped Lailu in a hug. "Let me get you some food, and then you shall fill me in on all the gossip from Ruhann."

Lailu was speechless. Ratatoskr living outside of Ruhann was unheard of, although she was fast learning that she knew of very little of what went on beyond her homeland. She still didn't know where she'd landed the first time her portal malfunctioned; it wasn't anywhere like the land she'd just trekked across with Ramus.

Cashe bundled Lailu off into a snug little booth, where well-worn seating was adorned with soft, red cushions. A jam jar filled with wildflowers sat on the table, the white daisies catching her eye. It had only been a few days since she had parted ways with Daisy, Lima, and Faelan —it felt so much longer. She wanted to know if they'd found out anything else. As discombobulated as she was, she'd almost forgotten the storm she'd fled from. She thought of Hazel and Balu, hoping they were safe and sound; that the strange weather passed quickly.

Other than the magic being unfamiliar here, Lailu didn't see anything wrong with it. She didn't doubt the Faidhean in the caves were worried—they knew their magic best. If they said there was a pull, she believed them, yet... there were no crackles of blue light, no ominous flames, no storms threatening their lands. Her portal had been there when she needed it. In fact, her portal was the only time she'd seen the visible blue flicker of magic at all.

Perhaps it was their distance from Ruhann. From Kirkhyrst, even. Perhaps their magic had a different flavour here.

Cashe busied back and forth, and soon a steaming vegetable broth, crusty bread, a jug of spiced cider, and a plate of chestnut buns were laid out before Lailu. She looked around for her companion; Ramus had vanished without a word. If he didn't return, she could bear living in this cosy tavern for a while.

Lailu cleared her throat, and Cashe scurried over.

"Everything all right dear?" Cashe asked.

"It's all just a little..." Lailu flapped her paws, "Disorientating."

"Ah. I guess you haven't left Ruhann much?"

"Never. Well, not until this week."

"I always found the nest suffocating as a kit, couldn't sit still for very long at all. My parents despaired—they were very traditional. I longed to discover where portals could take us. The very boundaries of the magic, you understand?"

"And that brought you here?"

Cashe laughed. "Oh no, Reulta is quite close to home!"

Lailu gasped. She hadn't even known Reulta existed. How big was the world? She'd travelled the farthest she had ever been and yet was practically on her doorstep. She recalled the big waxy leaves and humid air of that unknown place.

"What were the other lands like?" Lailu asked.

"Fantastical! But also lonely and scary at times. Let me brew us a tea, and I'll tell you some stories. There are plenty of them!" Cashe chuckled. Lailu gazed into space, the clatter of crockery signalling when her tea was ready.

Cashe slid into the booth opposite Lailu, a mug cradled in her paws. The aroma of familiar herbs and spices tickling her nostrils was a comfort. Her host clearly hadn't forgotten her culinary roots while gallivanting around the world.

"Where shall we start?" Cashe asked, sipping her hot tea.

"Have you ever been to somewhere where the air is thick with moisture, and the plants have leaves larger than anything seen in Ruhann?"

Cashe wrinkled her brow in concentration.

"Perhaps you mean Chahkrira. Prickly bug inhabitants—kind of hard to understand anything in their clicking tongue. They were very organised. The humidity was not to my liking, though. Made my fur all frizzy." Cashe patted her head.

Lailu hadn't thought to try and communicate with the insects she saw. She'd assumed they were exactly like the insects at home in Ruhann, who must have their own way of interacting, since they organised their colonies so well, but how that was done was unfathomable to the Ratatoskr.

"Not like Orfela," Cashe continued, looking wistful. "Of course, it's best that the humans don't know such places exist."

"Why not?" Lailu asked. She had been thinking the scientists at Kirkhyrst's university might have been able to help map these places, with their instruments and meticulous record keeping. No one would have reason to be lost again.

"Well, they ruin everything they touch, don't they?"

Lailu's brow furrowed. "I don't understand."

"We might live far, far away, but we all know something's not been right with the natural order of things for quite some time. There are Faidhean in this city who have lived for centuries. Magic was always stable until Kirkhyrst started harnessing it. It's not natural what they do."

The younger Ratatoskr bristled, wanting to defend her newfound friends. Something stopped her. How well did she know them really? She'd been charmed at the attention of strangers from outside; Lima's interest in Lailu's life was more notice than she'd received from anyone in her life, other than her own mother. Daisy made a good show of proving the Grid was innocent, but Lailu wouldn't have been able to tell if she was lying. Deceit wasn't something she was well versed in. Had she been blinded to the danger they presented?

# Lima

"It's getting dark already," Daisy said, checking the time. It was only mid-afternoon, but the sky had filled with steel grey clouds, casting the streets in gloom. After leaving the university, they found themselves wandering through the Meadows, lost in thought. On a normal autumn day, it would have been a pleasant walk, a chance to pretend the city was far away.

In reality the cacophony of the city was never silenced, a reminder that Kirkhyrst was still there beyond the trees. Today it was muted.

The paths through the Meadows were busy, full of people who had nothing better to do than go for a walk. The grassy areas were strewn with picnic blankets; friends and families enjoying the unexpected break from work. No point being cooped up inside when there was no intergrid to browse or television to watch.

Lima felt a knot of anxiety building up inside her. There was so much to take in—none of it was getting her any closer to helping Lailu, and she wanted to help the people in the rookeries just as much as her newfound friend. The corners of her lips turned upwards recalling the peace she's felt curled up with the Ratatoskr—just for a moment—before reality sunk back in. She was just an intern. A stupid privileged intern who couldn't even use that privilege for good. Her stomach churned.

Returning power to Kirkhyrst was crucial. Not so many people would be fortunate to be rescued by the Alder pack should they run into trouble in the dark. Lima was concerned that another night without power would tip the city over the edge. People were already starting to boil over, with petty arguments and short tempers on every street. And if the hospitals had to close...

She liked to think the people of Kirkhyrst were inherently good, perhaps naïve, but they all got along. Didn't they? Her mind flickered back to Daisy's encounter. That was just after a few hours of darkness, and plenty of shops had been broken into last night, the jagged remains of windows boarded up hastily. Lima didn't relish being caught out after dark again. She crept closer to Daisy, the close air setting her even more on edge.

"Do you think the engineers have found anything yet?" Lima asked.

"I hope so—people are being weird. I mean weirder than normal."

Just as the words left her lips a man walked up to them, standing far too close and told Lima, "Cheer up love, it might never happen."

"Screw you," Daisy pushed the man away as he muttered insults under his breath.

"Sorry about that. Just—last night..." Daisy said once the man was out of earshot.

"It's alright. It must have been scary. A vampire walked me home, otherwise I would have weed myself. It was so dark out."

"A vampire, huh? I never asked where you'd disappeared off to?"

"Um... I went up to the rookeries... I'd finished all my work. Hari said I could go."

"Don't panic, I wasn't checking up on you. Not like that. You're really worried about them, aren't you?"

"Who?"

"The people in the rookeries. The ones we've been ignoring."

"I guess. It's just not fair. Why do I get better treatment because I was born into a wealthy family?"

"Welcome to the real world, Lima."

As the first drops of rain fell, there was a burst of activity as blankets were gathered up and people started speed-walking towards the exits. Anyone would think the rain was acid, not simply water. Lima held out her hand to check. Stranger things had happened.

"Damn it, I didn't bring an umbrella," Daisy said.

"You can share mine." Lima of course, had come prepared. They slowed their pace as she searched in the darkest recesses of her bag, people streaming past them in a rush to escape the rain. After a few steps, Lima walked into Daisy's back. "What is it?"

The sound of thunder rumbled in the distance. Daisy pointed to the sky.

"Did you see that?"

"No, I was looking in my bag."

"Wait."

Heads angled upwards, they stared at the sky. The rain fell faster now, filling the air with the scent of petrichor. A fork of lightning illuminated the sky, the clouds glowing blue and crackling with an energy they'd last seen in Ruhann.

"Is that...?" Lima trailed off.

"Magic?" Daisy whispered. "Sure looks like it."

Around them people had stopped to stare, the novel sight distracting them from the rain in their faces. Lima supposed it was sort of pretty—if you didn't know what it was. Her stomach transformed into a deep pit with the knowledge she and Daisy shared; magic only looked like that when concentrated, say in the Grid's cores or a Ratatoskr's portal. Places where magic was controlled. Not set free, high above a city, cut adrift from its own source of power.

# Faelan

FAELAN WASN'T LOOKING WHERE he was running. The sky had just flashed blue, like someone had opened a massive portal in the sky. He half expected a giant Ratatoskr to fall out. So he didn't notice the humans standing in the path, not until he was inches away from their legs. They weren't paying attention either and didn't move out the way of the hulking wolf who crashed straight into them.

Their shouts drew attention away from the sky, and more humans ran over to help up the family who now lay sprawling in the dirt. The package Astrid had tied so carefully to him had come loose, the rain leeching into the outer wrapper. The rabble of humans faded from his attention as he tried to push the package back into the harness without much success.

A pair of shadows loomed over him, their scent familiar.

"You should look where you're going." Daisy smiled down at him. "Fancy seeing you here."

The package unravelled at their feet. Daisy leant down to gather the contents up before the sheets could fly away in the wind. Her smile faded as she took in the loose papers.

"Faelan, what are you doing with these?" She held up a sheet filled with diagrams and equations. Faelan couldn't make head nor tail of it and shrugged. He'd never asked what he was delivering.

"These are schematics... Grid property. Confidential Grid property!" Her voice rose as she checked the now torn wrapper. "What the fuck, Faelan? Is this what you were doing out in Ruhann? Stealing from us! Who is this Anderson?"

Faelan shrank away from her anger. He wasn't in a position to explain. Not with looks and gestures. Even if he wasn't lupine, his clients paid him for confidentially as well as speed and reliability, none of which he was providing at this precise moment. He looked helplessly at the package's contents, getting wetter by the minute.

"Are you even stuck? Is this some sort of trick? Pretend to be all helpless so we look the other way. Is this why Astrid had all those questions?"

Daisy tucked the papers under her arm and stormed off. Where was she going? He needed that package! Lima stood there looking between Faelan and the fast disappearing back of Daisy, her curls bouncing with each angry stride.

He set off after her, keeping a safe distance. He could run faster than her, but then what? He wasn't going to stand and snarl at her like a deranged beast, blocking her way, scaring her for a second time. She didn't deserve that; she was just doing her job. He didn't want to think about what Travis would do if he lost the package. He knew that guy wasn't above board from the start, but he'd turned a blind eye, happy to take his money. The Grid was hardly at risk from a few sleazeballs getting hold of their plans though; their dominance was absolute.

The rain was falling heavier now, beading off his dense fur. Behind him, he could sense Lima following, the scent of her anxiety sloughing off her in waves. They exited the Meadows through the ivy bound wrought iron gates. Instead of turning right towards the Grid offices, Daisy went left towards Fairmount following a route Faelan knew all too well.

# Daisy

Daisy hammered at the wooden door of the pack house. Kane was the one to greet her, surprised to see an angry, wet human on their doorstep.

"I demand to see your alphas!" Daisy shouted over the wind and rain. The storm had come out of nowhere and now raged against the city. She could relate.

"Hang on a minute," Kane mumbled, rubbing sleep from his eyes.

"No, I won't, a pack member has been..." Daisy fumbled for words. "Espionaging!"

"What?" Kane caught sight of Faelan lurking by the gates and shook his head. Lima stumbled into view, bedraggled and out of breath. "I suppose you should all come in."

Daisy might be angry but that didn't mean she wanted to get this beautiful house muddy. It didn't look the sort of place that would be full of hairy, muddy shifters lolloping about. She shuffled her shoes off and took the offered towel to pat dry her hair and clothes.

"The alphas aren't here," Kane said as he mopped up the puddles beneath their feet.

"They never are these days," Astrid appeared from nowhere. "What's going on?"

"You!" Daisy pointed.

Faelan barked defensively.

"Yes, me." Astrid raised a perfectly groomed eyebrow.

"Did you put him up to this?" Daisy brandished the package in Astrid's face.

"Delivering stuff? No. He insists on having an independent income." Astrid turned to Lima. "And you are?"

"Daisy's intern?" Lima ventured.

Astrid threw up her hands in mock despair and ushered the group into the den. Daisy dropped the soggy papers onto the coffee table.

"Those documents belong to the Grid. They're instructions for the infrastructure. To set up a Grid." She leafed through them at last. "The core, the network, all the wiring. It's all here."

"And they're not being delivered to a Grid outpost?" Astrid asked.

"Of course not. Would I be this pissed off if they were? I'm not an imbecile. They're going to some random lodge in Ruhann. Ruhann! Where they would never allow the Grid to function."

"Ah." Astrid shared a look with her mate. Daisy could see it now, the connection between them, a oneness. A link that wasn't there between Astrid and Faelan. Kane looked like he knew exactly what was running through his mate's mind.

"Ah what?" Daisy snapped.

"How much do you know about how Kirkhyrst came about?"

"Just what everyone learns at school. Place rich in resources, magic included. Once the magical revolution started, nowhere else could compete. Humans flocked here. I've seen the ghost towns."

"And the Grid?" Astrid prompted.

"Lightning struck a scientist's experiment, blah blah, history was made." Daisy didn't see how this was relevant.

"We all have the stories we tell ourselves—myths and fairytales. What humans call history," Astrid said.

"I'll have you know our history is very well documented. Just some things, they're kind of top secret? Where are you going with this?"

"There are tales that the shift was once tied to the lunar cycle. That this stopped around the time humans started experimenting with magic."

Daisy scoffed.

"Luna's mum believes it."

"Who's Luna?"

"Our alpha female."

"What? The alpha's mum's still alive?"

"Yes, honestly, do you think we work our alpha's to the grave? Luna's not that old. She can choose to stand down whenever she likes—she'd need Jacob to agree. You can't really have one half of a bonded pair running things." Astrid glanced at Faelan and shrugged.

"We're getting off topic," Kane interrupted.

"Sorry. Well. If another Grid was being made..." Astrid trailed off.

"Isn't shifting when you want better?" Daisy asked.

"Yes. But if true it would have been a huge disruption in how our magic works. We can't risk that happening again. What if we all got stuck like Faelan, and not necessarily in the form we would choose if we had the chance?"

Daisy looked down at Faelan. Was his lupine form what he'd chosen? She felt a pang of pity towards him. Not that it excused his criminal activities.

"Maybe all this weirdness is the result of someone experimenting with their own Grid. Except they've got a head start," Astrid said, nodding towards the papers.

"Out west?" Kane asked.

"Maybe. You know certain groups are desperate for their own Kirkhyrst. A lawless society wouldn't think twice about borrowing the plans." Astrid made air quotes around the word borrowing.

Daisy went still for a moment. She couldn't begin to imagine the kind of resources you'd need to set up a new Grid, completely from scratch. What was the point in doing it out in Ruhann where there weren't many customers? No, things weren't adding up.

"Sabotage!" Daisy said out loud. "Maybe they're not experimenting. They just want this knowledge so they can break it. Seems like they might have succeeded. Seems like something someone who has their own magic would do."

She glared at the shifters.

"I promise you, as future alpha, Faelan's not a criminal. An idiot maybe." Astrid smiled in the wolf's direction. "But he's loyal, and the Alder pack would never condone stealing magic. No pack would."

"And we all benefit from the Grid. It's not like my magic can be used to light this room or cook dinner," Kane added.

"He loves dinner. He speaks the truth," Astrid said.

"I should report this," Daisy stammered.

"You could, but... As soon as whoever it is gets wind the Grid is onto them, they'll scarper. You'll never know where they're located. It's not going to be this boarding house. Let Faelan deliver the package—pretend nothing's happened. We'll all go with him, scope things out."

Daisy had to battle her instincts to tell someone official. She looked through the papers. If she could just remove some key pieces, would that be better? Or would that just lead to further disaster? It all depended on how far they'd got in recreating the Grid. If that's what they were doing.

"Can I think a moment, please?"

She didn't know what to believe. She didn't know these shifters, and sabotage made so much more sense... She pictured going to Hari with this. He would get the authorities involved; Faelan wouldn't be able to speak for himself, and they wouldn't be able to see beyond an opportunistic wolf stealing from them.

And if Astrid was right? If someone was doing something so stupidly dangerous as creating a core by themselves, then they needed to know where it was. Get it shut down.

"I want to come," Lima said. Daisy had forgotten she was there. "I just can't sit around here doing nothing while Lailu is lost. If I can help... maybe... I can see her again..."

Lima looked so sad. Oh gods, Daisy thought, she was really going to do this, wasn't she? She let out a breath and nodded at the group.

"And our ragtag bunch of heroes assemble," Kane quipped, rubbing his hands in glee.

# Lailu

LAILU AWOKE TO THE scent of the unfamiliar: waxed pine and a floral aroma she could not place. Opening her eyes, she remembered she was at *The Thirsty Squirrel*, aching and bruised from the previous day's exertions. She was safe at least, bundled in strange cloth sheets on a soft pad. Waking up in strange places was becoming a regular occurrence. She missed her oak.

It astonished her that there were Ratatoskr living outside Ruhann, she had never thought to expand her sphere of existence beyond the reaches of the Great Forest. She was happy there, but she was starting to see that their portals could offer so much more. Of course, she didn't want to impose on other cultures if they didn't want her there. Her limited experience as an adventurer hadn't given her that impression so far. In Chahkrira, someone had fed her. The cave dwellers of Tionnfell had scared her, but they'd still given her a bed. Ramus had endured a long trek to bring her here, a place she could only agree was better suited to a Ratatoskr. Cashe was nothing but hospitable.

She lay back and tried to imagine the forms of other, unknown to her, species. Ramus was imposing but still had something of Ruhann about him. Deer were a common sight, even if they didn't walk on their hind legs. Not all the Faidhean she'd glimpsed had been quite so easy to place.

She thought of the story she'd told Lima only a few nights ago. It seemed so far away now. The animals in Yggdrasil were all common to her, so if it was a story true of all magic then where were the Faidhean? In the roots of the tree, where light didn't reach, the people would be hugely different from the canopy dwellers—she could tell that much from comparing moles to magpies. She was itching to go out and explore the streets of Reulta, but she also needed to get home.

So many questions swirled around her head. Was her portal the only one to malfunction? Had the storm died down? Had another Ratatoskr alerted the scurry to the impending danger? The magic, would surely return to the trees, wouldn't it? Without it there was no regeneration. She felt a little sick at the vision of a barren, treeless wasteland where once the Great Eldur Forest grew.

When things calmed down, she would come back. A good Ratatoskr should know their neighbours. That should go for Kirkhyrst too, no matter Sylvain's isolationist values. Had the humans been better informed about the nature of magic, maybe they would have been more careful. Or maybe not. Maybe Sylvain was right, but would it hurt to try?

A gentle knock sounded at the door.

"I brought you some tea," Cashe called from the other side.

"Oh lovely," Lailu padded over to the door. "Good morning."

Cashe carried in a tray with a pot of fragrant tea and a selection of pastries and fruit. What a treat! Lailu had skipped so many meals since her portal started failing and was grateful for Cashe's abundance of hospitality. She would find a way to pay her back somehow.

"Do you think I could look round town after breakfast?" she asked tentatively.

"I don't see why not. Unless your friend has other plans..."

"My friend? You mean Ramus?" Lailu laughed. "I don't know if he was my captor or protector!"

"Well then. You are welcome to wander freely, just don't stray too close to the Goblin Market."

"Goblins?!"

"Hah. Not really, it's just what we call it. Some unsavoury characters do business down there. If anyone ever goes missing in Reulta, they're always involved."

Lailu gulped down a mouthful of tea.

"Is that not a bit unkind to goblins?" She wasn't sure what was real any more.

"No such thing, my dear. It's just a name." Cashe patted her knee. "Oh, and there's a Morrigan downstairs for you."

Lailu spat out her tea.

"Why didn't you start with that?"

"Breakfast is the most important meal of the day. The Morrigan's in no rush. I gave her some spoons to look at."

"What... never mind, I don't want to know."

Cashe stood aside as Lailu catapulted herself down the narrow stairs.

At one of the tables the girl from the caves sat gazing intently into a soup spoon, twisting the utensil back and forth as if it was the most fascinating thing in the world.

Lailu cleared her throat, and the girl, the Morrigan, looked up with her blank black eyes.

"Do you have news?" Lailu asked, fearing the worst.

"So much destruction," the Morrigan croaked. Lailu's heart sank. "The storm moves east."

"The scurry? It's..."

The Morrigan blinked and her gaze sharpened on Lailu. "Your scurry is untouched, wet but safe. The dark furred warden was there, I checked. He accused me of stealing nuts."

"Why does no one round here start with the important bits?" Lailu was too relieved to be truly annoyed. If Sylvain was telling off visitors, everything was fine.

"The storm leaves ashes in its wake. Is that not important?"

"Yes, of course, I saw the Great Forest with my own eyes. Hang on, you said the storm moves east? To Kirkhyrst?"

"The human city is not my concern. It has always been unbalanced. The storm won't harm it more than it has harmed itself."

"Unbalanced?"

"Can you not feel it? The world is changing." The Morrigan paused, searching for words. "It makes my feathers itch."

* * *

Sunlight glinted off the cobbled streets, a darker shade of stone than the shards surrounding the city but just as sparkly. Lailu basked in the warmth of the morning. A niggle of guilt pressed at her mind, but she would always have time for a bit of self-care. The Morrigan's news had settled her nerves somewhat. Cashe hadn't said anything about leaving yet, and Ramus was nowhere in sight. Other than trying her portal again, she wasn't sure what she was expected to do next. She didn't relish the thought of getting lost. Again.

Instead, she would get lost the old fashioned way, by walking down the wrong street.

Cashe had suggested she stick to the main thoroughfare and city gardens. When a glimpse of colourful fabric caught her eye, she turned down a narrow alley full of stalls. The colours were so vibrant—she wanted to know what dyes were used. And the patterns, they were so pretty. She complimented the traders on their wares, walking further and further away from the main street.

Everywhere she turned, another delight met her. They traded goods in Ruhann of course, but everything was so rustic, made of what the forest offered. One elderly woman happily engaged her in conversation, explaining how they mixed madder, goldenrod, and birch bark with minerals from the hills, setting it with a dash of magic.

Another explained how a smooth, luxurious fabric was woven from caterpillar threads. Rougher textiles came from the fleeces of animals farmed in the valley. She stepped quickly away from the woman when she started assessing Lailu's furry exterior. However much she admired these fabrics, she didn't want to be turned into a coat.

Perhaps she could collect the scurry's shed fur and return to trade. They did sometimes make small items with it. It was a beast to weave with; mostly they used it for padding. The craftspeople of Reulta might have better luck.

Distracted, she stepped out into a wide road lined with shops. Had she got turned around and ended up where she'd started? These streets were such a warren. She peered into a shop window full of crystals, admiring the pretty colours.

A hand came out of nowhere, and Lailu squeaked as it landed on her shoulder.

"Spare some magic for a poor old woman?" a gravelly voice asked.

Lailu shook herself free and stared at the woman, her face lined with pale scars. In her hand she was holding a purple crystal.

"You want my magic?"

"Fetch a pretty price it would."

"It's not for sale!" She spun around and strode down the street, resisting the urge to run. She desperately wanted to use her portal but couldn't quite trust it to get back to the tavern.

As she skittered round a corner, a large figure loomed in the shadows. It growled and the footsteps behind her faltered.

"You would be wise to return to your shop, Elspeth."

"I did not know she was marked," the woman replied.

"She is not."

Antlers emerged from the gloom. Ramus, come to collect her and her tainted magic. Lailu didn't know whether to be relieved or scared. She very much wanted to see Cashe again, if only to say her goodbyes and thank her for her kindness.

"Marked?" Lailu asked.

"Later. Not where prying ears abound." He looked pointedly at Elspeth, who scurried off with a flippant wave of her hand. She was a lot spritelier than she'd been in front of the crystal shop.

Lailu had even more questions than she'd started the day with. She had the sense to stay quiet as she hurried to follow Ramus back into the heart of the city.

"Favours are currency. It is an unwritten law among our people that one shouldn't touch a person who owes a favour," Ramus said.

"But don't I owe you a favour? You've been helping me, or..."

"By bringing us news from Ruhann and beyond, you fulfilled it. It would be best not to protest."

"Isn't it safer for me to be marked? I mean, if I'm not, why did Elspeth leave me alone?"

"So many questions. I led you here, it would be... discourteous to allow you to be preyed upon. Elspeth has survived this long in a Faidhean city by knowing when to back down. As for safer? An unfulfilled favour can weigh on the soul."

"What was she doing with that crystal?"

"No doubt she wished to extract some of your magic and store it inside. Elspeth deals in enchantments that need magic, yet she has none of her own. You are ripe with it."

Ripe? Lailu scrunched up her nose, and Ramus glanced at her. He made a noise that could have been interpreted as a laugh, foreboding as it was. Lailu guessed that was just Ramus being Ramus.

"Can I go back to The Thirsty Squirrel?" she asked.

"Of course. Where else did you think we were going?"

"I don't know. I thought maybe I was... your prisoner?"

That noise again.

"What would I want with a nosy little Ratatoskr?"

# Faelan

The five of them were trying to look inconspicuous which meant they ended up looking extremely suspicious as they headed down to the docks. An illustrious career in espionage was unlikely for any of them. There were long queues as people sought out what little power the steamers could offer. Others looked ready to emigrate, luggage piled high around them. It wasn't looking good for them finding passage to Ruhann today.

Honestly, it hadn't even been a full day without power, and people were acting like the sky had fallen in. Yes, the sky was doing a weird blue flashy thing, but everyone would be better off staying at home. Himself included, but what Astrid wants, Astrid gets.

He'd had a long hard think last night about the morals of delivering stolen material. With magic acting the way it was, they were better off leaving it alone, not fuelling some madman's experiments. If that's what this was. He would deal with Travis—he could always bite the man's hand off and flee to Ruhann. No one would ever find him.

That's not true, the Ratatoskr could. He had a feeling they wouldn't turn him in. Not if he told them he'd bitten someone implicated in the destruction of their forest. He'd spell it out in the dirt with his claws if he had to.

He needed to placate Astrid though; she had dived headfirst into this scheme, determined to save the day. She wanted to prove herself—he understood that. It made sense to find out what they were doing and where. However, he could just as easily deliver a wad of paper instead of the real deal. He wasn't sure how he was supposed to communicate this plan to the others, but he'd cross that bridge when they got to it. First, they had to get there.

Humans were ridiculous. Rushing to leave town when in a few days this would all blow over. Daisy had been closed mouthed over what the problem was; either she didn't know or didn't trust them enough to share. Faelan doubted those in charge would stand for a prolonged outage. In the meantime, it would do everyone good to go a few days without.

He was a little hurt by Daisy's accusations—that she'd gone from smiling at him to cursing him in seconds. OK sure, he was caught with stolen documents, but does the postie know what's in every letter they deliver? He was starting to like her, had thought of those silly shifter romances on her shelves and wondered if she'd be up for a drink if he ever shifted again.

Faelan sniffed the air, head held up to the wind. The press of unwashed bodies around him was almost overwhelming, but there was one body in particular he was searching for. There. He yipped and wove off through legs, earning him a few shouts of protest.

"Faelan, wait up!" Daisy called after him, pushing against the wall of people blocking her path. Astrid let out a snarl, every bit the alpha wolf she was about to be, and the sway of the crowd went still. Those who were brave enough to turn to look were greeted with a polite smile from a beautiful woman. Surprise etched onto their faces.

"Excuse us, coming through." Astrid opened up a path through the crowd, as easy as that. Onlookers stood dumbfounded, but no one risked questioning her, the authority flowing off her in waves.

"I want to be you," Daisy said in awe to Astrid once they'd reached the steamer's berth.

"It is quite good being me, I agree. Now where did little wolf get to?"

They stood before a yellow and red steamer, a handwritten Out of Order sign attached to the gangplank. Wet paw prints led up and onto the deck.

"I'll go fetch him. You find us a working vessel." As Astrid went to board, Daisy grabbed her arm to hold her back.

"Wait. I think this steamer will do nicely."

"We're not going to row to Ruhann," Kane objected, but Daisy scurried off onto the steamer and out of sight. Astrid sighed, this was going to be her life now, running after rebellious wolves who can't follow orders.

"How many times do I have to say, we're not taking passengers right now," an irritated male voice boomed from inside. "Oh, it's yah."

"Adam! How's Selene fairing?" Daisy greeted the captain.

"Can't get anyone at the Board of Transport to come look at her. Something tells me that's not why yah are here." He glanced towards Faelan who was sat at his feet looking as innocent as a wolf could, tongue lolling out the side of his mouth.

"We need to get back to Ruhann, on important Grid business. You'd be in our debt. It's crazy back there."

"Yeah. Everyone suddenly wants to get out of town." Adam ran his hand over his face. "I don't wanna risk stranding people on the Tarac, if she's gonna be stopping an' starting."

"Of course, but we're not just any people. We're the Grid."

"And the Alder pack," Astrid butted in.

"Where did you come from?" Adam asked, surprised that his steamer had filled up with passengers without his knowledge. Astrid smiled sweetly at him.

"You'd be in our debt too. Never know when you might need a wolf's help."

Adam looked over the bedraggled group assembled in front of him. Staying berthed in Kirkhyrst was risky. It looked like he'd been sleeping onboard, probably to deter looters. Three shifters would be perfect security. He nodded once.

"Awright then. All aboard!" Adam offered them a toothy grin and turned towards the bridge.

# Lima

Rain lashed at the steamer's deck as the group huddled inside. There was no sign of the weather easing, and the sky continued to flash unnatural blue. At least *Selene* was powering through the storm with no signs of stopping. Daisy sat in the bridge with Adam, an attempt to ease his mind as they sailed through what could only be described as a magical storm. None of them were truly equipped to deal with magic malfunctions, but Adam didn't know that. Fortunately, the journey had been incident free. So far.

Lima pressed her nose against the window, her breath fogging the window with each exhale. The wolves had fallen silent, some sort of unspoken vibe passing between them. Faelan curled up in a damp ball, his nose tucked in beneath his tail. The others sat on the benches, staring into the distance. She hoped they had a plan. A non-violent plan.

The steamer lurched suddenly, catching Lima off guard. She slid against the table, catching herself before she fell to the ground. All three pairs of shifter eyes focused on the door to the bridge. The steady chug of the steamer continued unabated.

Regaining her seat, Lima's attention turned outside, half expecting a blue ripple to be whirling around the steamer. The usually calm waters of the Taric were churning ominously. Waves battered the hull, rocking them back and forth, as if they were at sea. Not on an inland river whose usual fare was sedate barges and steamers, boats unprepared for such conditions.

She couldn't see any other vessels following them; perhaps they had turned around and returned to Kirkhyrst. Visibility wasn't great though—they could all be out there, obscured by the rain.

"What the…" Kane's knuckles grew white as he gripped the table, leaning over Astrid for a better view. Lima glimpsed scars tracing his fingers before he pulled his hand away. The web of lines fading as the blood returned.

"What is it?" Astrid asked, taking hold of his hand, lacing her fingers through his.

"Nothing. I thought I saw something in the water, cresting."

"A log perhaps? There's nothing but fish in this river."

"Yeah… a log," Kane nodded to himself.

A crack echoed from below, and the steamer tipped to one side. Lima scrabbled for purchase as her body slid sideways, the water below visible through the windows. Her hands slipped. Her legs didn't have the strength to brace herself for long, and she tumbled downwards, just as the steamer crashed back into position. She braced for impact, covering her head, waiting for the pain to come.

Instead, a strong arm wrapped round her, breaking her fall. The angle was awkward, and for a moment she hung between safety and falling. But the force had gone out of her fall, and her head flopped down onto a soft mass.

"Idiot," Astrid playfully snarled at Faelan, now sprawled under Lima's limp body. "I would have caught her properly if you hadn't jumped in the way like a lupine crash pad."

The door banged open, and Daisy rushed through.

"Is everyone OK?" she asked, taking in the scene.

"Where did these waves come from?" Kane asked just as the steamer rocked in the other direction. This time they were ready for it, sliding a little on the floor, but less at risk of head injury. Daisy clung onto the door for dear life.

"Adam's never seen anything like it," Daisy responded, eyes wide. "Lima, are you hurt?"

Lima looked down at her limbs. Four, all accounted for, no fluids leaking out. She shook her head.

"Faelan broke my fall."

Astrid huffed but let it go. There were bigger fish to fry.

"Right. Everyone, life jackets on," Daisy instructed.

"I can swim fine," Astrid protested.

"Me too," Kane added. Faelan huffed in agreement.

"In this?" Daisy gestured to the window, a wave rising as if to perfectly prove her point. The steamer rose to one side again, crushing Astrid, Faelan, and Lima up against the window. Astrid carefully shielded Lima from the weight of their shifter bodies.

"Point taken," Kane said and grabbed a life jacket from under the bench, throwing it at Astrid. "Darling?"

Astrid donned the bright orange monstrosity and helped feed Lima's arms into hers.

"Leg straps too." Daisy pointed to the dangling straps no one had thought to secure. "No point in wearing these if you just drop straight through the moment you hit the water."

"Is the steamer really going to capsize?" Lima's lip trembled. Like everyone, she'd had perfunctory swimming lessons at school, but that pool hadn't had five meter waves. Nor magic humming against the edges.

"It's just a precaution," Daisy said, although she didn't sound all that confident.

Astrid held a jacket up against Faelan. "I don't suppose there's a... dog version of this?" She pulled an apologetic face at Faelan who was doing a good impression of scowling. No shifter liked being called a dog.

After another ten minutes of being thrown from side to side, Adam stuck his head around the door.

"We gotta look around for a place to dock. Can't keep going like this. Things are gonna fall off her."

Everyone looked out of the windows. All Lima could see was water; rain from above, the Tarac from below. Scratch that, she felt like the Tarac was coming at her from all directions, the water looming above her as the deck tilted beneath her feet. She clutched onto Faelan's fur.

"Over there!" Daisy strained to be heard over the roar of the storm, flinging her free hand in the direct of the riverbank. As they crested another wave a dock flickered into view. Adam squinted against the driving rain, weighing up his chances.

"Here goes," Adam mumbled. "Prepare for a crash landing." He stumbled back toward the bridge, leaving everyone clinging on for dear life.

# Daisy

"I GUESS WE'RE WALKING the rest of the way," Daisy said, squeezing water from her clothes. The dock and surrounding area were completely deserted, the storm keeping everyone at bay. "How far is this boarding house?"

"Frontier Lodge, Greynoll, West Ruhann," Kane replied, inspecting the package. "So somewhere between here and the wild west."

"Hah bloody hah," Daisy grumbled, giving up on ever being dry again. Her jeans were waterlogged, and her hair was plastered to her face. The rain was still coming down with as much force as her shower, maybe more, and the dense clouds blocked out all signs of the sun.

If this was the dock they'd arrived at last time, turning left would take them west. She wasn't one hundred percent sure. If they were on the southern bank, they'd be going in completely the wrong direction.

Adam was busy inspecting the damage to *Selene*, alternating between angry mutters and stroking her sides. She had a long gash down her hull and wouldn't be going anywhere soon.

"Adam," Daisy called over. "Do you know where we are?"

The captain looked up at Daisy and then took in his surroundings. "Huh," he said.

"Is that a good huh or a bad huh?" Daisy asked.

"These Ruhann docks all look the same, but there's not many of them. It's either Celandine or Aquilegia on the north side... or could be Crocus, which is on the south. We coulda got turned round in the waves."

"So, they don't have signs or anything useful like that? How do you know where to stop?"

"They usually have flowers set out front. I guess they've been swept away."

Daisy looked around for any sign of crumpled flowers with no success. She appreciated the simple charms of Ruhann, but it wouldn't kill them to carve a nice sturdy sign and attach it securely to the building. The flowers didn't even bloom all year round.

"What about in winter?"

"We only go as far as Holly—the most easterly one. It's Buttercup in summer."

Daisy shook her head. They didn't have time for this.

"Do you have a compass on board?"

"Nah, never need one. I just go up the river and back again."

"Soooo," Astrid drawled. "We don't have the foggiest where we are or where we're going. I guess Faelan leads the way—he at least knows what it smells like."

"I'm no walking anywhere," the captain grumbled, turning back towards his vessel. "Yah all welcome to camp out here until the storm clears up though."

Daisy and Astrid exchanged glances. The storm had come out of nowhere, and there was no way of knowing how long it would go on for. They were tired and wet, with no change of clothes. While a rest was tempting, walking would keep them warm at the very least. Daisy was starting to shiver. She felt bad that the shifters were staying in human form for her benefit. Faelan looked much more at home in this wild weather than Astrid and Kane did.

Maybe Faelan was just more of an outdoor kind of guy than his packmates. Daisy was still mad at him. From the look of the pack, he can't have been so desperate for the work not to do due diligence. He could be working for terrorists for all he knew. When he shifted back to human form, he was in for a right telling off, that was for sure.

There was a two in three chance that left was the right way. Faelan sniffed the ground, picking up a scent which reassuringly went left. The group followed behind.

Each step was an unpleasant squelch as they made their way down the track. The downpour had washed debris loose from the ground, shards of rock and fallen branches thwarting what seemed like every step. It was going to take forever to reach Greynoll, wherever it was.

Meteorology had never been Daisy's strong point. She didn't know what an obscene amount of rain to fall in a day was, but she was sure the ground should be more resilient. Great swathes of earth were missing, roots exposed to the air after years growing underground. Pools of water could be seen for miles. She supposed that was what flood plains were meant to do. Flood.

Yet this didn't seem like one day's worth of damage. She cast her mind back to the weather of the past few months. She'd been too preoccupied with her increased workload to really notice. It had been a hot summer; she'd had some regret for not spending much time outside. Hot summers happened sometimes. There was still food in the shops and water in the taps. Anything extreme would have had some impact on her life, even as distanced as it was from the natural world.

The sky rumbled ominously overhead, promising another round of soaking. A gust of wind rattled the leaves of the canopy, moving from tree to tree as if delivering a message. Then another sound joined the cacophony: a low throaty growl. Daisy spun around to face Faelan. His ears were laid flat, and his teeth bared. Some ancient instinct kicked in, and she froze.

"What's got into you?" Astrid swatted at him, earning herself a less than playful nip. A flash of purple illuminated the forest, threads of light tracing across the shifters. Kane let out a yelp and fell to the ground, his back arching. Astrid's eyes widened as she took in the scene, a shudder working its way across her body, her canines lengthening.

Faelan lunged towards Daisy. His jagged teeth, inches from her face, were lit up with tendrils of magic and dripping with saliva. Her brain stalled—being eaten alive was not a concept it could comprehend. Her flight, fight, or freeze reflex opted for the less-than-helpful freeze method. Faelan's jaws snapped down, narrowly missing her neck. A strong arm wrapped around his throat, holding him back. Astrid clung onto her packmate with a sudden urgency.

"Run. Now!" Astrid hissed at the humans. Lima didn't need to be told twice, and she tugged Daisy away from the gnashing teeth, their feet slipping and sliding in the fresh mud. Daisy came to her senses and turned to follow, running clumsily in a direction she hoped was the right one.

# Lailu

In a flash of light, two Ratatoskr stepped out onto the hillside above Reulta. Cashe's portal blazed behind them, as if mocking Lailu for her lack of control. Cashe had been wary about travelling too far, fearing the same fate as Lailu, but had agreed to take her a short distance from the city in order to practise.

The other Ratatoskr had been using her portal to do her chores around Reulta and hadn't experienced any untoward effects, always ending up at her desired location. Lailu might have been a tad jealous. Cashe had a theory that Lailu's proximity to the Eldur Pines had caused a disturbance in her magic.

"You wouldn't find me portalling straight into that mess. But it's your life," Cashe advised.

"The Morrigan said the storm's passed."

"She also said it left destruction in its wake. If it's eaten up all the magic, your portal won't want to open there. You might end up exactly where you started."

Lailu was frustrated with herself for not asking more of the Morrigan. She'd been scared, worried for her friends, not thinking they might have been afflicted with the same problem. Who else had been lost beyond the bounds of Ruhann?

"What about Kirkhyrst?"

Cashe raised a furry eyebrow. "Now why would you want to go there? If anywhere will mess up your magic, that city will be it."

"I could focus on Lima. Get help. Or at least a ride back home."

"Well, let's just focus on The Thirsty Squirrel for now," the other Ratatoskr said, with pity shining in her eyes. "Go on, try and access your portal. Think of the lovely tiffin we'll have when we're successful."

Lailu steadied her breathing. She could do this. Images of the tavern filled her mind and sparked a tiny fizzle of something in her heart; she could feel it, just. She would not think of the magic abandoning her. Of being lost and alone. Of stranding Cashe somewhere terrible. The fizzle went out.

"Your fear is paralysing you," Cashe said. "You're all up in that pretty head of yours. I should have got you drunk."

"Cashe! Alcohol isn't the answer to everything. Besides, I need to be in control."

"True that." Cashe thought for a moment. "I know. Throw your portal over there—don't try and go through it."

"What? Where? Is that even possible?" Lailu spluttered. She had only ever opened her portal in her own personal space.

Cashe pointed to a spot a hop and jump away, not very far at all. She scrunched up her face, and a circle of solid blue light appeared, floating above the grass. With a click of claws, the portal vanished into thin air.

"Now you try," Cashe coaxed. "Remember. We're not going anywhere."

Lailu focused on a small, white boulder. Once she'd got past the strangeness of Reulta's landscape, she started to appreciate its beauty. At home there were no glittering rocks, and even she could admit winters were a bit drab when the snow didn't fall. Here the land provided its own blanket of white. When the sun shone, it was spectacular.

Concentrating on the sparkles in the stone, her mind cleared. It was just her and this land... and her magic. A portal popped into existence, sitting atop the boulder. Lailu squealed with glee.

"It worked!"

"Right. So close it up. And repeat ten times."

She was happy to oblige. Each time her portal sprung to life, her heart lifted higher. Pushing her power out further and further each time, it was almost fun. On her tenth attempt, she spun round with a flourish and danced an on-the-spot victory dance as the portal flashed into existence.

"Ready to head back?" Cashe asked. "I can take you, or..."

"I feel good, centred. I'll try." Lailu hesitated. "I understand if you don't want to come with me."

"Nonsense. If we end up in the back of beyond, I'll be there to portal us right back, won't I?"

Lailu smiled back at Cashe, flooded with relief. Someone had her back. With that thought, Lailu's portal opened once again, strong and bright and welcoming. Stepping through filled her with calm, and when she opened her eyes, she was greeted by the hearth of *The Thirsty Squirrel*.

Cashe quickly busied herself with preparing tiffin. The tavern was empty once again. Other than Ramus and the Morrigan, she hadn't seen anyone else pass through the door.

"Is it hard, being the only Ratatoskr here?" Lailu asked when Cashe returned with a spread of sandwiches.

"I like my own company well enough."

"But the tavern, it's so quiet."

"Ah." Cashe settled herself in the seat opposite Lailu. "Some Faidhean are set in their ways, don't want to mix with anyone the slightest bit different. I'm happy they don't set foot in here. Mostly I take in travellers, like yourself. I know what it's like to be far from home.

"I also brew a mean moonshine. I only make so much at a time; it's hard to get the containers to ferment it in. Let me tell you, when a new batch is ready, the queue goes out the door!" Cashe laughed. "Everyone loves this Ratatoskr when the moon shines."

"We make mead for Tapping Day. Is it similar?"

"I haven't had a good mead in decades. My moonshine isn't as sweet, more herbal. Some people might mix honey in if they don't like the taste."

"I'd invite you to Tapping Day, but I fear it won't be happening this year."

"It'll bounce back, my dear, nature always does." Cashe patted her paw and returned to the bar.

Now Lailu was feeling more herself, she wondered if it was only her own mind causing her trouble. The trauma of seeing her beloved trees burned to nothing—it sent her off-kilter. That must be it. Coincidences did happen sometimes. She needed to get back to inspect the damage, start planning for the next season. For all she knew, it was entirely normal that the weather cleansed unruly magic, storm clouds carrying the stray threads where they would do no harm.

If the Great Forest was completely destroyed, there was nothing she could do anyway. Her heart hitched. No, that wasn't true, they could replant. It would take time, and a huge amount of effort. If the magic was stable there was no reason not to try. Some Eldur Pines grew further afield, and with her newfound knowledge, she was certain they could call on others to help. There were those outside Ruhann who wanted nature, and magic, to flourish just as much as the Ratatoskr.

After tiffin, she decided. It was unwise to travel on an empty stomach, and Cashe had gone to the effort of making it just for her. She thought of Lima, a smile returning to her face. They'd only spent a short time together, but Lailu sensed the goodness in her, a kernel of someone amazing waiting to flourish. She just needed to grow into her confidence. Yes, she would try and find Lima first. A test of her portal. If she focused on something—someone good, her mind couldn't sabotage her.

It was time to go home.

# Lima

LIMA'S LUNGS BURNED AS she raced through the trees, her legs growing tired despite the surge of adrenalin running through her veins. Daisy was half dragging her by the sleeve, making their progress clumsy, but at least Lima couldn't let up without being dragged through the undergrowth.

"The cliffs," Daisy panted. "If we can climb..."

Lima could barely climb at the best of times, let alone as knackered as she was right then. She nodded anyway. The grey rocks were sharp against her hands as she pulled herself up. Her ascent was far from graceful, more of a scramble; her survival instincts taking over her motor functions. Somehow, she found herself several metres from the ground. Still alive. Not eaten.

They paused momentarily, straining to hear signs of pursuit over their ragged breathes.

"I think we're OK for now. If we can get a little bit higher..." Daisy craned her neck scoping out the rock face for hiding places. "Maybe that's a cave?"

Lima squinted at a dark blot against the side of the cliff, the shape swimming in front of her eyes. The rain had started up again, and they'd hardly had a chance to dry out from previous soakings. Perhaps the idea of a cave was just wishful thinking, but it gave her a burst of energy all the same. At the very least, being higher up would make it harder for the shifters to reach them.

If she could get that far. She struggled to get purchase on the steeper slope, hindered by the rain slicked rocks.

"Here." Daisy offered Lima her cupped hands. Tentatively, she stepped up, wobbling a little as she found her balance. She needed to find a handle to grab onto—not the vines which could easily give way. Something that would bear her weight. She did her best not to look below her. She wasn't that high up, but a fall backwards onto rocky ground risked broken bones. Risked bloodying herself and making it easier for the shifters to scent her. Or was that just sharks?

A ledge to her left caught her eye, and she lunged before she lost her nerve. For one horrible moment she felt herself sliding backwards... Luck was on her side, and she held on. She hauled herself up, scraping a layer of skin off in the process and slid into the gap in the rocks. It wasn't much of a cave—if it could be called a cave at all—more of a hollow. It would do. She held out a hand for Daisy.

"If we survive this, remind me to go to the gym more often," Daisy wheezed as she dragged herself up. Lima laughed, but there was no humour behind it.

They huddled together in the narrow opening, watching the curtain of rain pouring off the cliff. She told herself autumn storms were perfectly normal, yet Lima had never seen so much rain in one day. The dampness went down to her bones.

"I'm scared," Lima whispered in a small voice. Tears gathered in her eyes, and she tried to blink them back.

"Come here." Daisy pulled her into a hug. "I'm so sorry I dragged you into this. My job isn't usually like this. It's usually very mundane and repetitive, with lots of coffee. Not to mention a whole lot drier. There was this one time... a contractor broke a toilet. It gushed everywhere!"

Daisy was trying to distract her. Lima was grateful for it—the life of an office-worker so very far from their current predicament. The distraction wasn't entirely working.

"Do you think they'll come after us?" Lima asked.

Daisy stared out into the rain, thinking.

"I don't know. If they're more wolf than human, what reason would they have to keep chasing? We're probably not very tasty prey, not when there are plenty of deer and rabbits about."

The alternative was not worth thinking about. The shifters they'd met had such an easy-going nature. Even Faelan in his lupine form had become a familiar sight, a far cry from the primal fear he'd induced when he lunged for Daisy.

Yesterday, Daisy had accused the shifters of sabotage in a moment of anger. Lima hadn't thought she'd meant it, but if it were true, they could have lured them out here with an ulterior motive. One where a convenient accident happens. Astrid had told them to run, but to where? They were two unprepared humans running loose in Ruhann.

The sooner the magic surges were fixed, the better, but Lima had an awful feeling that just switching whatever it was off wouldn't solve everything. The Ratatoskr had shown them there was a delicate balance to nature and magic, one that needed to be respected to stay on an even keel. What the Grid did was hardly respectful; it was all take and no give. Even if they stopped whatever was going on out here, they were still complicit in sucking magic out of the world.

Unnatural. That's what Sylvain had called it.

Synapses in her brain fired, connecting fragments of her thoughts.

"Daisy?"

"Hm?"

"If you just turned the core off, where does the magic go?"

"The energy feeds out into the Grid network until it's used up. It'd just stop generating—I mean collecting, more."

"So, if it wasn't connected to a network?"

"Like a makeshift core cobbled together in the back of beyond you mean?"

"Yeah."

"Theoretically... there are two options. It releases into the atmosphere or stays in the core."

"And if it's not turned off and not connected to a network?"

"You'd see a lot of magic building up—gods, the whole thing could blow up!"

Brilliant, now she had to worry about exploding cores as well as being eaten alive.

"Do I even want to know what happens if it does?"

"It's never happened in the history of the Grid, so I don't know—nothing good. An explosion wouldn't explain all this." She waved her hand vaguely. "The fire, Lailu, Faelan, the blackout, this awful weather—it didn't happen all at once."

"Unless it exploded and started off a chain reaction of weird shit? Starting with the fire?"

"Then I have no clue how we end it."

They sat in silence for what felt like hours, alert for any sound of approaching wolves. At one point Lima thought she heard howling. It turned out to be the wind, picking up for another round of battering. Her body was exhausted, but her mind was too busy to let her sleep.

"What now?" Lima asked, not wanting to abandon their mission despite her fear. Some good should come from this ill-fated journey. Daisy hesitated before answering.

"I have an idea."

# Daisy

"I HAVE A DELIVERY here for Mr Anderson. I shall just leave it—her... here. For him to collect. Uh, bye!" Lima stammered at the boarding house receptionist before making a hasty exit, hiding her blushes behind her hair. Don't give them time to ask questions, Daisy thought.

Daisy stood before the receptionist with a beaming smile pasted to her face. Was this the stupidest idea in the history of stupid ideas? She belatedly realised they might think she was a prostitute, ordered in for Mr Anderson. She wasn't up to speed on the law regarding sex workers out here. She gulped. The things she did for her job.

"I'm the package!" She resisted the urge to add *Tada!* The receptionist looked her up and down and clearly decided they weren't paid enough to care what happened under this roof.

"I'll show you to his room. This way."

She'd tried to tidy herself up a bit after coming up with this madcap plan. There was only so much one could do without a shower; she must look a right state. Bedraggled and dirty, with a wild panic in her eyes. Thank gods *Frontier Lodge* didn't have standards.

The documents were with Faelan. Who knew if he was in the right state of mind to even remember who he was let alone that he had a package to deliver. The package was damaged enough start with; it could very well be completely destroyed by now. She couldn't risk this Anderson bloke getting spooked before they had more information. Not now Lima had put the thought of exploding cores into her head.

The receptionist rapped on the door to room 5, informed the occupant they had a delivery and promptly returned to their position at the front desk.

"About time," a brusque voice said as the door opened a crack. The man looked startled to see Daisy standing there. "You're not the usual courier."

"He couldn't stay, busy couriering jobs to tend to. I'm the package. I mean, the delivery. I er..." she trailed off, trying to come up with a convincing lie. "Your associate wanted you to have the very best assistance. I know things about the Grid that would make your hair curl."

"I—What?"

"Not everyone who works there thinks they should hold all the power, if you know what I mean. Sending me is intended to speed things up around here. All that toing and froing with bits of paperwork. Why wait when you can send the horse's mouth?" Daisy kicked herself internally. She needn't have worried; the suspicious look on Anderson's face turned to curiosity.

"We shouldn't stand out in the corridor all day—we might be overheard," she prompted and was rewarded with an open doorway. She stepped through with a deep breath. She was really doing this.

Inside it looked like the Grid's spare parts room, lots of boxes of wires and numerous connectors were laid out on the table as if Anderson had been working on them before he was interrupted. Daisy moved a half-dismantled console off the desk chair and perched gingerly. On the surface were numerous schematics with the Grid's logo on. She wished she had a hidden camera like the spies in movies had but would have to make do with her memory.

Her mind had conjured up all sorts of ideas of how outlaws would look and act, but Anderson appeared rather average: mousey brown hair thinning at the temples, creases in his forehead from too much worry, and a slight build with a rounded belly. He wore a rumpled striped shirt, rolled up at the sleeves, and trousers that wouldn't look out of place in the office.

He didn't look too dissimilar to her dad, now she thought about it.

"What appears to be the hold up?" she asked, asserting a confidence she didn't feel.

"The capacitors, they just won't hold the charge. They do for a few minutes, but then they overload, and poof. We lose the magic."

"And you're following the Grid designs to the T?"

"As much as we can. Look we can't get the same refined materials out west. Our contact at Blackthorn hasn't delivered everything she promised."

Daisy tried to keep her face blank. Had no idea how she could press for more information on Blackthorn without seeming suspicious. She glanced around at the boxes. Some were stamped with Blackthorn Industries but that didn't mean much. She probably had a few of those boxes herself at home. They were so ubiquitous.

"And your supplier? Are they giving you the same grade of products as the Grid gets?" Daisy bluffed.

"I knew it!" Anderson scowled. "She told me they use the same off-the-shelf products that anyone could buy, that it would be suspicious to re-route batches destined for the Grid."

"Do you have any of your capacitors here?"

"No, I don't like being near them. All that magic contained, it could do anything, especially with the lack of quality control we have right now. I'll take you out on site."

She breathed an internal sigh of relief. This was exactly what she needed. Her knowledge of how the capacitors actually worked was slim, but she knew enough to give off an aura of competence, just as long as no one expected her to rewire the things. Once she knew where the site was, she'd get back to Kirkhyrst pronto and report the breach.

When Anderson turned back to face her, Daisy caught a glimpse of metal beneath his coat. Something she had only ever seen in movies, wasn't entirely sure they existed in the real world. Perhaps it was just a tool of some kind, she tried to tell herself. Too right, her panicked brain yelled back, a tool of death.

Anderson had a gun.

# Lima

Parked behind the boarding house was a black Blackthorn Dagger, a top of the range all-terrain vehicle favoured by the rich and famous. Lima suspected most of them never left the city.

She ducked behind a bin as Daisy and Anderson came out of the building and got into the car. Either Anderson was loaded, or the Blackthorns were supporting this endeavour. A nice car as a sweetener. Daisy would need solid proof before accusing them though. As Lima understood it, they were the major supplier of the materials used by the Grid, and they weren't exactly prohibited from selling to others.

She didn't want to just hang around in the bushes until someone returned. Part of her knew that the shifters were still out there, knew where Daisy and Lima were headed. They could turn up at any moment, and she was completely defenceless. She picked up a branch and tested its weight in her hands. It wouldn't do much damage to a fully grown shifter; she could wedge it in their jaws if they came for her. Maybe. That would deal with the first one; she didn't have a plan for all three.

There was no way to follow the car either. It had sped off the minute the doors had closed, taking a grim-faced Daisy with it. She'd rather stay close to the boarding house than be out in the open, somewhere with other humans to call upon and doors to barricade against gnashing teeth.

Walking around the building, she peeked into the rooms on the ground floor. Beds were made up neatly, covered in green sheets and plaid throws. Someone had put in above minimum effort to make the place look homely. About half the rooms had signs of occupancy, luggage or clothes strewn about, a teacup left out on the bedside table. The moment she looked in on room 5 she knew it was Anderson's. The place was a mess.

The building was of a simple construction with no locks on the windows. Cautiously, she tested the frame. The window wobbled, but she couldn't get purchase to push it upwards. She tried jabbing it with her branch to no avail. What she needed was something thin and sturdy to prise open a gap. Scanning the ground, she could only see mud and leaves. More branches like the one she was uselessly wielding.

In all the chaos she had lost her bag. She knew there would have been something useful in there, but there was no way she was backtracking to find it. Bags were easy to replace, as was all her stuff.

Her Grid pass! She had forgotten all about it, new as it was. It was wedged deep in her pocket, a rectangle of flexible plastic. It would have to do. She inserted it into the thin gap under the window, jiggling it back and forth, praying to gods she didn't believe in that it wouldn't snap.

After a tense few minutes the window moved, just enough for her to get her fingers under and slide it open. Despite her aching limbs and grazed skin, she managed to pull herself over the sill and into Anderson's room. It was bigger than the others, with a dedicated living area separated from the bedroom. Picking her way around the boxes, she went over to the desk first.

Lima could see plenty of diagrams similar to those Faelan had been delivering; those wouldn't tell her anything new. She sifted through the papers, finding invoices and purchase orders for various materials and equipment. They all seemed above board as far as she could tell. No one was going to care that Anderson bought 500 metres of insulated cable, even if it was odd to ship it out to Ruhann.

Inside the desk drawers there was the detritus of a life lived in a borrowed room: receipts, medicines, loose coins, a stash of chocolate. Lima was tempted by the chocolate, ravenous after the long walk. She wasn't a petty thief; she was riffling through Anderson's belongings for good and righteous reasons. She pushed the chocolate aside and kept on rummaging. At the very bottom there was a notebook.

She sat on the bed and opened it at the first page. The handwriting was a mess—a sign of someone who had spent a lifetime typing instead of perfecting their cursive. She made out lists of materials, some crossed out, others marked with question marks. Another page had a crudely drawn map, showing the Tarac and the borders of Ruhann, with a large blank area circled.

If she could cross-reference it with a more accurate map, it might be useful. Perhaps it was where Anderson had taken Daisy. Argh! Why hadn't she thought to listen at the window? She carried on flicking through the notebook, scanning the text for any clues. Anything concrete they could take back to Hari.

A folded sheet of paper fell to the ground. It was a sheet from a printed contract: a list of investors for a "new power initiative" signed and dated by each. Celia Blackthorn's name at the top. Gotcha, Lima thought. Then her blood ran cold. Another name stared out from the paper, in black and white: Matthias Samson

# Daisy

THE RUTS IN THE road jarred Daisy's spine as the car bounced down the track away from the boarding house. She gripped onto the door, trying to steady herself, hoping Anderson knew what he was doing behind the wheel. As they travelled further into Ruhann, the branches became barer, the smattering of leaves brown and shrivelled. Autumn was imminent, but the trees had only just been turning when she was at the scurry.

Something felt off. The trees were grey, desiccated rather than dormant. Even the evergreens looked sad in the unsaturated light. The car turned a corner, heading out into the open. Daisy gasped. The once green, rolling hills were filled with skeletal trunks. Nothing but deadwood for miles around.

Anderson looked over at her.

"Eyes on the road," she said, as a wheel hit a pothole, sending her flying forward in her seat. Anderson tutted but turned back to the front.

They couldn't have driven as far as the Great Forest. Daisy tried to get a better look as the car sped along the track. The trees weren't scorched; it wasn't fire that had done this.

"How long have the trees been like this?" she asked.

"Like what?"

"Dead?"

"Huh. Hadn't really noticed. Must be what winter is like up here," Anderson brushed her off, swerving into what could only be described as an industrial estate.

The Grid did their best to conceal their rural outposts, but no such attempt had been made here. The hillside looked like a giant hand had clawed its way through the ground, leaving ugly scars in the landscape. The recent storms had made it worse, with mud coating every surface. How could the Ratatoskr have missed this on their doorstep? It was a while away from their settlements, sure, but they had portals for gods' sake.

A basic concrete structure had been set into the mess of hill, a small concession to dampening the interference caused by whatever it was they thought they were doing. Multiple sheds huddled around it in varying states of disarray. Daisy tried to suppress a shudder at all the health and safety transgressions as she stepped over thick ropes of cable snaking along the ground.

Anderson was picking his way across the waterlogged ground as if it was a personal affront to him. His shoes were more suited to the city than trekking through the countryside, and now he was out in the open, he looked increasingly out of place in this environment.

On the way, Daisy had done her best to memorise the directions. She wished she could find a moment alone to scribble down a rudimentary map. The Grid might be able to detect all this if pointed in the right direction but if they didn't, she couldn't live with herself if Anderson got away because her memory failed her.

Of course, she had misgivings about the Grid's monopoly on power, but checks and balances were essential. Magic was too dangerous for just anyone to go around messing with. Once this was nipped in the bud, she would see what she could do about the rookeries. It's not like Anderson's project would even be helping them anyway. What good was magic captured out here, far away from the poorest in Kirkhyrst? Those who set out to the frontier towns were generally those with some savings, people who still had energy left after a day's work to dream of a better life.

She hadn't had much time for dreaming of late either, but at least she didn't have to worry about where her next meal was coming from. She had a secure home and family that cared; the least she could do was try and help those less fortunate. Like Lima wanted to do.

Daisy wasn't the ambitious type. It wasn't until this past week that she'd noticed quite how stale her life had become. All she'd needed was an environmental catastrophe and a near-life experience to give her a wake-up call. She would march back into the office, evidence in hand, and get the Grid back on track. Sort out the power irregularities and make sure everyone got the service they were promised.

A howl echoed through the quiet.

"Bloody animals," Anderson muttered and picked up his pace. Daisy wasn't sure whether the sound was a reassurance or not. If they were regular, run-of-the-mill wolves, there was nothing to fear. There was always a chance the shifters had regained their senses. But if not... the sight of Faelan's teeth snarling before her face was still fresh in her mind. It had to be the magic controlling him.

Despite her grievances, she didn't want him shot. Nor Astrid and Kane.

Anderson pushed open a metal door and beckoned Daisy into the darkness beyond. Inside, static crackled through the hot air.

"Is it running all the time?" Daisy asked.

"Oh no, this is just the after effects."

Daisy was glad the gloom hid her shocked expression. The fact she could feel something even when it was turned off was not a good sign.

"How long are you switching it on for each time?" She tried to keep her voice level against the rising panic.

"We've never kept it stable for more than thirty minutes, tops. The guys get antsy."

This had to be the cause of all their problems. Such short bursts causing so much disruption, even as far away as Kirkhyrst, was troubling. Something had to be seriously wrong with the assembly or configuration. The Grid's cores were running non-stop and never created a magical storm. She would have noticed.

"Is there a reason we're stood in the dark?"

"Sorry. Conserving power. Light switch is behind you, to the right."

She gingerly reached behind her, feeling across the wall. The light flickered on, and she waited for her eyes to adjust. She very much hoped she was seeing things.

For starters, there was no shielding to the counterfeit core, the whole thing was open to the elements. Anyone with access to the building could lean over and touch it, touch the raw magic that would flow through when it was on. It was smaller than the Grid's main core, which potentially limited its capacity for chaos. The cables were crudely welded into place, and the casing was stuck together with tape, failing to hide the scorch marks beneath.

She was hesitant to touch the thing. As the silence stretched on, she knew she needed come up with something in line with her cover story. She didn't want to inadvertently help them either.

"The proper shielding will help stop interference," she said truthfully, albeit referring to the interference they were causing to the outside world. It'd probably help the erratic behaviour of the magic too. If they were to continue down this path, she'd do her best to instil a bit of safety to the project, at least until the proper authorities got here.

"And this welding will need redoing. It's a mess." She gingerly poked one of the cables. "Ideally you should have interconnecting high-voltage couplings with a safety cut off on each connection. You risk damaging your equipment otherwise." Not to mention the damage to everything else. She hoped she sounded convincing as she prattled on, throwing in words she recognised from support tickets. Anderson appeared to be paying attention.

"And clear up some of this mess while you're at it." She pointed at the detritus lying around the open space surrounding the core. "It's a huge fire risk."

"Right, well, you had better see it in action," Anderson said, and before Daisy could utter her objections, he waved over a large bearded man in overalls. "Tyler, do the honours."

Tyler, presumably, flicked a switch. A deafening hum filled the air. Just one switch, Daisy thought in horror. This was too easy to just turn on and off willy nilly. What if someone tripped and landed on it by accident? This had to stop.

But what could one woman do? She had to engineer a way out of this and get back to Kirkhyrst. Hand it over to someone who knew what they were doing. Anderson was shouting at her, but she couldn't make anything out over the machine's din.

Staring into the heart of the core, Daisy saw shapes moving around, they looked almost like... no, she rubbed her eyes. She was tired and stressed, seeing things. Like those ink blots psychologists used. Or a cloud, just a formation of water vapour that sometimes looked like a dragon. This was just a formation of magic.

Yet, the Grid's core never had shapes moving around inside it. It was always a steady blue glow, an occasional swirl when under high load, a crackle around the edges.

There was a commotion outside, and the door blew open in a huge gust of wind. Boxes blew across the room, flying into the core. They crumpled into nothing as they hit the magic. Branches and rubbish were picked up as the windspeed increased, traces of blue light flickering across its path.

There. She saw it again. A ghostly figure in the concentrated magic. It almost looked like a wolf.

# Lailu

Bracing herself for the noise and chaos of a city, Lailu stepped out of her portal, only to be met by forest. She took a deep breath, the familiar scents of home filling her nostrils. Ruhann. She was so relieved to have found her way home, she wasn't too worried that her portal had backfired once again. Before her stood a human-made structure, which placed her quite far from the scurry. Even several days walk through her homeland was not enough to dampen her spirits. Ruhann was still here; the fire hadn't engulfed the whole country.

Above her, the eerie storm continued to flicker. The Morrigan had told her it moved east, yet it still lurked on the borders of Ruhann. She'd hoped to be rid of it. The last time she'd stood in its midst, her portal sent her far away, as if it knew she should be far from its influence.

A clatter came from inside the building. To her astonishment a human was climbing out one of the windows. Just as she was about to make herself scarce, she saw the human's face.

"Lima!" she exclaimed, a bubble of happiness forming inside her chest. Her portal had brought her exactly where she needed to be.

Lima fell the rest of the way out the window and gaped at Lailu.

"Sylvain told us you were missing!"

"I was! I guess I still am from Sylvain's point of view. I doubt that Morrigan told him anything."

"What?"

"My portal malfunctioned. I couldn't control where I went, and then it just stopped working at all."

"Oh Lailu, that must've been terrifying." Lima gave her a hug. Lailu let herself hold on for a few seconds longer than necessary. Lima's body was damp and muddy against her; she found she didn't care.

"I can't wait to tell you about the places I've been! I met Faidhean! And a Ratatoskr who runs a tavern! That was after the caves—I didn't like them much. But wait. What are you doing here?"

"I, uh... long story."

"I have time."

"Shouldn't you be getting back to the scurry? Let them know you're fine?"

"I'm not entirely sure I trust my portal enough to get me back. Not with this storm. I thought I was aiming at Kirkhyrst, but I found you anyway."

Lima blushed.

"If you're sure," Lima took a deep breath. "You know Daisy said the Grid had been experiencing more problems lately? After we got back, the power went out in Kirkhyrst, like everywhere.

"The weather went mad, and it turned out Faelan was delivering top secret Grid stuff to here." She pointed at the building behind them. "So, we came back to try and find out what's going on. Faelan's still a wolf. And now there are two more. Shifters, who are wolves. I mean they shifted without wanting to. And then—" She gulped. "It's like they forgot they were human. We had to run away.

"Then Daisy came up with a plan. She got into a car with a strange man who may or may not be building a dangerous magical machine."

"Woah, slow down. Remember to breathe. What do you mean, a magical machine?"

"A core, like the Grid. Lailu, they're trying to bring a Grid to Ruhann."

"Like the one at that hub?"

Lima nodded. "But bigger? Maybe. I don't know. And we went to the university—they had this machine that extracts magic, and, oh gods Lailu, it kills things! What if this core was the thing stealing your portal magic?"

Lailu blanched. She'd convinced herself her problems were psychological, was perfectly happy with that conclusion, but if Lima's theory was correct, it wasn't over. She thought of Elspeth begging for small scraps of magic, offering coin in exchange. If humans could just steal it from afar, nothing would stop them.

And that they had come to Ruhann, had waltzed into her home and wrought destruction, all the while stealing from them? It made her blood boil in a way it never had before.

"And gods, my dad," Lima said.

"Is he hurt?"

"No. He's involved. I found his name. In there. He, he's an investor."

"Investor?"

"Like he gives them money to make it, and they give him money when—if it's successful. I never really bothered about his work. I should've paid more attention."

"Shush. You are not responsible for the actions of others. Even your own kin." Lailu enveloped Lima in a hug to rival any bear. She didn't know why they always got the credit for hugging. Ratatoskr hugs were infinitely superior, and much less deadly. As she held on, Lima let the tears fall.

Lima was proof that not all humans were rotten. Lailu was glad she had her on her side, even if she had no influence on what her father or their Grid did, it made her feel better all the same.

"If you don't mind getting lost with me..." Lailu mumbled into Lima's hair.

"I'd never be lost with you by my side," Lima pulled back to smile at Lailu, tears staining her cheeks.

"What direction did Daisy go in?' I can't promise this will work, but we'll try and find her together."

# Faelan

THE WOLF RAN, HIS pack by his side. No, that wasn't right, there were only three of them. His pack was... he couldn't think. Their prey had got away. They still ran. Through the rain and mud, nipping at each other as they strayed too close. His alphas. He was here with his alphas.

Sheets of rain hammered down, soaking his pelt. Movement caught his attention, rabbits skittering from the bushes. No, not his prey. What was he hunting again?

Ahead, his female alpha stopped, blocking the path, her teeth bared. He slid to a stop, the ground slick beneath his paws. The other male, he jumped at her, but she stood her ground. Forced the other wolf to show his belly. A shiver ran across his skin, he was no alpha, what was he doing standing here, staring. No, the other wolves weren't alphas either. Not yet.

Something niggled in his mind. A name. Astrid. A look of recognition sparking in his eyes. His name was Faelan, the other wolf Kane. His prey was... Oh Fenrir. They'd been hunting humans.

In an instant, Astrid shifted, standing in the middle of a road in Ruhann as naked as the day she was born.

"Fuck," she said. "Are you two in there?"

She stood with one foot on Kane's flank, resting lightly but ready to push him away if he tried anything. He whimpered and shifted.

"I feel weird," Kane mumbled. "Shit. Did we eat…?"

"No, thank Fenrir."

Faelan shoved at his lupine form, willing his bones and muscles to shift. Whatever just happened he didn't want it to happen again. Ever.

"Don't strain yourself, little wolf," Astrid said. "Whatever we do next, it's going to be easier if we've not got our human bits hanging out."

"Nothing on you hangs, honey," Kane drawled.

"Now is not the time. But thanks." She smiled at her mate and turned back to Faelan. "That's not like what happened with you? On the steamer?"

Faelan shook his head. It would have been carnage.

"Right. Now this doesn't look good if word gets out that shifters are losing control."

"Do you want me to make them stay quiet?" Kane asked.

"No! We're not gangsters."

"I was thinking more of a bribe. You think I'd hurt them?"

"Kane, I'm sorry. It's just… argh!"

Faelan very much hoped this was a one off. There was no way shifters would be allowed to roam free in Kirkhyrst if they couldn't be trusted around humans. They might not even be allowed freedom at all.

"Now, do we risk going back to Kirkhyrst knowing we could go feral at any moment, around millions of humans? Or do we risk going to find Daisy and Lima, who we traumatised, knowing that we could go feral at moment?"

"I vote for finding the bastards who caused this trouble and tearing their throats out."

"Kane! We don't even know the reason for this. It could be, I dunno, solar flares."

"Come on. Do you even believe that?"

"No. It seems too much of a coincidence. I also don't want to be put on trial for murder. No matter how tempting it might seem."

"I suppose." Kane pouted.

"Still. Finding Daisy and Lima is the better option. Less people around if we do... you know." Astrid scrunched up her face and held up her hands, her fingers curled to imitate claws.

Kane kissed her on the nose. They were back to normal. For now.

# Lima

LIMA JUMPED OUT OF the way as vomit splashed at her feet.

"Lailu! Are you OK?!" Lima asked, though clearly she wasn't.

Her portal was still lit behind her, threads of blue magic unwinding at the edges, as if being pulled by an unseen force. Where they held hands, a blue haze shimmered.

"I—I think I'm going to faint." Lailu collapsed in Lima's arms, her portal going dark. Lima couldn't shake the memory of the lichen at the university, shrivelled and lifeless. She checked Lailu's pulse; it was there, but weak.

Their newfound location was bereft of life. In the distance, a large, box-shaped building sat against a bank of mud of rock. Daisy was nowhere in sight, but everything Lima saw around her made her certain she was in the right place. Nowhere else in Ruhann would feel so empty.

She couldn't just leave Lailu lying there, out in the open. Lima scuttled over to a shed, trying the door. She was running on empty, and her limbs were weary, but she tugged with determination. It wouldn't budge. She tried another. They were either locked or warped so badly by the damp that she didn't have the strength to unstick them. The only other hiding place was a line of scraggly bushes, their stems bare.

Whispering her apologies, Lima grabbed Lailu under her arms and dragged her over to the bushes, draping her with a few strange branches. Her russet colouring blended in a little with the clay-like mud, and as long as no one looked too closely, she would be fine. Nothing would let Lima believe otherwise.

Once Lailu was tucked away in her hiding place, Lima ran over to a stack of crates near the building, scanning the area for signs of life. A terrible hum was emanating from behind a dented, metal door, sending throbbing pulses through her head. Just like the hub they'd visited days ago, only ten times worse. No wonder Lailu had passed out.

If Daisy was here, she must be inside that building, but Lima could hardly waltz in there uninvited. She didn't have a plan, she'd been relying on seeing Daisy, making some sort of signal, and then portalling out of there. Lailu wasn't in a fit state to do anything, let alone rescue them, and Lima couldn't see a way to make herself known to Daisy. Not unless she knocked on the door.

She made herself small and inched around the other side of the building. The car from the boarding house was there, now splattered in mud. A getaway vehicle she thought, except she couldn't drive, and Anderson hadn't helpfully left the keys behind. She tried the handle, just in case; it was locked.

There were no windows in the concrete structure and no convenient back entrance. No escape route if the core exploded.

As she was weighing up her options, a shadow fell over her.

# Daisy

THROUGH THE DOOR ANOTHER man in overalls appeared dragging a dishevelled Lima into view. Daisy's stomach dropped. She shouldn't be here. How had she been so stupid to bring her intern into this mess? These people were dangerous, not just through their incompetence. Anderson had a gun for gods' sake. She hadn't even told Hari where she was going. Stupid, stupid!

"I found her lurking by the car," the man said, gripping Lima roughly by the arm. She was soaking wet, with debris in her hair and a scowl on her face. So far, she seemed unhurt. Daisy had to keep it that way. If something happened to them, no one back home would ever know their fate.

"She anything to do with you?" Anderson asked.

Her heart leapt up into her throat. She was no good at thinking on her feet, not when it meant spinning a believable lie. Her hesitation stretched into an awkward silence, all three men staring at her.

"She's my personal security," she ventured. "I tried to leave her behind, but she is paid to protect me at all costs. You wouldn't think to look at her—she has special skills."

"Right." Anderson didn't look convinced. Fortunately for her, the core decided to use that moment to spit out blue sparks. One landed a hair's breadth from Anderson's foot. He leapt in the air and shrieked. "Turn it off. Turn if off!"

Tyler fumbled for the switch but was too late. The power surged, lighting up the room with a wash of bright blue. Tyler was flung through the air, hitting the ground with an awful crunch. Anderson unholstered his gun, aiming it at Daisy.

"Fix it. Now!" he yelled, arm shaking.

"I—it's not—it's not shielded, I can't…"

Fear lanced through Daisy as she squinted against the glaring magic flowing from the core. The shapes were back, shifting from serpentine to wolf to a tangle of antlers to a shoal of fish darting straight towards her. She flinched, throwing her hands in front of her face.

"You said you were from the Grid!" Anderson yelled at her.

"I am! Your core, it's different. It shouldn't have those things."

"What things?"

"Look!" She pointed, her fingers a hair breadth's away from the current. She pulled them back quickly, inspecting them for damage. She'd got lucky, but magic was still pouring out the core, she could see it now. The smaller core was extracting magic at far too rapid a rate, and it had nowhere to go, nowhere except the air around them.

Daisy tried to inch away from the core, but Anderson caught her movement. In the doorway a figure appeared; the magic surged around Daisy, reacting to the intruder. It brushed past her skin, raising goosebumps despite its warmth.

"How dare you!" a voice bellowed at the same moment Anderson pulled the trigger.

# Lailu

THE SIGHT WOULD HAVE taken her breathe away had it not been so needlessly cruel. Within the light of stolen magic were the echoes of her trees. Their essence. Their very souls. Between the ghostly branches, traces of other creatures flocked, reacting to Daisy who was illuminated by their magic, a halo of sparks around her hair. As the echoes sensed her presence, they turned towards her, reaching out, changing shape.

"How dare you!" Lailu screamed with all her might. As the anger burst out with a flash of bright light, a loud crack sounded in her ears. Instinct took over and she lashed out with her portal. It unfurled right in front of Daisy's shocked face, taking the projectile with it. Be damned whoever was on the other side.

The man wielding the weapon turned towards her. A horrid, harsh thing—minerals forged into unnatural form. A kernel of sense broke through her anger, and she snapped the portal back to her. She wanted to send this man far away—she faltered. How could she unleash him onto an unknown place? She needed focus, to send him somewhere he could do no harm.

She could send him back to Kirkhyrst, of course, but she wanted him punished. She couldn't trust the justice of humans, not after this.

The monstrosity of a machine was still pulsating, visages of its stolen magic lighting the room. Lailu's stomach churned, and her head was on fire. She wasn't going to pass out again. This was too important. Too horrific. Was this what they did in Kirkhyrst too?

One of the humans ran towards the doorway, she barely noticed him. He fell, struck down by an invisible force.

"Lailu," Lima's pleading voice reached her through the roar. She had struggled free from the grasp of her captor, distracted as he was by the unconscious body on the ground. Lima held out her hands to Lailu, palms up.

Lailu glanced down at her paws, sparks of magic flying from her claws.

"I—" What was happening to her?

# Daisy

DAISY DIDN'T KNOW WHO was more dangerous, Anderson with his gun, or Lailu with her palpable anger, flowing off her in waves and making her magic do things Daisy didn't realise Ratatoskr could do. She had underestimated them all this time.

Then there was the core behind her. She hated having her back turned to it. The thing was nothing like the ones at the Grid. OK, the rudimentary design of it was the same, but it wasn't meant to have things whirling around inside. Things that looked like creatures. Things that made a soft-spoken, kind, Ratatoskr blaze with outraged magic.

When Lima spoke, a fleeting expression of confusion—of doubt—flickered across Lailu's face. Anderson took this as his opportunity to stride forward, brandishing the gun as a shield, shoving it right into Lailu's face. Brave or stupid, who knew.

Lailu swiped out at the hand holding the gun, her sharp claws scraping four gashes across his outstretched arm. Anderson cried out in pain, letting go of the gun. It clattered across the ground, landing at Daisy's feet. She froze.

She knew she was just as likely to shoot herself, or her friends, if she picked it up. She had no idea how they worked, just that they were instant death. At least if television was to be believed. Unless she was the hero of this story; then she would miraculously come back from the brink of death to save the day. No, she was not going to gamble her life based on fiction.

The core. She was closest; she needed to turn it off. It might not have a true kill switch, but she was grateful for the ill-conceived on-off design. As she reached out with a trembling hand, something surged towards her, blinding her. Coming at her from all directions. A solid weight barrelled straight into her, knocking the breath from her lungs.

Her last thought was that she had flicked the switch. She had saved the day, hadn't she?

There was a great pressure on her chest. So, this was how it felt to die.

* * *

It turns out a fully grown, albeit naked, shifter male weighs quite a lot. Faelan was draped across Daisy, unconscious in his human form, a nasty looking burn running down his back. She gently pushed him off her, careful not to touch the raw skin.

She rubbed her sternum as she sat up and looked around. Lima stood clutching a sobbing Lailu. The men were nowhere to be seen.

"Where's Anderson?" she croaked.

"As soon as Faelan burst in, they ran," Lima answered. "Gods, I thought he was going to eat you."

Daisy probably tasted pretty rank by now: a mix of sweat, adrenalin and mud. Probably a potent aphrodisiac to a rabid shifter. But Faelan was no longer lupine.

"Human men, eh? Can't stand a bit of naked masculinity," Astrid panted in the doorway as Kane wrapped a tarp around her. More for Daisy and Lima's benefit than the shifters'. Humans were notoriously weird about nudity.

"Sorry we're late to the party," Kane said. "Looks like you handled it all by yourself anyway."

"Oh Fenrir, I am so embarrassed. Savaging your newfound friends is not the shifter way," Astrid apologised.

"It's not like you actually savaged us, but thanks," Daisy said. "Um, what happened?"

"With us, or...?" Astrid gestured at the core.

"Either? Both?"

"You turned it off, Daisy," Lima told her. "But these ghostly tentacle things were reaching for you. Like they had escaped from the core. Faelan pushed you out the way."

"Soul catchers," Lailu whimpered.

"Uh, yeah. Lailu says the core was sucking in the essence of magic beings, not just the magic in the air. Whatever hit Faelan—it triggered his shift. I guess you passed out for a few minutes. Did you bang your head?"

Daisy reached around and prodded her skull. Still intact.

"I don't think so."

"This lumbering fool probably squished all the air out of you," Astrid said, prodding Faelan with her toe.

"Is he going to be OK?" Daisy asked.

"Oh, a severe case of bruised ego, I expect." Astrid crouched down to inspect him. "We're fast healers; I'm sure he'll come round soon."

"I hope so, because it's muggins here that has to carry him otherwise," Kane complained with a wink at Astrid.

"I don't suppose any of you spotted spare clothing lying around? It's getting a bit nippy in here." Astrid brought attention to her tarpaulin clad chest.

"Sorry, had other things on my mind. You could check in the sheds out there?" Daisy suggested. "Or there are some sacks you could poke holes in. I'm sure you'd look very fetching."

"Astrid can carry it off. I can't. I'll go look," Kane offered and slunk off.

"We can't just leave this here," Daisy said, turning her attention back to the core. "Those idiots will just use it again when we're gone."

"Can you pull out the crucial bits?" Astrid asked, peering at the machine.

"I can try."

"We can scatter the parts with my portal," Lailu piped up. All her tears had been used up, but she still clung to Lima. "It doesn't really matter where they go, as long as they're separated."

"Wait, how did you get here? I thought you were lost in the Great Forest." Daisy was confused.

"My portal failed me. I guess I was lost, far, far away. This thing," she spat, "Must be to blame. I found Lima, and then we found you."

"Can you just shove stuff through it? I mean, that thing with the bullet was impressive."

Lailu's fur fluffed with pride, and she nodded. "I feel like I understand my portal so much better now. Cashe taught me so much."

There would be time for questions later. So many questions. Lailu's plan was the best they had, and they needed to hurry before Anderson came back with reinforcements. She studied the core for a moment before yanking off a handful of cables.

"Can I help?" Astrid asked. "I don't want to accidentally pull out the thing that stops it exploding."

"I don't know what I'm doing either—the more hands the better," Daisy said, carefully pulling out a silvery coil. "Here, Lailu, get rid of this first."

The Ratatoskr nodded and took the item. She opened a portal, smaller than before and threw the coil in. "Good riddance! Anything else?"

Daisy passed over a bunch of cables that had no way of connecting to the coil. Perhaps a resourceful person would find them and make them into something useful. She wasn't going to feel guilty about fly-tipping, not today.

"Do you know where you're sending them?" she asked.

"Those? They went to a cave," Lailu said, closing the first portal and instantly replacing it without another. "This, I hope, is a tavern. Pass me those barrel things."

Daisy handed over elements taken from the base, and Lailu carefully fed them into the portal.

"If they don't break on the way, I know someone who'll make use of them."

They carried on like this for another thirty minutes, Lailu muttering ambiguous statements about where items were going. Daisy was just glad they had dismantled the core. Replacement parts would be hard to source, and

Anderson wouldn't be able to use this site now the location was known.

It would slow him down at least.

# Lima

LIMA CHEWED ON HER fingernails, wondering how to bring up the papers she'd found in Anderson's room. She had to tell Daisy. With Blackthorn funding it would start up all over again. Daisy could get the information to the people who mattered: the Grid board, Kirkhyrst council, the city guard.

A small part of her wanted her dad to be ignorant of what he was funding. Sweet talked into some business venture at a party. He'd said he'd lost some contracts lately, this would have been too good to resist. The promise of a competitor to the Grid.

She kept stealing glances at Lailu, who must be so hurt and confused right now. With every portal she opened, her demeanour brightened. Lima wanted to tell her how sorry she was, that this wasn't what she had signed up for at the Grid—how wrong her dad was. Her need for forgiveness was selfish. Lailu had important work to do, and then would return to her scurry to deal with the consequences of everything humans had done.

Lailu had been as shocked at the rest of them that her magic could be used as a weapon. As soon as the core was turned off, she'd broken down in tears. Lima had tried her best to comfort her but was so out of her depth; hugs were all she could offer. Ratatoskr always land on their feet, as they say, and Lailu seemed to be doing OK now she had a task to focus on.

The parts of the core disappeared bit by bit, carried away to places Lima had never heard of. Kane returned, sporting grey overalls and sturdy work boots, a hardhat perched jauntily on his head.

"Do you think I'm sexy?" Kane half sang, sidling up to Astrid with a growl.

"Of course. But also ridiculous," Astrid said as Kane deposited a bundle of clothes on the floor. More of the same, minus the boots and hat.

"Sorry, couldn't find any lady sized boots. Must only hire bears."

Astrid wriggled into the overalls and rolled up the sleeves.

"Help me get these onto Faelan. If we have to carry him home, it'll be one less set of awkward questions," Astrid said, holding open the legs of the remaining overalls. "Here, you grab his leg, and I'll shimmy this on."

Lima had been trying to her avert her eyes from Faelan's naked body, but Astrid and Kane had clearly never dressed another being in their lives. The overalls kept slipping off.

"Did you guys never have dolls?" Lima asked. Both shifters shook their heads. "Urgh, give him here."

Lima bunched up the left leg of the overalls and fed Faelan's foot through, doing the same for the right leg. "Can you lift him please?"

Kane scooped Faelan up in is arms, and Lima pulled up the overalls in one movement. Despite his lack of awareness, she was careful not to touch the angry, red marks across his back. She was tucking his arms into the sleeves when Anderson's notebook fell out of her waistband. Bouncing quietly onto the floor.

It lay open, its pages accusatory.

"Hey, you dropped something," Astrid said, picking it up. Her brow furrowed as she took in the writing. "What's this?"

"I found it in Anderson's room. There's a contract in there. It's signed by Celia Blackthorn and... err... my dad." Lima stared at her shoes, unable to meet anyone's eyes. She felt so guilty, and this would be the end of her internship for sure. Not that it mattered in the greater scheme of things.

Daisy looked up from dismantling the core, her hands grasping a metal bar.

"Blackthorn?" she asked.

"Uh... yeah. And dad. I'm so sorry I had no idea..." Lima rambled. She didn't want to cry, but her lip began to wobble. Lailu turned and grasped her hand, grounding her.

"Shhh. I'll take a look when we're back in Kirkhyrst." Daisy said, taking the notebook and tucking it away. Out of sight, out of mind. She wished.

Once the machine had been stripped bare, the room empty, Lailu opened her portal once more. So, this was it. Lima thought this might be the last time she would see the Ratatoskr's sweet face.

"Be right back," Lailu announced before stepping through. The portal snapped shut behind her.

Kane whistled. "That is some party trick."

"She's amazing," Lima said, and the shifters exchanged knowing looks.

Moments later Lailu returned clutching a misshapen object in her paws.

"Oh wow. Is that my bag?" Lima gaped at Lailu, her tears forgotten for now. "How on earth did you find it?"

"I've been practising." Lailu bowed. "It's a bit muddy, sorry."

"Why are you apologising? It was me who threw it in a puddle." Lima peered closer at her bag. "Or in a bog."

"It's all bog out there," Lailu said, shaking the mud from her feet.

"Look. I can probably portal you all to the outskirts of Kirkhyrst. I don't know why Sylvain has refused to do it all these years. Stuck in his ways I guess."

"Are you sure?" Daisy asked.

"Yes. Let's get you home."

# Daisy

IF DAISY LAY DOWN, she knew she wouldn't be getting up again today. She very much wanted to lie down. Exhaustion washed over her, but she still had things to do.

Lailu had dropped them off at the bottom of Charnel Hill, the closest she was willing to get to the city, meaning it had taken them another hour to reach the tramlines that would carry them home. Astrid had insisted they make multiple copies of their evidence and forced Daisy into a printshop. Fortunately for them, the power had returned, and the bored assistant barely gave their dishevelled appearance a second glance.

Each time they passed anyone, they put of a show of Faelan being drunk, his arms slung across the shoulders of Kane and Astrid. Their strength lifted his feet from the ground so that he wasn't dragged—not that anyone was paying close attention. Not now the power was back on, and everything was good and right in the world. If only.

Daisy couldn't go into the office in her current, mud-splattered state, despite the important information she was carrying. She leafed back through the notebook. Some of it was nonsense: rows of numbers and crossed out ideas. Other pages were frighteningly familiar though. Lists of essential parts to keep a core maintained, energy level calculations, names... dates of experiments she would love to cross-reference with her cases at work.

A gentle knock on her door made her jump. She dragged herself out of her chair and peered out into the hallway. A tall, cloaked figure stood there, holding a steaming mug of coffee.

"Sweetie, I heard you shuffling around. I was worried, what with the power being out and... What on earth happened to you?" Etienne handed over the mug, and Daisy inhaled deeply.

"You're an angel. Hang on, let me draw the curtains."

Once the room was suitably shaded, the vampire came and perched on Daisy's sofa, taking her in.

"You appear to have mugwort growing in your hair," he said.

"Urgh, I need a shower."

"Never a truer word said."

Daisy stuck out her tongue before turning serious.

"I'm fine. Promise. It's just been a lot. And I need to go into the office, I'll fill you in later?"

Etienne nodded and got up to leave.

"I know you think I'm just some ridiculous old vampire, but I do care about you Daisy."

His footsteps faded away, and she let his kindness fortify her. Drink coffee. Take shower. March on down to Grid. She could do this.

* * *

"Daisy! Thanks gods you're back. I've got to go report in on this debacle with the board in ten minutes. Your presence would be appreciated," Hari said.

"Can I speak to you first? In your office?"

Once the door was closed, Daisy handed him the contract.

"What am I looking at?"

"A contract. To build a core. I saw it."

"Do you have evidence?"

"Is that not enough Hari?"

He shook his head. "We can't go around accusing Blackthorns based on a muddy bit of paper. Where's this core?"

"Ruhann. Well, not anymore—we dismantled it, scattered the pieces."

Hari groaned.

"You mean to tell me you destroyed the evidence?"

"For gods' sake, you didn't see it. Lailu called it the soul stealer."

"Lailu? Soul stealer? You'll need more than this to convince the Grid to take on the Blackthorns. You know what they're like. They don't like to ruffle feathers."

"The Ratatoskr who helped us. There were creatures—people," she corrected herself, "Inside their core. It's been making people sick. What if the Grid is doing the same?"

Hari studied the paper in his hands. "You know what, that girl is always signing autographs isn't she? I bet this is forged. She's hardly a criminal mastermind."

Daisy resisted the urge to scream. The funds were coming from somewhere, and the bulk of it was coming from whoever had signed as Celia. It had to be Blackthorn money, even if they were using their frivolous heir as a scapegoat.

"You were at Celia's the other day... How did she seem?"

"I don't know. Like a disinterested socialite looking down her nose at a servant? She barely spoke two words to me. She definitely didn't casually mention building a rival Grid."

She was running out of time, had to get him back on track.

"There's more," she said taking out the notebook. "There's things in there only a Grid engineer would know. And someone was sending them our blueprints."

"Matthias Samson... that's Lima's father, right?" Hari was still focused on the contract.

"Don't even start. Lima hasn't a bad bone in her body."

"You must admit, it looks suspicious."

"No, Hari." Daisy gave him her death stare, and he relented.

"I suppose the timing's all wrong," Hari looked at his watch. "Can you try and weave a coherent story in the time it takes to walk to the boardroom? We have to go."

Daisy did her best to relay the events in Ruhann: the effects on the shifters, how the core made Lailu ill, Anderson trying to shoot her. She told him her theory on the surges being caused by the core not having anywhere to safely discharge. She held back the fact that it was collecting excessive amounts of magic. That might explain their flow rates and blackout, but she didn't want to give anyone ideas. Not if they'd just go ahead and make their own soul stealing machine to increase yields.

She was out of breath by the time they reached the boardroom door. Hari looked like he was about to say something, but they were quickly ushered in by an executive assistant, eager to get the meeting on its way.

"Ms Miller, please take a seat." A balding man twice her age pulled out a chair. She hadn't realised the Grid's board was quite so grey. And male. Six pairs of eyes scrutinised her as she sat down, Hari sliding in beside her.

"Mr Griffith here tells us you have information pertaining to the magic disturbances of late?"

Daisy nodded.

"We found evidence of an unauthorised core being built in Ruhann. We dismantled it this morning." She paused. Took a breath. "The project appears to be funded by Celia Blackthorn, among others."

"It aligns with the time the Grid came back online," Hari added.

"So, Blackthorn has finally decided to stop playing nice with us. We knew this day would come," one board member said. Daisy was trying to remember their names; her head was too full to focus.

"We're taking this woman's word for it are we?" another asked.

"Now, now Dean," the balding man turned back to Daisy. Carter—that was his name. Phineas Carter. "May I see...?"

She handed over the contract and notebook, hands shaking.

"I doubt Celia has the brains for this. Someone's using her," Dean said. "This isn't enough to go on."

Daisy felt herself shrink in her seat. Why did she think this was going to be easy?

"Matthias Samson on the other hand..."

"Yes, we'll let the council deal with him, and this Anderson fellow. Trading stolen proprietary technology. Of course we'll need to find the leak too," Carter said. "This Samson, the daughter. She was working here?"

"Her internship has been terminated immediately," Hari interjected.

"She had nothing to do with this. I swear," Daisy pleaded. They weren't going to let Lima into the building again, she knew that much. Investigating her father was punishment enough; they didn't need to drag her name through the mud too. To have these pompous men look at her like she was dirt.

Poor Lima. She hadn't stopped to think what this mean for her. The Samsons were well-off, but if that wealth was all tied up in criminal activities, did that mean they would lose their home? Gods she felt sick.

"Another thing," she squeaked. Hari gave her a warning look, but she ignored it. "The core. It was drawing magic out of magical beings, not just the air. Hurting the Ratatoskr. Shifters. The Alder pack can testify."

"I'm sure they can," Carter turned to his assistant. "Draw up an NDA for her. Make sure she signs it before she leaves."

"What?" Daisy spluttered.

"You've done good work. Keep quiet and there'll be a promotion in it for you. Maybe you can lead the energy reduction taskforce." They all laughed at this. Daisy was stunned.

"What just happened?" Daisy turned to Hari in the stairwell. She'd been numb reading through the pages of the NDA, but she had no choice other than to sign. Not if she wanted to keep her job.

"I'm so sorry Daisy. You saw them. They knew—they just don't care."

# Faelan

Hot, clean water had never felt so good. The steam billowed around Faelan as he stood in the shower, letting the water flow over his sore skin. He could put up with the magic burns if they meant he had use of his human body again.

He'd woken up face down on his own bed, disorientated and sore, wearing strange overalls. A note told him everything was fine, and no one was dead. Short and to the point. Astrid was quick to hear him stirring and had tiptoed in to his room to fill him in on the details. She'd offered to help him bathe, but he'd brushed her off.

He was so embarrassed. Not about his nudity—he had very little shame for his naked body, even if he had been sprawled all over Daisy. Astrid told him it was Lima who dressed him in the end, that Kane was flopping him around like a ragdoll before the reserved, young human stepped in. It was more the fact that he had nearly torn Daisy's throat out. Would have done if his future alpha hadn't stopped him.

Downstairs, Astrid was pacing the kitchen, waiting for Luna or Jacob to show their face. It was clear now that they couldn't just leave it in the hands of humans. Grid business was shifter business now, and the business of every other magic-bearing creature in this world.

"I'd offer you coffee, but you appear to be jittery enough as it is," Faelan said.

"You know, I think I preferred you as a wolf," Astrid replied. "But yes, I will take a coffee if you're making."

"Me too," Kane said, appearing in the doorway.

Keys jingled at the front door, followed by a stampede of small feet, as Luna returned with some of the pups. Dark shadows under her eyes, a weary look on her face. She definitely wasn't going to appreciate what they were about to unleash.

Faelan nodded a greeting and helped her with her bags.

"Faelan, thank you. I feel like I haven't seen you in weeks," Luna said, pressing her lips to his cheek.

"Ah. I've been... busy. Astrid has something she wants to speak with you about," he said, deferring to Astrid. She would say it better anyway.

"You might want to sit down," Astrid said. "This blackout, we think we know what caused it?"

Luna raised a perfectly manicured eyebrow and Astrid launched into an explanation of everything that had happened, from Faelan's spontaneous shifting to the discovery of the essence inside the core. Faelan had missed most of that part, but the tentacles reaching towards Daisy were real enough. He had no reason to disbelieve Lailu if she said it was full of trapped souls.

"You don't seem surprised?" Kane said when Luna's expression remained neutral.

"It was bound to happen eventually. It's the price we pay for all these conveniences." Luna waved to the kitchen in general. "Of course we know magic is siphoned off, but we have assurances from the Grid to keep it within agreed levels.

"You knew about this? This atrocity, and just let it happen?" Astrid snarled. "It's our magic!"

"We didn't authorise this project in Ruhann if that's what you mean. I will speak with the directors, make sure they tighten security."

"You're alpha. You're meant to protect us!" Astrid shouted. "What is even the point of your fancy law degree if you don't use it to help us?"

"You know perfectly well I help all you pups. You have good lives, are allowed to roam this city freely. The laws that protect you exist because of me."

"It's not enough! Faelan could've been—" Astrid's voice broke. "You think I'm going to be alpha of this pack after this? You can keep it."

She stormed out. At the gates, she stalled; storming off was all very good when you had somewhere to go to, but this was her home. She made do with kicking over a stupid gnome. Kane slunk out after her, giving her a hug.

"So hot-headed. It's such a shame you won't be alpha. Kane does nothing to put her in her place..." Luna murmured.

"Now is not the time, Mother," Faelan snapped. "And for what it's worth, Astrid is right."

# Lima

LIMA HAD USED UP all her tears hours ago. The city guard came to the house, asked countless questions. Her dad demanded a lawyer, but that didn't prevent them from taking him away in the end. Her tears weren't for him, not really, more for the loneliness setting into her bones. She'd even sent Angela away, not knowing if she could afford to pay her wages. The house was eerily quiet without her.

Tap, tap, tap. Something was hitting her window. The branch of their ornamental cherry tree, she thought, blowing in the wind. It would irritate her all night if she left it. Remind her of the trees her family had been complicit in destroying.

There were already rumours going around about a painkiller shortage, that some calamity had befallen the crop this year. Suddenly all of Kirkhyrst was interested in the Great Forest. She hadn't read far—her gridmail had pinged with her official dismissal from the intern programme, followed by Daisy emailing an apology absent any real explanation of what had happened. Lima could guess well enough.

The power had been restored; soon enough everyone would forget about the blackout, relegate it to anecdotes and bedtime stories. While Lima didn't care so much about losing her internship, she did regret the chance to find out what the cores were really doing. She doubted the university would welcome her now, even if she had theories worth investigating.

From what they'd pieced together, the makeshift core alternated between emitting pent up magic into the atmosphere and grabbing whatever magic it could find. No wonder the magic system fell into chaos. The Grid's core was obviously more controlled, but Lima wanted to find out if it was still slowly leeching magic from the living. She owed Lailu that much.

There was that tapping again. She shouldered the sash window open, only to be hit square in the forehead by a small pebble.

"Ow! What…"

"Psst! Down here," the voice was music to Lima's ears.

"Lailu? What are you doing in my garden?"

"I needed to know you're OK."

Lima's lip wobbled, the words *I'm fine*, for once refusing to be spoken.

"Not really," she whispered.

"Do you want me to come up there? Or can you climb down?"

Lima was momentarily speechless. Then a bubble of laughter escaped her lips. "Or I could use the back door?"

"Oh. Your houses are so strange." Lailu craned her neck, seeking out the aforementioned door. "I see it now. I'll wait for you."

Lima's footsteps echoed through the deserted house, picking up speed as she hurried down the stairs. No one was here to tell her off for running. She longed to say her proper goodbyes to Lailu, to ask for her forgiveness.

She wrestled with the tangled ring of keys, fumbling with the lock, and threw the door open to be met with a smile.

"Hi," she said.

"Hi," Lailu replied.

Seconds passed and they stood there staring. Grinning at each other.

"I thought—" Lailu started at the same time Lima said "I need—"

They both laughed.

"You go first," Lima offered.

"I thought, if you weren't OK… that maybe you'd like to come back with me?"

Lima didn't know what to say.

"It would be weird I know, a human among Ratatoskr, but the wardens told me they wouldn't oppose it if it's what I wanted."

"And is it?" Lima asked, her voice little more than a breath. "What you want?"

"Yes. But only if you want to?"

"Oh my gods, yes!" Lima flung herself at Lailu, enveloping her in a hug. "Help me pack? Gods, what do I need?"

Lima pulled Lailu inside by her paws, the Ratatoskr laughing at her eagerness.

"Clothes. Unless you want to adopt Ratatoskr styles." She waved at her unclothed body.

"Yes. Good idea. You said you have a library? Would you like some more books?"

Lailu's eyes lit up. "Oh yes please! If a tree must die, then let it be a carrier of knowledge forever more. And ridiculous love stories—I like those too."

Weighed down with as many suitcases as she could find, Lima surveyed her worldly belongings. Not a lot, and mostly books. Her console wouldn't work in Ruhann; not that she wanted to be associated with anything the Grid touched anyway.

She thought about leaving a note, but even if her dad returned to see it, he didn't deserve it.

# Faelan

FAELAN WAS IN HOLDEN Hill to find somewhere to rent, at least until things blew over. If they ever did. There weren't many properties suitable for three fully-grown shifters, not within their budget. He wasn't going to sleep on a sofa while Astrid and Kane did—whatever—in bed, a thin wall away.

Staying with the Alder pack would mean a stipend for the future alphas, but Astrid would throttle him if he went behind her back to ask for it. They hadn't officially quit. Luna was wilfully ignoring what was, in her mind, a tantrum and expected the pair to return to their duties in a week or two. Faelan wasn't so sure.

Deep in thought, he found himself walking past a familiar sign. *Etienne's*. He could do with a drink, that's what he told himself anyway. If a certain Grid worker just happened to be there, maybe he could say sorry for almost eating her.

The décor was not what he expected, but then they'd hardly be dangling blood bags from the ceiling. It was kind of homely. Behind the bar, a tall vampire polished glassed, his suit a vibrant purple. Etienne, he assumed, and at the bar, a curly-haired figure sat hunched over an untouched coffee.

Etienne glanced up, catching sight of Faelan's eyes.

"Oh," he muttered, putting down the glass. "Don't suppose you can tell me what happened to her?"

Daisy didn't utter a word. Fenrir, had he done this? Kane had made it sound like she'd laughed off the near mauling in the end. Perhaps she'd just been in shock. Faelan gingerly took hold of her stool and spun her around to face him.

"Daisy? Look at me," he said, trying to coax her out.

"They made me sign an NDA," she mumbled, meeting his gaze. Her eyes were red and puffy.

"She's been like this since she got back from the office yesterday. Said she's so glad I wasn't dust then clammed up. It's always the same answer. An NDA! Like she's signed away the ability to talk about what she ate for dinner last night!" Etienne threw up his hands in exasperation.

"The Grid made you sign something?" Faelan asked and Daisy nodded. "Did you lose your job?"

"No. But Lima—she's gone..." she whispered, barely audible. Faelan leaned in closer. This was not the confident woman he'd been trailing after in Ruhann. Bloody corporates and their legal nonsense. He shouldn't be surprised that Luna was part of it.

"Gone where?"

"I don't know. She's not on her socials; she didn't reply to my gridmail. I tried her house, but it's empty. Her father's apparently in custody. I don't think her mother... I dunno, she never mentioned her."

"We'll find her. I have my nose." Faelan smiled at her. "And Lailu found her before, she can do it again. We'll send a bird."

He didn't know where he'd find one, but he'd try. He looked over at Etienne who shrugged.

"She was worried about the rookeries," Daisy said.

"OK. We can start there."

"There's no point to any of it. If I make a fuss, if they even listen, they'll increase power generation, and if I can't tell people why that's bad..." Daisy put her head back in her hands.

"You know, I was there. Unconscious for some of it sure, but I know enough. I saw enough. The Grid can't stop me talking. In fact, I'll start now."

Faelan jumped up onto the bar, the wood creaking beneath his weight. Etienne raised an eyebrow but did nothing to stop him. Faelan cleared his throat loudly, attracting the attention of the other patrons. Three vampires, two humans, and a shifter skulking in the corner. A small audience, but it would do.

"Who wants to hear a story about the Grid?"

# About the Author

Ellie Warren has been blogging about other people's books for over a decade at Curiosity Killed the Bookworm. When she's not reading and writing, she pokes holes in software for a living. She grew up in the Scottish Borders and now lives near the New Forest, with her partner and a very hungry Labrador.

You can find her on Bluesky, Instagram, Threads, and Twitter/X as @patchworkbunny, and on Mastodon as @patchworkbunny@ellie.social.

www.curiositykilledthebookworm.net